MURDER WITH MERCY

MURDER WITH MERCY

Veronica Heley

This first world edition published 2013
in Great Britain and the USA by
SEVERN HOUSE PUBLISHERS LTD of
19 Cedar Road, Sutton, Surrey, England, SM2 5DA.

British Library Cataloguing in Publication Data

Heley, Veronica.
  Murder with mercy. – (The Ellie Quicke mysteries ; 14)
  1. Quicke, Ellie (Fictitious character)–Fiction.
  2. Widows–Great Britain–Fiction. 3. Detective and
  mystery stories.
  I. Title II. Series
  823.9'14-dc23

ISBN-13: 978-0-7278-8281-3 (cased)

All Severn House titles are printed on acid-free paper.

Severn House Publishers support The Forest Stewardship Council [FSC],
the leading international forest certification organisation. All our titles that
are printed on Greenpeace-approved FSC-certified paper carry the FSC logo.

Typeset by Palimpsest Book Production Ltd.,
Falkirk, Stirlingshire, Scotland.
Printed and bound in Great Britain by
MPG Books Ltd., Bodmin, Cornwall.

ONE

Ellie Quicke had problems enough before she was asked to look into the untimely death of first one neighbour, and then another. Not to mention a third. Each one getting closer to home . . .

Tuesday afternoon

There really was no need for anyone to suffer nowadays, was there?

The important thing was to keep a list of people who needed her help. When she heard of someone she entered their name in her diary and, when she was having a good day, she went to see them.

She'd just heard the sad news about an old friend, confined to a wheelchair after an accident. He was taking it hard, poor man. She must make time to visit him soon.

The list never seemed to get any shorter, which was a bit worrying because she was not getting any younger. She told herself to think of all the people whose names she'd been able to cross off over time, and that made her feel better.

Looking back, there was only one death which had really upset her. Many times he'd said he wanted to die, and she'd done what she could to help him out of his misery. She'd pounded up the tablets and dissolved them in his whisky. He'd necked the lot down, but then . . . she didn't understand why . . . he'd changed his mind and begged her to call the ambulance. She'd been so flustered that she hadn't known what to do for the best and she'd left him to die alone. No one had questioned it, because he'd said so many times that he wanted to end it all, but it had upset her.

She'd crossed through his name in her diary with a red biro, to remind her not to help anyone unless they really, really wanted to die.

The only thing was, she couldn't remember where she'd put her diary. She must have another look for it after supper.

Tuesday afternoon

One of the pleasures of Ellie's life was a trip to a garden centre.

She'd planted masses of wallflowers in the herbaceous border in the back garden so that even in the nastiest of weathers the effect was not entirely grim. Soon the viburnum and the witch hazel should be showing colour, though her winter-flowering pansies had stopped blooming when the wind had turned to the east. As far as she was concerned, it was a penance and not a pleasure to go into the garden in November.

There wasn't much doing in the conservatory at the back of the house, either. In the old days their elderly housekeeper had regarded this as her territory, but lately she'd allowed Ellie to potter there, picking dead leaves off the overwintering geraniums, spraying the azaleas and coaxing the Christmas cactuses into flower.

Titivating wasn't the same thing as planting so, when Ellie received yet another importunate letter from a woman she'd tried to help, she'd tossed it into the waste paper basket – knowing it would have to be retrieved and dealt with at some point – and decided to take the rest of the day off.

She ordered a minicab and trundled off to the nearest garden centre, where she picked out half a dozen of the biggest, fattest amaryllis bulbs she could find. Bringing them home in triumph, she didn't even bother to see if any messages had accumulated on the answerphone. Instead, she assembled everything she needed for potting the bulbs up in the kitchen: terracotta pots, a large pack of peat and the trusty trowel that had once belonged to her mother. Ellie knew that you could buy dormant amaryllis bulbs in ornamental pots complete with cylinders of peat, but that felt like cheating to her. She believed that if you wanted to do a job, you should do it properly.

She donned an old apron and a pair of bright yellow latex gloves, cleaned out the sink and half-filled a washing-up bowl with the crumbling, black peat. She made a well in the middle, poured in some water, and began to mix and knead. It felt rather like making pastry – just as satisfying and just as messy.

She put a layer of wet peat into the bottom of each pot, placed a bulb on it, and began to fill up the space with more of the soggy black stuff. The mess in the kitchen sink was truly amazing. She grinned. This was better than making mud pies as a child and, as she was an adult, it was doubly enjoyable. Wasn't there some song about Glorious Mud . . .?

The front doorbell rang.

She was up to her elbows in muck.

It was true that their elderly housekeeper Rose was in her bed-sitting room next to the kitchen, but Rose always had an afternoon nap with the television on and wouldn't hear the bell.

Ellie's husband, Thomas, was . . . where? Out for the day. He'd retired from parish work to run a small but influential Christian magazine, but was often called upon to help out in emergencies at local churches. He could be anywhere in London. As for Vera, who helped Rose to run the household, neither she nor her schoolboy son were due back yet.

The house was quiet, except for the susurrus of the television coming from Rose's room.

The bell rang again.

Ellie rinsed her gloves under the tap and went to answer it. The wind caught the front door and the visitor swept in on a gust of rain.

Ellie knew her caller well enough to say, 'I'm just in the middle of something. Take off your wet coat and hang it over the chair. You'll have to come into the kitchen. Mind the cat, I know he likes you, but he can trip you up if . . . No, I'm not cooking. Well, in a way I am. I'm potting up some bulbs, and if I don't get the sink cleared up before Rose wakes from her nap, I'll be in trouble. Would you like a cup of tea?'

Detective Constable Milburn said, 'Brrr. Horrible weather. Shall I put the kettle on?'

'Please do. You want something to eat? I hope you don't want cake, because I doubt if we've got any left.'

'No, no. A cup of tea and five minutes of your time would be splendid. Those aren't daffodil bulbs, are they?'

'A sort of lily which flowers indoors. I pot them up and put them in a dark place for a while. When the flower buds appear, I bring them into the light. Some people leave them in the light all the time, but I think the bulbs like being fooled into thinking it's winter when they're put in the dark, and it's that which makes them start growing again.'

She finished putting wet peat around the bulbs, and placed the pots on the draining board to let the excess water run off. The mess in the sink was indescribable. There was black powder everywhere she looked: up the sides of the washing-up bowl, and slopping over into the sink itself. And the draining board. And over her apron. 'Mugs are in that glass-fronted cupboard. Milk in the fridge. Sugar? No? The biscuit tin is on the end shelf.'

'I would have thought you'd have a greenhouse. Save you doing it in the kitchen sink.'

'Mm. I know. Rose will kill me.' She managed to scoop out nearly all the remaining peat and began to swill the rest around the sink and down the plughole, hoping she wouldn't block up the drains. 'I've been thinking about putting a greenhouse against the garden wall where it would get the sun, but I haven't got round to doing anything about it.'

She stripped off her gloves and her apron, bracing herself for what was to come. Which member of her family was in trouble now?

'The family's all well?' DC Milburn poured boiling water on to tea bags in the mugs and added milk.

So it wasn't Thomas. 'Fine.'

'Your daughter Diana? Her baby must be about due, now.'

Ellie pulled her mouth into a smile, belying the anxiety which she always felt when she thought of her only daughter. 'Due any day now. Getting a bit tired.'

'The girl you took in as a lodger to help your housekeeper? With her young son? That was good of you.'

'Vera. Such a blessing. It took a lot of persuading to make her enrol at college, but the hours fit in with Mikey's schooldays, and she's doing well. Rose doesn't seem to mind her running the kitchen, either.'

Had Mikey been truanting from school? But Ms Milburn wouldn't have come visiting for that, would she?

'Relax,' said Ms Milburn. 'No one in your household has been crossing the line, as far as I know.'

Ellie smiled naturally this time. 'Shall we take our mugs through to the other room? You bring the biscuits.' She had smudges of peat on her sweater. She tried to brush them off, failed and decided to deal with them later.

As they passed into the hall Ellie nudged a wedge under the door to the kitchen, to keep it open. Then, if Rose should call for help, Ellie would hear her.

Once in the big sitting room, Ellie drew the long velvet curtains and picked up some of the newspapers which Thomas had dropped on to the floor that morning. The room felt chilly, despite the central heating, so she switched on the gas 'log' fire.

Midge, the family's marauding ginger cat, followed them in and plumped himself down in front of the fireplace. He kept a beady eye on DC Milburn as she did sometimes let him have a titbit. He ignored Ellie, because he knew from experience that she wouldn't feed him outside mealtimes.

'So, are you very busy at the station?' Ellie, making conversation.

'The usual. Budget cuts. Redeployment of personnel. But the crime statistics are down, so the boss has been on holiday and gained five pounds.' She frowned. She was no fan of her boss.

Neither was Ellie, who had unfortunately made an enemy of the Detective Inspector. In a moment of distress Ellie's brain had slipped a cog and she'd referred to him as 'Ears', since his appendages turned bright red when he was angry. The nickname had spread till even he had heard about it. To make matters worse, Ellie had shown him up for poor police work. Ears had been heard to say that if he could only have one wish, it would be that Ellie Quicke should be shut up in a nunnery. In a silent order.

'He's in a good mood for once?' said Ellie. Hope dies hard.

'Well, no worse than usual.' Ms Milburn attempted, and failed, to sound nonchalant. 'I don't know if you've heard. A girl came into the station to lodge a formal complaint. She said her cousin had murdered her aunt for her second-hand Prada handbag.'

Ellie wanted to giggle but, looking at Ms Milburn's solemn face, decided that this would be inappropriate. 'Ms Milburn, we've known one another for ages. Would you mind if I called you by your first name? I'm Ellie, of course.'

'Ellie. I'm Lesley.' A pause. It would take time for them to become accustomed to the use of Christian names.

Ellie took a biscuit and held the tin out to Lesley. 'Go on. A girl called at the station wanting to report a suspicious death. Ears took one look at her – I assume she wasn't pretty? Oh dear, I really ought not to say such things.'

Lesley managed a smile. 'Well, perhaps if she had been a beauty he wouldn't have dismissed her out of hand, but yes, he passed the buck to me. I took her statement and made some enquiries. Aunt Ruby had been in a bad way, was due to go into a home, took too many sleeping pills one night. The doctor said he thought she'd taken a double dose because she was in pain and had become confused. There was no one else in the house at the time.

'He'd visited the previous week to discuss Ruby's going into a home and said she'd hated the idea but hadn't seen any alternative. He signed the death certificate with some jargon that meant her heart had stopped. They use that form of words sometimes with elderly patients who are likely to pop off at any minute. No one would have taken any notice if the niece hadn't started shouting that it was murder.'

'Actually shouting?'

'Shouting. She was irate. Indignant.'

'Not grieving?'

Lesley shook her head. 'The cousins had disliked one another from birth. The accused had an alibi. She'd been away on a hen party weekend. Manchester. I checked.'

Ellie was amused. 'So who gets the Prada handbag?'

'Ruby had made a will some years ago after her husband died. She hadn't updated it, so everything goes to the cousin who's accused of murder.'

Ellie noticed her slip-on house shoes had trekked peaty footmarks all over the carpet. Oh well. 'You don't really suspect foul play, do you?'

'The official line is that Petra – the complaining niece – is off her rocker with jealousy because her cousin gets not only the Prada handbag but also the contents of their aunt's council flat, which, by the way, now reverts to the borough. I suppose what the aunt left might fetch a few hundred, if that.'

Ellie took another biscuit, brushing crumbs off her skirt. 'So how did Aunt Ruby come to be in possession of a Prada handbag, even if it was second-hand?'

'She used to work as a cleaner. One of her ladies gave it to her as a Christmas present.'

Ellie shrugged. 'So?'

'Oh, nothing. Nothing at all.' Defeated. Irritated. 'I thought the tale might amuse you.'

'Pull the other one. More tea?'

'No. Enough, thank you.' She put down her mug with a snap. 'There's another case. Similar. Elderly lady, not doing too well after a cancer operation, took too many sleeping pills one night. Different doctor. Verdict: misadventure.'

'It happens.'

'Yes, of course it does. I'm babbling. Take no notice.'

Ellie was puzzled. Lesley was wandering all around the point. Or was she? 'Who benefited in that case?'

'Some distant relation. The deceased left her a terraced house overlooking the park. That won't be on the market for long.'

Ellie half laughed. 'Two old ladies get confused and take too many tablets. Where's the problem? Are you afraid there's going to be a third?'

Lesley's colour rose. 'I suppose that's it. One old lady takes the easy way out, and another thinks, "Well, why not?" and copies her. Who can blame them, if the pain gets too much or they're threatened with being taken into care?'

Ellie sat back in her chair and thought about what Lesley had said. 'You are a good detective, Lesley. Better than your boss, though we won't go into that, will we? Do you really think Petra or her cousin knocked off Aunt Ruby in order to inherit her Prada handbag?'

Lesley avoided Ellie's eye. 'Yes. No. Oh, I don't know what to think. Ears wants me to stop Petra making a fuss and suing everyone in sight, which is what she threatens to do. What it is . . . I have no right to ask, but do you think you could have a word with the girl, see what you think?'

Midge turned his head to the door, his ears pricked. His hearing was far sharper than Ellie's. He stretched, elongating himself to twice his normal size. So what had he heard? Rose, getting up from her rest? The boy Mikey returning from school? Mikey had a special relationship with Midge. Where one was to be found, the other was bound to be not far away.

Ellie looked at the clock on the mantelpiece. Mikey was late. She frowned. He was often late, coming back from school. But that was another matter. Meanwhile, to deal with Lesley. 'What good would that do?'

There was a distant scream from the kitchen. Was it Rose finding her precious sink awash with peat, or had she hurt herself? Ellie stumbled to her feet, her mind projecting a visit to the nearest Accident and Emergency department.

Lesley followed Ellie to the door, saying, 'Petra was sacked from her job in a burger bar at Ealing Broadway six months ago and hasn't worked since. I know you've got shares in that hotel that's just about ready to open in the next road. They must be taking on new staff. I thought you could make an excuse to have a word with her about it, offer her an interview for a job there or something?'

Another scream from the kitchen.

The doorbell rang. A long, insistent peal. Only one person rang the bell like that, and Ellie grimaced, knowing who it would be.

Lesley was not ready to leave. 'I sound desperate, don't I? And I'm not making much sense, either. It's just that something is very wrong, and it's bugging me.'

The doorbell rang again. Mistress Impatience was out there, demanding attention, demanding that her mother do this or that.

Distracted, Ellie handed Lesley her coat, her eyes darting first to the kitchen quarters, and then back to her visitor. 'Thanks for calling, Lesley. I'm sorry everything seems to be happening at once. Perhaps when things have calmed down . . .?' She opened the front door to let her daughter in.

'You've taken your time!' Diana stalked into the hall, forcing Lesley to step aside.

Lesley grimaced, shrugging herself into her coat. 'Yes, yes. I'm on my way. Sorry. I know I shouldn't have, but Ellie . . . I gave her your address and suggested she call on you.'

The slim figure of a boy erupted into the hall from the kitchen like a stone from a catapult, narrowly avoiding Diana and forcing Lesley to take a step back.

'Mikey, you come back here!' Rose, shouting from the kitchen.

Mikey swerved round Ellie to reach the stairs and thundered up them, oblivious to everything but flight. The cat Midge followed him. They disappeared around the landing. A door opened and banged shut. They were on their way to the flat at the top of the house.

Lesley righted herself, half laughing and half annoyed. 'What's that boy been up to now?'

Ellie had spotted that Mikey had had a huge wodge of fruit cake in one hand and a bottle of Coca Cola in the other. He wasn't supposed to have Coca Cola because it gave him a sugar rush, and Mikey definitely did not need more sugar to give him a high. 'I think he must have found Rose's hidden stash of cake.'

'Mikey!' Rose, frail as a sparrow and looking rather like one, all brown and grey, appeared in the doorway to the kitchen. 'That young limb!'

'Quite,' said Ellie. 'Lesley, are you all right?'

'No harm done. I'll be on my way, but you won't forget . . .?' She stepped out into the wind and the rain, and Ellie shut the door on her.

Diana had already divested herself of her heavy overcoat. She handed it to Ellie and checked her appearance in the hall mirror, running a finger across her scarlet mouth, before stalking through to the sitting room and lowering her swollen body on to a high-backed chair. 'I could do with some tea. Earl Grey, no milk, one lemon slice.' Black hair, cut short. A stick-thin body with an outsize bust and protruding belly. She looked as if she were about to give birth any minute.

Before becoming pregnant and getting married to the biggest
of the local estate agents – yes, in that order – Diana had
always worn black. Since the wedding she'd gone in for navy
blue, with chalk white trims. The colours didn't suit her particularly, since she'd failed to inherit Ellie's fine skin and cornflower
blue eyes. She'd adopted the colour blue because she'd read
somewhere that babies liked it. As if you could have a baby
by the book.

Ellie hoped this change of dress colour meant that her
daughter would be a better mother to the expected baby than
she'd been to her son by her previous marriage. Well, she
could always hope.

'Mother!'

'Coming, dear.' Ellie wished she'd had time to change out
of her gardening clothes and shoes, and to clean up in the
kitchen. Oh, horrors! The mess in the kitchen! 'I'll see to your
tea. Won't be a minute.'

She hurried through to the kitchen to find Rose, arms akimbo,
glaring at the still dirty sink and the flower pots on the draining
board. 'Sorry, Rose. I meant to finish before you woke up.
Leave everything, will you? I'll clear up when I've got rid of
Diana.'

Rose refilled the kettle with vicious haste. 'What does
Madam want this time? And don't say it's only a social call,
because that one doesn't "do" social.'

Ellie clattered a fine bone china cup, saucer and teapot on
to a tray, and delved into the fridge for a lemon to slice. 'I
didn't realize there was any cake left.' An empty cake tin was
on the table, the lid on the floor underneath. Ellie retrieved
the lid and replaced it on the tin.

'I kept a piece back for your tea but Mikey got to it first.
He'd have had my hand round his backside if I'd got to him
quicker.'

'He's a growing boy.' Ellie put tea bags into the teapot and
poured on some boiling water. 'Diana won't eat cake, anyway.'
She carried her tray through the hall and into the sitting room.
Diana was leaning back, eyes closed and hands clasped over
her stomach.

'Here you are, then. How are you feeling today?'

Diana's pregnancy had not been an easy one, and she'd felt sick for most of the time.

'As if you cared.'

Ellie didn't reply. It was never any good arguing with Diana. 'Nasty weather. How's your husband? The last I heard he was hoping to get out of his wheelchair soon. I never knew a knock on the head could set you back so much.'

A twist of Diana's lips. 'He's given up, won't make the effort any more. Sinking into self pity. "My life is over," that sort of thing. I can't be doing with him when he gets like this. He wants attention twenty-four seven. If I stay home with him he frets about the office and says we're heading for bankruptcy. If I go to the office, he's ringing me every five minutes, wanting me to come home.'

Ellie didn't care for Evan but she said, 'Oh dear. How awful,' and tried to mean it. 'I thought he'd feel better once he was back in his own house. It must have been fun for you, decorating and refurnishing it to your own taste.'

An arsonist had set light to Evan's substantial detached house some months ago. Worse, the arsonist had been his mentally unstable son. A double whammy, you might say. It had taken months of work and a complete redecoration of every room before the place had been fit to live in again.

'Yes, yes,' said Diana. 'I haven't been able to find a housekeeper and gardener to live in yet. Every time I arrange for Evan to interview someone, he turns them down. One drinks, another is too fat. He doesn't know what he wants.'

Perhaps, thought Ellie, he needed a loving, attentive wife. Ah well.

'As for that daughter of his,' said Diana, with some animation, 'she says she loves him to bits and wants to look after him, but she's studying for her exams, and when she *is* at home, he doesn't want her helping him to the toilet, or in and out of the bath.'

'Mm,' said Ellie, 'she's a good kid, but I can see he wouldn't want that.'

'Another thing; she studies with her headphones on, so when he calls for help, she doesn't hear him. And, let's face it, a schoolgirl can't give him the companionship he needs. He needs someone older, more responsible, to be with him every minute of the day.' Diana put down her cup. 'He's depressed, but won't go to the doctor about it. I have to get my priorities right. The business needs me.'

'And the baby.'

'Yes, of course.'

Business would come first with Diana. The new baby, second. Evan definitely came third now that she had to support him in his convalescence, rather than him supporting her in the style to which she had become accustomed.

Diana said, 'That's what I came to see you about. He's developing paranoid tendencies, doesn't trust the district nurses. I can't blame him; you never see the same one twice. And with me attending to his business, and his daughter at school all day, he's pretty vulnerable. The other day he let some Jehovah's Witnesses into the house, can you imagine? They were still there an hour and a half later when I got back. To put it bluntly, he needs a minder, someone I can trust. Heaven knows why but he trusts you, and I want you to take him on, perhaps mornings only for the time being.'

Ellie hadn't expected this. She shook her head, wondering how to soften her refusal. 'I've got so many meetings, so much to do. Surely you can find an old friend who'd be willing to sit with him?'

'I wish I could, but he's so "down" that it's . . . To tell the truth, ever since one of his old friends took an overdose, he's been talking about suicide, and I can't have that, can I? I know you've got things on, but surely you can do this for me?'

TWO

E llie's mind zigzagged to and from various possibilities. Could Diana be referring to the case which had brought Lesley Milburn to see her that morning?

No, Evan Hooper would never be disturbed by the death of a cleaner. But hadn't Lesley mentioned another woman who'd overdosed recently? 'You mean the woman living up by the park?'

Diana stared. 'The park?'

Ellie gestured to her right, then realized the park lay in the opposite direction, and pointed to her left. 'Pitshanger Park? A terraced house backing on to the park?'

A frown. 'Don't be ridiculous. Terraced house, indeed! Anita lived on the Argyle Road in a detached house similar to ours. She was captain of the women's team for some years. You must have met her?'

Ellie's first husband had been a member of the golf club. She'd gone to various social events there with him but not made any real friends. Did she remember Anita? Yes, she did. A lively, good-looking woman with a pleasant husband.

Diana continued, 'Conservative, of course. She and her husband were very old friends of Evan's family. Was he best man at their wedding? Something like that. A tragic case, cancer. She took too many pills one night. Misadventure.'

Not the same woman, then. But, perhaps, another case to add to Lesley's file? No, no. If an elderly lady becomes confused and takes too many of her pills, where's the crime in that?

Mm. Wasn't suicide considered a crime in itself? Ellie was not sure. It used to be considered a crime, didn't it? But perhaps it was so no longer? It was, she supposed, understandable that someone in great pain, or with a terminal illness, might be tempted to embrace death early. On the other hand, hadn't she heard a minister at church say that it was wrong to shorten the span of life which God had intended for you? She must ask Thomas.

Diana snapped her cup down on its saucer. 'Well? I can count on you to help me out in this, can't I?'

Ellie told herself that she was not going to be blackmailed into doing something she didn't really want to do. 'I could do one morning a week, and that's more than I should offer. I suggest you get a paid companion for him. Perhaps someone who can help him with his physiotherapy?'

'He goes to the physio twice a week, complaining all the time. Since he can't drive, I either have to take him, or pay for a cab.'

Ellie wanted to ask if Diana considered her mother to be cheaper than a cab, but a prolonged ring on the doorbell stopped her. 'Now who . . .?' Vera had a key, and Mikey was already home.

Diana inched her way out of her chair. 'Tomorrow morning, then. Nine sharp. I'll let you in and give you a key before I go to the office.' She balanced herself on her feet and made for the hall as the bell rang again.

'Coming!' Ellie helped Diana into her coat and opened the door to the wind and the rain . . . and a strange man. No, not a stranger, but someone she hadn't expected to see on her doorstep. She made the mental shift into business mode. 'Hugh?'

Some time ago Ellie had inherited Pryce House, an attractively ugly turreted mansion in the next road. There had been strings attached to the sale, and those strings had caused Ellie many hours of worry. She'd sold the house to a hotel chain, while reserving some shares in the business for herself to give her a financial cushion in case the aforementioned strings got out of hand.

Somewhat to her surprise, the managing director of the hotel chain had wanted her to play an active part in transforming the Victorian monstrosity into a first-class hotel, and she had found herself consulted on all manner of things from the layout of the garden to the placing of the new lift shaft and even the choice of interior decorator.

Hugh was the company's highly efficient project manager

and they had frequent site meetings, but he had never called on her at home before.

He usually greeted her with a smile, but today he looked grim. 'I hope it's not inconvenient, Mrs Quicke?'

Ellie said, 'Come on in, Hugh. My daughter's just leaving. What a horrible night.'

Diana pushed past Hugh as if he were a lad on work experience trying to sell dusters, inserted herself into her car and drove off.

Hugh stepped inside, taking in the spacious hall, the doors leading to the dining and sitting rooms, the colourful stand of plants in the conservatory at the back of the hall and the polished wood of the grand staircase.

'A cup of tea? Coffee?' Ellie wondered, uneasily, if Mikey were responsible for this unexpected call, although she couldn't think why he should be.

'No, thanks. A quiet word with Mikey's mother . . .?'

So Mikey *was* in trouble. Ellie tipped her head towards the kitchen, listening for Vera's alto. The radio was on, but she couldn't hear any other voices. So, Vera hadn't yet returned from college. 'I can't remember what day of the week it is, but if it's Tuesday that means she won't be back till later.'

'It's Tuesday, yes.' He hesitated, unsure of himself.

'You'd better come on in and tell me all about it.'

Hugh followed her into the sitting room with its mixture of antique and modern furniture. He didn't miss the luxury of the lined velvet curtains, the flowering azalea on the piecrust table, the good china Diana had used . . . or the mugs for Ellie and Lesley. 'You're busy?'

'Never too busy for you. Do sit down.'

He was reluctant to say why he'd come. He sighed, deeply. 'The boy.'

She nodded, anxiety mounting. 'What's he done now?'

'Don't get me wrong. I've got a lot of time for him.' He shifted his feet. He was not enjoying this. 'You know he comes over the wall into Pryce House at all hours of the day and night?'

She was startled. 'No, I didn't. At least, come to think of it, I did spot a track over the garden bed to the wall, but I thought it was foxes. How does he do it? That wall must be three metres high.'

'He's got a knotted rope attached to a laburnum tree on your side. One branch of the tree overhangs the party wall. When he gets to the top, he straddles the wall, lets the rope down the other side, and Bob's your uncle. I've known about it for some time. We all have. The men didn't used to mind. He was quite a favourite with them, useful for crawling into small spaces, retrieving dropped tools and the like.'

'I dare say. But he shouldn't—'

'That's boys for you. He says he does his homework in five minutes flat, and I believe him.'

Ellie faked a smile. Mikey's homework was a source of contention. He ignored the work he was supposed to do in some subjects, and Vera had twice been summoned to the school to be scolded about it. According to his form master, Mikey was heading straight for a life of crime, while if you believed the IT teacher, Mikey was the brightest brain in Britain and should go far. Take your pick.

'I wondered if he felt he'd been done out of his rights, with his father – adopted father – having been a member of the Pryce family that used to own that house. But he never spoke of it. The men say he knows his way around the place better than they do. Only, it's become a matter of sabotage . . .' Hugh gave another heavy sigh.

'I'm shocked.' And she was. 'Mikey can be mischievous, but he wouldn't . . . Wait a minute, there was some trouble a while back which caused your schedule to slip a few days, but you said that was down to someone you'd had to sack for cutting corners.'

'He'd been ordering more copper wire than was needed and selling the surplus off down the pub, so he had to go. He knew he'd been stupid, never argued when I sacked him. I can take that sort of thing in my stride. But after he'd gone, we discovered a leaking joint on one of the jobs he'd done: a job which had been signed off days before.'

'But if he'd left by that time—'

'He came back for a jacket he'd left behind. Or so he said. I was off site that day; the men hadn't liked to argue.

So we reckoned it was him, paying us out for sacking him. It would only have taken a couple of turns with a wrench to start a slow leak, but it took us two full days to check every joint . . .' He gestured his frustration.

'So that was down to him. We thought. Then four nights ago one of the electricians went back upstairs for a tool he'd left behind and heard water splashing out of a basin. Everyone else had gone. Someone had put the plug in and left the tap running. He shut the water off, reported it next day. It wasn't the man we'd blamed for the first problem. I know, because I checked. He was playing darts in the pub that night, and he didn't have a key to get back on site. We don't have a night watchman but the place is secured with heavy padlocks every evening, and a security firm comes round and checks everything at four-hourly intervals.

'No one put their hand up for it. Then I was delayed in a meeting up in town yesterday and didn't get back till everyone else had left the site. I wanted to check that some light fittings had been delivered, so I let myself into the house about nine in the evening and heard water cascading down the back stairs. Someone had turned the taps on in a newly installed bath on the top floor. I turned the taps off, and we've had heaters going all day to dry the place out. That's the third problem this month.

'My foreman says Mikey was hanging around yesterday till they threw him out but I'm perfectly aware that, in spite of all our precautions, the lad can get into the building whenever he wishes. Goodness knows how.'

She lifted her shoulders. 'What can I say? I'll have a word.'

'There's no father around, is there?' said Hugh, heavily. 'The girl's brought him up herself? A nice girl, by all accounts, trying to make something of herself. It seems to me she's got enough on her plate to be going on with and I don't want to add to her burdens, but he's got to be stopped. It's not just the water. Once I started to make enquiries, the men told me about some other incidents: mislaid tools, switches left on when they should have been shut off, a small fire started with a short-circuit—'

Ellie paled. 'You mean that Mikey's been responsible for . . .? No, I don't believe it.'

'I don't want to believe it, either. Neither did the men. That's why they didn't tell me. But recently they've started looking over their shoulders, watching to see where he is. It's bad for morale. And I don't need to tell you that it's going down badly with the management because it's made us fall behind schedule again. Not by much. Maybe another two or three days. But it affects the men's bonuses. So, with reluctance, I'm forbidding him the site from now on.'

'I'm appalled. Of course I'll have a word with him. You're right about Vera carrying a heavy burden at the moment. It's a shame, but I'll have to tell her, too. How about cutting that rope he's using to get over the wall?'

'It's on your side of the wall at the moment. If you're in agreement, I'll get someone to take a ladder tomorrow morning first thing and cut it off at the top.' He stood up, a solid, practical man. 'You have my word for it that this won't get any further, provided he stops playing games. Right? But if not . . .' He left the threat dangling.

The doorbell rang again. This time on a tentative note.

Whatever next? 'I understand. Thank you, Hugh.' She led the way back into the hall and opened the door to let him out only to find a stranger standing in the porch, trying to fold up a broken umbrella.

'Mrs Quicke?' The newcomer was a big girl with straight blonde hair and a heavy bosom. She was wearing a waterproof poncho over a sweatshirt and jeans. Bovver boots. 'The woman at the police station told me to see you about a job.' Without being invited, she moved into the hall so that Ellie had to take a step back. A cloud of stale cigarette smoke came in with her.

'Is your name Petra, by any chance?' Ellie shut the door on the outside world. At that moment she heard another door bang and Vera's voice raised in the kitchen. If this was Tuesday, then this was the one day on which Ellie ought to have organized some supper. It had completely slipped her mind to do anything about it, and she'd left the kitchen in a mess. Vera didn't cook on Tuesdays because it was her long day at college.

Ellie decided to deal with one thing at a time. 'Come in, do. Leave your wet things on the chair. I won't be a moment.'

She hurried into the kitchen. There was Vera, looking as if she'd just been fished out of a river. She couldn't have taken her umbrella that day. Her hair dripped, her jacket dripped, and so did her jeans. She was shivering convulsively.

Rose was emitting little cries of dismay and trying to help Vera peel off her jacket. The amaryllis pots were still on the side of the sink, and nothing had been done about supper.

Ellie said, 'Vera, upstairs with you this minute, and into a hot bath. It's my turn to do the supper and I'll get to it in a minute. Rose dear, can you look in the freezer, see if there's anything I can throw together for a meal? I have a visitor, but I can bring her in here while I cook, right?'

'Brrrrr,' said Vera. 'B-b-but—'

Ellie clapped her hands. 'Off with you now! No arguments!'

Rose dithered. 'I was wanting to see the six o'clock news.'

'So you shall. You go and watch the news and I'll see to everything.' Ellie hustled Vera off up the back stairs and asked Petra to come into the kitchen. 'Sorry about this, but I have to cook. Want a cuppa?'

Petra shook her head. Her skin looked soft and pasty, as if she spent most of her days in front of the television, smoking and eating junk food. She was carrying far too much weight for her height, and her default expression was sulky. She was wearing a tiny diamond on her ring finger, bright blue studs in her ears and a tattoo on her left forearm. A dragon? A snake?

Ellie reached for an apron. 'Petra; that's a pretty name. Do sit down.'

'My mum thought it up. She said my dad had been called Peter and she wanted something of his to remind her of him, seeing as he'd walked out on her before I was born. She wanted to call me Petronella, but that's a mouthful so it came down to Petra.'

Ellie nodded. She ferried the pots to the utility room, cleaned the sink again, and investigated first the larder and then the freezer for something to eat. A large packet of mince seemed to offer the best hope of getting something on to the table in time for them to eat. Onions, pasta, seasoning, a couple of eggs. A pack of frozen peas. The largest saucepan, olive oil.

Petra said, 'This is just like my nan's kitchen. At least, hers was a lot smaller, of course, but it had the same old cupboards in it. Don't you want to get it updated? Or perhaps it would cost too much?'

Well, that was a nice put-down, wasn't it?

Ellie chopped onions and put them into the biggest mixing bowl with the mince and the seasoning. She considered explaining that she'd inherited the house from an elderly aunt, whose equally elderly housekeeper – Rose – had decided to stay on to look after Ellie and her husband when her employer died. Rose liked the kitchen as it was. So did Ellie. Petra wouldn't understand that.

Ellie broke eggs into the mince and stirred. 'Tell me about yourself. What made you go to the police?'

'Well, it's Auntie, see. Over Chiswick way. It's a bit of a trek but I used to go over there maybe three times a year, for Christmas and her birthday and mine. She was a widow, had carers come in to get her up and put her to bed and someone else made sure she had a meal in the daytime, but there was always trouble with the upstairs people, unpleasant they are, always complaining about something, but what could she do, she could hardly get out and do something about the garden herself, could she? There was this man used to fetch her to church on Sundays in his car, which I think they, the church, wouldn't have bothered if they'd known how little she had to live on, but there; I mustn't speak ill of the dead, must I?'

'Er, no.' Tip some flour into a bowl. Set the big frying pan on to the gas, dump in some oil, let it start to sizzle. 'But she had other relatives, right? Didn't they keep in touch, too?'

Petra grimaced. 'Florrie, that is. My cousin. Born about the same time as me but she's one that would sour the milk in your tea, and she didn't stir herself to visit Auntie more than a couple of times a year, if that. Only, the last time I saw her, and that wasn't so long ago, my birthday was coming up, and Auntie always had a little something in cash put by for me, and she wanted to meet Dwayne, so we went over there together before we went clubbing, but he agreed with me then that Auntie was losing the plot. She was only a bit of a thing and Florrie had been to see her and she's a right bully, and poor

Auntie had got it in her mind that Florrie was going to get the Social to put her in a home, and she'd been in that flat for over forty years, hadn't she, and didn't see why she should have to move? And what if she couldn't do the garden any more, it was no more than a paved area, and my Dwayne said he'd see to it for her now and then, and that cheered her up no end, because the people up above wanted the garden, see, because of their dog.'

Ellie nodded, putting spoonfuls of the mince mix into a bowl of flour before dumping them in the fat in the pan. 'How much did she give you for your birthday?'

Petra blinked. 'What's that got to do with it?'

'Sorry. Yes. Go on. Dwayne's your fiancé? Have you moved in with him or the other way round?'

'His mum wouldn't hear of my moving in with them, so he moved in with me and Phee, short for Philip – that's my little boy that I had when I was still at school. He's old enough that I can leave him with my best friend in the flats, and then I have her little girl back when she goes out clubbing in her turn. He's not Dwayne's but they get on all right, and the flat's not too bad though there's only one bedroom and it's stuck at the back of the shops up an alleyway. I did think we might get Auntie's place, but they say not.'

Ellie filled the kettle and switched it on. 'So Auntie had nothing to leave.'

Petra shifted on her seat. 'Well, there were all her bits and pieces, her furniture and the like. And she had money in the Co-op, and that's to pay for her funeral with a bit over.'

'And the Prada handbag.'

'Which is what she promised me I should have. I didn't mind about the other things, the silk scarves and the fine soaps and that, though I wouldn't have said "no" to the sherry which she kept on the sideboard to look at, for she didn't drink, not a drop. They were all presents from the ladies she used to work for. And that bitch Florrie has got the lot.'

'Because your aunt had made a will?'

'She made it . . .' Petra concentrated on remembering, '"while the balance of her mind was disturbed". She and I had had a bit of a set-to, you see, years ago, about Phee's dad not sticking to me, and she said it was my fault for not wanting to wait and get married in church, which I said to her was so old-fashioned, no one believed in that nowadays, but she took against me for . . . maybe a year or more. Only then I thought, poor old soul, she's all alone in the world, and I made it up with her.'

'Only, she'd made a will in Florrie's favour in that time?'

'I didn't know nothing about it. She never said, not even when I asked her if I could have the Prada handbag when she was gone. Only, when Florrie rang me to say Auntie had passed over, I went round there to collect it, and Florrie wouldn't give me the time of day. Went all high and mighty, said I could get a solicitor if I wanted, but it was all watertight and I should save my pennies to give myself some liposuction for my hips. Jealous of my body, she is! Skinny bitch!'

Ellie poured boiling water into two pans, added salt. She threw frozen peas into one and lowered a big handful of spaghetti into the other. She reached for a spatula to turn the rissoles that were cooking nicely. 'So why did you go to the police?'

'Well, we'd popped over to see her about ten days before—'

'For your birthday present? With Dwayne?'

'All three of us. Phee went to play in the garden, while Dwayne was cutting back the laurel bush that had grown across the window, and that's when Auntie asked me if I had any sleeping pills. She said the carer would only let her have one each night and she needed at least two to give her a good night. And I said, "I don't need sleeping pills, do I?" and she said would I go and get some from the chemist's for her, and I said I would but then Dwayne said he was going to be late if we did that, and the district nurse or the doctor would give her some next time they came round, wouldn't they? So I gave her some painkillers which was all that I'd got in my bag, and we left. That's what upset me. She hadn't enough pills to kill her, so where did she get all those pills that she took?'

'I suppose the district nurse brought some round for her. Or your cousin Florrie.'

'They said not. She wasn't supposed to handle her pills herself. The carer put the pills for each day in a special box, and she never had the willpower to save them up, which is what they said she did, and I don't believe it for a minute. So it had to be Florrie feeding them to her, didn't it? Because if Auntie had had to go into care, then everything she had would have had to be sold up to pay for it, and Florrie wouldn't have had anything at all, whereas now she gets the contents of the flat and the money from the Co-op and the Prada handbag.'

Ellie poured a tin of tomatoes into the pan and added some tomato ketchup to give the sauce some bite. 'Well, Petra; I can't see that you can do anything about it if the police refuse to act. With what you've got, I can't see that they would.'

'Dwayne's been on at me to drop it but it riles my stomach to think of Florrie getting away with murder. Auntie wanted me to have that handbag, not her.'

Ellie sighed, glancing at the clock. She turned the gas down under everything.

Petra forced a smile. 'But the policewoman did say you could help me to a job at the hotel in the next road? They're taking on staff now, aren't they?'

'I don't have anything to do with that side of things, but I could ask when they are interviewing people and let you know, if you like.'

The sulky look returned. 'I thought you could do more than that. At the station, they said you could put in a good word for me.'

'Have you worked in a hotel before?'

'No, but it can't be that hard, can it? I wouldn't want to do the cleaning or work in the kitchens, but I can see myself in a little black suit behind the reception desk.'

'You're good with a computer, then?'

'Not my scene, that. But it's all smiling at people and handing them their keys, innit?'

Ellie held back a sigh. 'I think you have to be able to take telephone bookings, make out bills and deal with credit cards. Everything has to be done on a computer nowadays.'

'Well, I'd soon pick it up, wouldn't I? If you put in a good word for me, I'll wing it. The only thing is the hours. Dwayne did say he'd pick up Phee when he comes out of nursery – and a right shocking amount I have to pay for that every week, I can tell you – but now he says he needs to be free to pick up some limo work, because his cousin is thinking of starting up a hire-car business in North London, so he won't be able to do that any more.'

'Can't he get a regular job?'

An uneasy movement. 'Well, it's the CRB checks, he's got a bit of a record and there's no jobs anyway. So I'd only be able to work mornings, and no weekends, because that's the only time we have to go out and enjoy ourselves.'

Ellie despaired. 'Give me your contact details, and I'll let you know when they'll be interviewing. In the meantime, why don't you get yourself on a computer course to brush up your skills? I don't think they'll take you unless you can prove you're computer literate.'

The girl bridled. 'Oh, thanks for nothing! I thought you were going to help me!'

Ellie wanted to say, *Why should I?* She wanted to tell the girl that unless she stopped making bad choices in life, she was never going to amount to much. 'Let me show you out.' In the hall, she handed Petra her poncho and broken umbrella and opened the front door. It was still raining hard.

Petra quailed. 'You wouldn't spring to a cab for me, would you?'

Ellie shook her head.

The girl's colour mounted, and her mouth turned ugly. 'I was right about you, you're all the same, filthy capitalists stealing from the poor, but when Dwayne gets going we'll be living in a big house and you'll be down at the Council, begging for a squat! And don't think you can brush me off, you and those toffee-nosed police, because you haven't heard the last of this, I'll have my rights and you can all go and suck yourselves silly!'

Thomas's car swished to a halt in the drive. A big, bearded man, he got out, putting up his umbrella, smiling his pleasure at reaching home at last. 'What a day!' He spotted Petra and looked a question at Ellie.

'She's just going,' said Ellie, knowing that, unless directed otherwise, Thomas would put aside his workday weariness to offer Petra a lift.

'Any chance of a lift to the tube station?' said Petra.

'No,' said Ellie. 'In with you, Thomas. Supper's ready. Goodbye, Petra.'

'You'll be sorry for this!' Petra put up her umbrella and splashed off into the night.

Thomas gave Ellie a hug and a kiss. 'Who was that?'

'Trouble,' said Ellie. 'And the worst of it is, I think she's got a point. Who did give Auntie all those pills?'

THREE

Tuesday evening

She remembered yesterday. At least . . .
      She checked today's newspaper. Tuesday. She'd picked it up off the mat that morning, so yesterday had been Monday.

Was it really a fortnight since her last visit to Ruby? Poor Ruby, so frail and in so much pain. How many years had they known one another? Eighteen? Nineteen? Perhaps more. It was hard to remember which year it was that they'd met, but it was long before both their husbands died.

Almost every Monday afternoon they'd have a cuppa and a chat, and maybe there'd be some chocolate biscuits too, if Ruby's carer had remembered.

Ruby had said, 'I really don't want to be here any longer. I want to be with my darling husband again, and our lovely son. But it bothers me; I was only twenty-eight when our little one died in my arms, and I was forty-three when my husband copped it. Now I'm past sixty-five. Will they know me again, do you think?'

A tricky question. They thought about it.

'What I think is that your little son will see you as you were at twenty-eight, and your husband will see you as you were at forty-three.'

'Even at forty-three, I was beginning to creak in my bones. I certainly don't want them to see me as I am now. I did tell you that the doctor wants me to go into a care home, didn't I? I can't be doing with that. You brought the pills for me? I've tried to save some of mine, but the pain gets too bad so I have to keep on taking them. It's a poor night on the telly.' She winked. 'Maybe I'll go to bed early and get a good night's sleep for once.'

Dear Ruby. At least she's free of pain at last.

Tuesday evening

Ellie put the food on the table and called out, 'Come and get it!'

Vera sat down to eat with them, but could only manage a few mouthfuls before pushing her plate aside. She looked dreadful and, on being questioned, admitted that her head ached and her throat was raw. 'I'll be all right. I must have caught a cold.'

Ellie took Vera's temperature and sent her up to bed.

Mikey sat at the far end of the table with the cat Midge at his side. They 'talked' to one another, but to no one else. Rose was fidgety, complaining there was still dirt in her precious sink. Ellie apologized. Again.

Thomas took a third helping before Ellie could suggest he finished off with a salad – not that she'd prepared any but it was the principle of the thing. Thomas was always 'forgetting' that he was supposed to be on a diet.

Fruit and cheese for afters.

Mikey disappeared; one moment he was there, and the next he'd vanished. Rose broke a plate as she cleared the table, so Ellie sent her off to watch the telly in her own room.

Thomas patted his stomach in thoughtful fashion. 'The weather forecast doesn't look good, and the furrow in your brow tells me the storms are not only outside the house. Let me help you clear up, and you can tell me all about it.'

Ellie said, 'I'll clear up while you make some coffee for yourself.' She didn't drink coffee after four in the afternoon, but she treated herself to a piece of chocolate instead. Back in the sitting room, Ellie looked at the dirty tea cups and mugs she'd forgotten to take out to the kitchen, and pushed them aside. 'Your day went well?'

'Fine. Yours didn't?'

Ellie thought of all that had happened that day. Which should she tell him about first? Diana's latest demands, the odd request from the police, or Petra's visit? Or perhaps the worrying interview with Hugh from Pryce House?

Those could all wait.

She went to retrieve the letter she'd received that morning and which she'd dumped in the waste-paper basket in her study. She said, 'Read this. There's many a day I've wished I'd never met Mrs Pryce and been landed with her appalling stepchildren. Inheriting Pryce House was one thing. It takes up a chunk of my time, but I suppose it's better that it be turned into something useful like a hotel rather than be demolished to make way for another block of flats . . . but honestly; if I'd known how much trouble it was going to be to keep Edwina Pryce out of the bankruptcy court, I think I'd have declined to act.'

'Nonsense,' said Thomas. 'You know you've a flair for dealing with the oddities of life. I'll grant you Edwina is odder than most. Have you seen my reading glasses anywhere?'

'In your top pocket?'

The Pryce children, spoiled in infancy, had assumed they could live out a life of luxury without lifting a finger to help themselves, until at last their father said, 'No more!' He set each one up in business and bought them flats in a good neighbourhood. The idea was that they would take responsibility for themselves in future. Fat chance! They squandered the lot and asked for more.

After Mr Pryce died, his widow, following his instructions, had tried to limit the family's excesses with varying results. Impressed by Ellie's handling of her charitable trust fund, the good lady had left the bulk of the estate – including her white elephant of a house – to Ellie in return for keeping the surviving members of the family out of the bankruptcy court.

The eldest daughter, Edwina, thought she had a right to shop at Harrods although she hadn't the income to support such a habit. As soon as she found herself in debt, she passed the bills to Ellie for payment. Ellie seethed, but paid. And paid.

Thomas found and put on his glasses. 'Granted that Edwina has been nothing but a pain to deal with, it was worthwhile your helping her brother, wasn't it?'

Edgar had been by far the best of the bunch, eventually straightening out long enough to find a job and stick to it. Unfortunately, he'd contracted cancer. Vera had been his carer. She'd loved him and nursed him without expecting anything in return. Edgar had married her, adopted Mikey and, before he died, he'd asked Ellie to look after them both. It had been

Edgar's wish that Vera should pick up on the college education she'd had to forgo when a drunken school-leaving party had left her pregnant – and on her own.

True to form, Edwina had tried to make Vera hand over the little money which Edgar had saved and left for her. Ellie had put a stop to that, which naturally had infuriated Edwina further.

There was a third Pryce. He had a job of sorts, and though by no means a pillar of the community, he hadn't shown up very often on Ellie's radar.

Thomas scanned the letter which Ellie had received that day and let it flutter to the ground. 'I've never heard of these solicitors. Are they "No Win, No Fee"? I see they're threatening to upset Mrs Pryce's will or, alternatively, to make you hand over your shares in the hotel by way of "compensation" for the loss of Edwina's inheritance. They've got a nerve, haven't they?'

Ellie sighed. 'Edwina doesn't really think she can upset the will. It's been through probate. It's been scrutinized up hill and down dale and, despite her screams of rage, it's been pronounced valid. No, what she's doing is trying to make herself such a nuisance that we'll pay her what she calls "compensation".'

'Give the letter to your own solicitor and forget about it.'

'I know that's what I should do and I will, but it doesn't stop me getting into a state about it. Oh, Thomas, I'm so worried. Hugh, the project manager at the hotel site, such a nice man, he came round to see me this evening, and I'm terribly afraid that Mikey's been playing tricks at the hotel. More than tricks; it's equivalent to sabotage. No, I really can't believe that Mikey would do what they say he's been doing, but he's been banned from entering the site. I promised to have a word with him about it but I can't do it behind Vera's back, and now she's ill and I don't know what to do.'

He reached for her hand. 'Ellie, light of my life. Don't lose your perspective on things. I can't believe Mikey has been up to anything dreadful, either. Have you asked him about it?'

'No, I got interrupted. Then I thought Vera ought to be the one who . . . But you are quite right. If it were just boyish pranks . . . But there's been real damage done and it's delaying the project.'

'Well, that's not Mikey.'

She thought about it. Was he right? How could they possibly tell? No, Thomas was right. Mikey wouldn't. Hadn't. Couldn't. 'I'll see if Vera's fit to come down and talk to us with Mikey. If not—'

'We'll do it ourselves. We can't have the lad's reputation traduced.'

Ellie climbed the stairs to the top floor, where all was fresh and clean. The builders had done a good job of creating a spacious, two bedroom flat in the attic. They'd put in masses of insulation to keep the place warm in winter and cool in summer. They'd extended the central heating, put in fitted cupboards, a bathroom and a kitchen. The only thing the builders hadn't been able to do so far was to create a separate outside staircase to make the flat completely self-contained, though one day Ellie hoped the council would pass the plans for that, too.

Vera was in her kitchen, swaddled in an outsize dressing gown which looked as if it might once have belonged to her husband. She'd made herself a hot lemon drink. Her eyes were half-closed, and she was swallowing painkillers.

'Bed,' said Ellie. 'No arguments. Thomas and I will have Mikey with us for a bit. We're told he's been neglecting his homework to potter around Pryce House.'

Vera's voice was hoarse. 'I hope you can get through to him. I can't. In my day we were in awe of the teachers, in primary school at any rate. He says they're all morons, except for the IT teacher. He sits there looking out of the window, and if they ask him what they've just said, he parrots it back to them in their own tones and that makes the other kids laugh. If you can think of a way to make him do his homework, then please do!' Her voice faded, and she started to cough.

Mikey appeared in the doorway with Midge the cat strung around his neck. Midge didn't like anyone else picking him up, but for some reason regarded Mikey as a different species and allowed him liberties he was not prepared to extend to any other member of the human race. Except that on occasion he did condescend to stretch himself out on Thomas's frontage when he lay back in his La-Z-Boy chair, and he would permit

Ellie to have him on her lap for a short time if she were stressed and he was after a treat.

'Downstairs, Mikey,' said Ellie. 'We need to talk.'

He shrugged but preceded her down the stairs, his back rigid.

Thomas had dropped off to sleep by the time they got down to the sitting room but blinked himself awake, yawned and paid attention. 'Mikey, how is your mother?'

Another shrug.

'Poorly,' said Ellie.

Mikey seated himself on a low stool. Midge jumped down and made for the warmth in front of the fire.

Ellie didn't know how to talk to Mikey. She'd never considered herself to be brainy, and people like Mikey who had an affinity for maths and computers were out of her comfort zone. She hoped Thomas would do the talking but he was rubbing his eyes, clearly ready for an early night. He'd probably had just as hard a time as she had. Maybe more so. It was up to her to speak to the boy.

'Mikey, you're over at Pryce House a lot. You know the public aren't supposed to go into the site. It's dangerous.'

A shrug. 'I go over the wall. They don't mind me. They show me how to use the tools. I help to hold things. It's good. Better than school.'

'Recently there's been some trouble. You know about it?'

A shadow passed over his face. 'Someone's playing tricks, hiding tools, causing leaks.'

'Some of the workmen think it might be you.'

Disgust personified. 'Morons!'

'Do you think you have a right to be on the site because your stepfather was brought up in that house?'

Mikey thought about that. Shook his head.

'I know,' said Thomas, exerting himself to remain awake, 'that it's hard to be suspected of something you didn't do. You've been going over there for some time, have got to know the workers. Do you think what's been happening is sabotage?'

'What's "sabotage"?'

'Accidental is one thing. Deliberate is sabotage. You know that very well. Mikey, pay attention.'

Another shrug. His attention wandered. Ellie could have slapped him. If he behaved like this at school, no wonder he was on the teachers' hit list.

'Hugh wants you to keep away from the site for the time being. It's just possible that the culprit is only making "accidents" happen when you're around.'

Mikey reached out to the telly to turn it on.

'Not now, Mikey. Have you done your homework?'

A grin. He hadn't, of course. 'It takes five minutes. If I bother.'

Ellie said, 'I'm very much afraid that you're going to get your mother into trouble if you go on like this. How many times has she been called in to talk to the teachers about your behaviour in class? Won't they make her life a misery if you don't do your homework?'

Another shrug. Another grin. He couldn't have cared less.

Thomas pulled himself upright. 'They haven't threatened you with a visit from Social Services, have they?'

A wide-eyed look. A frown. No, they hadn't.

Thomas looked worried. 'Mikey, Social Services take a special interest in single parent families, and if they see children from such families acting up at school, or not doing their homework, or truanting, they tend to get involved. They come down hard on the mothers if they think they're not acting as proper parents. They can even take the children away and put them into care.'

Mikey blinked.

'You hadn't thought of that? Mikey, pay attention. This is serious. They have every right to be worried.' Something in Mikey's demeanour made Thomas add, 'You haven't been truanting, have you?'

He shrugged. Did that mean he had?

Midge got up off the rug, stretched, and went to wind himself around Mikey's ankles.

Mikey slid off his stool and evaporated, taking the cat with him.

'That went well,' said Thomas, angry with himself. 'The lad doesn't frighten easily. I bet he's over the wall again tomorrow.'

'Hugh is going to take away the knotted rope the lad's been using.'

'Much good that will do. I was serious about Social Services, you know.'

Ellie sighed. Thomas had probably lied about the success of his day, understanding that she'd needed to talk more than he did. And she hadn't even had time to mention Petra and the visit from DC Milburn. Lesley.

She said, 'We've both had a tiring day. Let's have an early night.'

An 'early night' with Thomas might well lead to a good night's sleep for both of them.

'Just what I was thinking,' said Thomas, rising from his chair with alacrity.

Wednesday morning

Ellie swam up from the depths of sleep, wondering if she'd left a window open.

No, someone was breathing on her. She struggled to open her eyes. A chilly feeling on her right indicated that Thomas had got up some time ago and was probably sitting in his quiet room downstairs. She looked at the clock. Nearly eight, and she'd overslept. It was a dark morning and – yes, still raining hard.

Mikey was sitting cross-legged on the bed with Midge beside him. It was Mikey who had been breathing on her. He thrust a piece of paper at her.

Vera's writing. 'Sorry. Think I've got flu. I'm staying in bed. Mikey's had his breakfast.'

Ellie looked at Midge, who was licking his chops and pretending he hadn't just been fed some of Mikey's bacon. She sat up in bed, yawning. There was something she'd promised to do that day, only she couldn't think what.

Ouch! She was supposed to be babysitting Evan Hooper at nine. She sprang out of bed – well, lurched out of bed, actually – and headed for the bathroom. 'Give me ten minutes and I'll be up to see to your mum. I think Thomas had to go somewhere today. He must have left early. I've got to go out, but I'll take you to school on my way.'

Mikey slid off the bed and eeled out of the room.

Vera was indeed most unwell, running a high temperature. Ellie knew there was nothing to be gained by ringing the doctor for a simple case of flu, but made sure the girl had plenty to drink and some painkillers. She dashed downstairs to snatch up a banana and eat it while checking she had her mobile phone in her handbag, and her keys . . . and a notebook, just in case. She found a dry-cleaning ticket . . . She ought to have collected her coat two days ago. She must remember to pick it up. She reassured Rose that she'd be back at lunchtime, ignored the mess in the sitting room and phoned for a cab to take her to the Hooper household, dropping Mikey off at school on the way. She had never learned to drive but kept a tab with a local cab company.

The Hooper house was a large, detached, three-storey house in a road of similar well-to-do houses. All traces of the fire that had done so much damage had been banished with fresh paint and triple-glazing for the new sash windows. The double garage to one side had been completely rebuilt, but there were no curtains at the windows of the flat above it, so there was no live-in staff as yet. The place looked stark and unwelcoming on such a dark, drizzly morning.

Diana – who was Evan's fourth wife – didn't approve of frills, or of allowing greenery to soften the red brick of the frontage. Each of Evan's wives had wanted a different decor for the interior. Ellie wondered how Diana had risen to the challenge of removing her predecessor's image.

Needless to say, Diana was waiting for Ellie in the hall, looking at her watch. 'You're cutting it fine. His daughter's at school and Evan is in the sun room. He'd like some coffee and toast for his breakfast, as quickly as you can. I may be late back. I'll ring you if I am.' Off she went, pulling her coat up around her neck.

How long would Diana be able to keep on working? The baby was due next week, wasn't it?

Ellie admired the new William Morris wallpaper in the hall. It suited the house. She went into the kitchen – she might have guessed it would be all black marble surfaces – and through that into the large conservatory at the back of the house. From being a private gym in the time of Evan's third wife it had been returned to its original use as a sun room, but there were no plants in it. Instead there was bamboo furniture, screens and a water feature. Ellie wondered if Diana would install plastic plants; they'd fit in nicely.

The master of the house looked as beaky as ever. Even in a wheelchair he was an impressive figure of a man, but he had put on weight recently. Probably because he had nothing to do except eat and grumble? He greeted her without a smile – what had she expected? – and demanded the day's newspapers, his iPhone and coffee.

She said, 'Please?'

'What?'

'My daughter has asked me to keep you company this morning and, although I am very busy, I am happy to oblige. But I am not your servant, and when I've brought you what you've asked for, I hope you will remember to thank me.' Smiling as sweetly as she could, she returned to the kitchen. Once out of his sight, she stamped her foot and mouthed a bad word. Then went to do as he'd asked. Perhaps when he'd been fed and watered, he'd be in a better mood.

He started yelling for her even as she carried his coffee in to him. 'Ellie! Hey, you there!'

Ellie said, 'Do you treat my daughter the same way?'

'What?' He thought about that. 'It's no fun being in a wheelchair, it's enough to make a saint swear, and I'm no saint.'

No. She handed him his coffee and the newspapers. 'You don't have to stay indoors. You could get a cab to take you in to work. You must miss it.'

Silence. A reddening of puffy cheeks? 'At my age . . .'

She crossed her fingers. 'You're not old. You've a lot to look forward to.'

'You're as old as you feel.'

'Soon you'll have your son to look after.'

A grunt by way of reply. He opened the newspaper and hid behind it. 'I'm feeling the cold nowadays. Would you fetch my cashmere sweater from my bedroom? On the chair in the window, first right at the top of the stairs. You can look into the boy's room too, if you like. I've had everything sent in from Harrods. Only the best for my boy.'

But not, alas, for his only remaining daughter, who'd inherited his looks and had an even better brain, but whose sex had always ruled her out in her father's eyes.

Ellie went up the stairs and into the first bedroom; a huge double-bedded room, masculine in tone. En suite. No female fripperies in sight. Not that Diana went in for fripperies, but . . . yes, the adjoining bedroom was obviously hers. A walk-in dressing-room and en suite lay beyond.

Across the landing at the back of the house Ellie found what was obviously destined to be a guest room, followed by one for his daughter. It wasn't so much of a schoolgirl's room as that of a student who took life seriously. Books, computer, television, jeans, and sweaters. Also a somewhat worn teddy bear tucked between duvet and pillow.

Back to the landing, and Ellie found the room dedicated to the boy who would shortly, God willing, ease the hunger in Evan's heart. Poor little mite. Diana had never been good mother material, and Evan would probably spoil the new baby rotten. The room had been decorated in blue for a boy. Everything had been delivered for a young prince but was still in its wrappings. Perhaps Diana was superstitious enough not to want to unpack anything until the baby had arrived safely? Or perhaps she didn't care enough to do so?

Ellie shook her head at her thoughts, and then cheered up. It was possible that Evan's neglected daughter, who had always been the best of the bunch, might supply the loving care the baby would need.

Ellie took the sweater downstairs and helped Evan into it.

He said, 'I hate being like this. It's no sort of life.'

'The baby will give you a reason for living. You'll be back on your feet in no time when he comes.'

'Diana's doing well, isn't she?' He was pathetically anxious.

'She is, indeed.' Crossing fingers.

'I mean, if anything were to happen to her just now, the business would fall apart. But if I ask her to be careful, she snaps my head off.'

Ellie nodded. No comment was safest.

He huffed and puffed, and finally came out with it. 'I had an old acquaintance come to see me about you and what she calls your underhand dealings.' He looked to see how Ellie took this. 'She said you'd cheated her out of her inheritance. She knew I'd been involved in the early stages of selling Pryce House and wanted me to help her upset her step-mother's will, or to get you to hand over your shares in the hotel to her.'

'You told her to get lost?'

'Of course. After all, Diana will get them in due course, won't she?'

Ellie almost laughed. The poor deluded man. 'I'm afraid not. I put all my assets into a trust fund for charitable purposes. Diana gets diddly-squat. I thought you knew that.'

He glowered at her. 'Of course I knew.' Judging from his expression, he hadn't. 'I told the harpy I couldn't help her.'

'Let me guess. Edwina Pryce? She's a millstone round my neck. Under the terms of the will, I'm supposed to keep her out of the clutches of the bailiffs.'

'She was saying, hinting, that you're getting someone to sabotage the rebuild of the house so that the hotel won't open on time.'

'What! Why on earth would I do that?'

'To get a better price for the house from another company, perhaps? That was her thought, anyway.'

'That's rubbish, Evan, and you know it.' Edwina was drop-ping poison everywhere, wasn't she? Had she been hanging around Pryce House? How, otherwise, would she know about the recent problems there? What if Mikey really . . .? No, not possible. Ellie decided to talk to the boy again about it.

Evan cleared his throat, looking shamefaced. 'Diana hates me being like this, doesn't she? I worry that . . . if I never walk again . . .?'

'She's worried that you've stopped trying to get back on your feet. She's carrying a heavy burden what with the office, the baby and a husband who's in a wheelchair.'

Tears stood out in his eyes, and Ellie averted her head. He wouldn't want her to witness his weakness. He snuffled, searching for a handkerchief in his pockets. She looked around for a box of tissues, but didn't find one.

He wiped the back of his hand across his nose. 'Sometimes

I get so down, particularly when it's cold. I feel the cold nowadays. And old friends die . . .'

Ellie nodded. Yes, they did.

'Anita. You knew her, too, didn't you? From the old days. Always so active. You never really got involved in the golf club crowd, but you do remember her, don't you?'

Ellie nodded. Anita. Ellie remembered a lively lass with a mass of fair hair and a gravelly, gin-and-tonic voice. The sort of person who gravitated to being chair of whatever charitable committee was flavour of the month. 'Of course I remember her. Cancer, wasn't it?'

'In remission for years and then it came back not once but twice. Freddie, her husband – you may not have come across him so much, he's still working – he used to turn out as Father Christmas at the golf club parties, always good for a laugh. Anyway, he did ask me to visit, to cheer her up, but I'd only just come out of hospital and couldn't face it. I ought to have gone to see her, though what I could have done . . . You feel so helpless. Then it's too late, it's all over and you feel guilty, though that's stupid, too. I couldn't have done anything to help.'

Ellie shook her head. He was feeling guilty enough without her saying so.

'Tragic.' His hands clutched the arms of his chair and released them. Over and over.

'Freddie asked if I'd a photo of Anita from the last golf club trophy dinner, before she took sick again. Presenting the trophy, you know? We always use the same photographer, so I rang her and asked her to search her archives, see if she could come up with something for him, and she did. I meant her to drop it round to him, but she put it through my letter-box instead and now . . .' He gestured at his legs. 'I can't get round there. I asked Diana to take it round to him, but she's so busy . . . Do you think you could . . .?'

'Yes, of course.' Mentally rearranging her day to fit in this errand.

He gave a heavy sigh. 'She took a massive overdose. Waited till her husband was away for the weekend, so he wouldn't find her and try to bring her back. I'll give her this, she was efficient in whatever she did. She must have been hoarding the tablets for weeks. The doctor wouldn't give her many at a time, you know. It makes it worse to think of her carefully setting one tablet a day aside, enduring sleepless nights, so that in the end she would go into an endless night.' He tried to laugh. 'Ha! I'm getting quite poetic. An endless night. Does that come from a poem, do you think?'

Ellie wasn't much into poetry. 'It's a good way of putting it. I'll take the photo round to him at lunchtime.'

'It's like the Hamlet thing. Or is it Macbeth? What if it's not all over when you die? Suppose you wake up in a nightmare?' He checked her face to see if she were following him. She didn't know what to say, and her face must have shown her bewilderment and doubt.

He said, 'I'm getting maudlin. Diana tells me I'm dwelling on it far too much. But sometimes, I think . . . well, if Anita's life was unendurable, if the pain had got too much, and there was nothing more that could be done to help her . . .?'

Ellie made an effort to cheer him up. 'The doctors say there's no need for anyone to suffer like that nowadays.'

'Morphine, you mean? Ah, but would you have enough when you wanted it? No, I think she took the right decision. I salute her for it. I hope I shall have the guts to do the same if . . . Not that I'm anywhere near that.'

Ellie was bracing. 'Particularly as your son will need his father soon. Very soon.'

'Ah yes.' His eyes brightened, and then went dull again. 'It's the waiting. I've never been any good at waiting.'

FOUR

Wednesday noon

The doctor had said he'd make an appointment for her at the memory clinic, but she hadn't heard anything from them yet.

She remembered some things so clearly, they might have happened that morning . . . except, what had she done that morning? She couldn't find her diary. Had she written anything down on the calendar?

Oh. Yes, Surgery at ten o'clock, to see the practice nurse. Not a nice woman; not nice at all. Called herself Desiree, if you please. In the old days they'd never have employed someone as overweight and unhealthy-looking, but nowadays doctors didn't have much choice, did they? It was all committees and partnerships and she didn't know what. Unfortunately, since her dear doctor Ben died, she'd had to put up with seeing Desiree at regular intervals in the surgery.

Desiree was big and black and beautiful. Well, big and black; a beauty she was not. When Desiree took your blood pressure, you had to turn your head away. How could a practice nurse hold down a job with bad breath? Desiree called you 'dearie' and 'pet', and she didn't listen when asked to use your proper name. Desiree had no respect for senior citizens. In the old days Desiree would have called an older woman 'Madam'. . . There was a musical with that title, wasn't there, long ago? 'Call me Madam'?

Desiree said that they were all in a flapdoodle about Florrie killing her auntie.˙ Something to do with the number of pills Ruby took, and the niece . . . the fat one, what was her name? Silly name, something to do with a place older than time? Got it! Petra. A city half as old as time. Apparently, Petra was going to sue everyone in sight, saying the doctors had been careless, giving Ruby too many pills. Petra had always *been trouble, right from the word go. She remembered Ruby saying . . .*

Now what was it Ruby used to say?

It had gone. Maybe it would come back later.

Everyone at the surgery was upset about Petra. If she found a solicitor who'd take the case on a 'No Win, No Fee' basis, then the doctors would be in real trouble. That couldn't be allowed. After all, she knew who'd helped poor Ruby to have a good night's sleep for once.

She'd better call round and have a word with Petra next day.

Had she anything in her diary? Where was her diary, anyway?

Wednesday afternoon

Ellie hesitated. Was this the right place? It didn't look like a house in which someone had died recently. Far from it.

It was a substantial detached house, probably built about 1920, on a main road. A dropped kerb allowed cars to enter a paved forecourt through electronically-controlled wrought-iron gates tipped with gold. Ellie counted four cars on the forecourt: one luxury model with tinted windows, two smaller runabouts and a builders' van. One of the smaller cars was bright red. You couldn't change the colour of your car just because someone in the house had died, but it did strike an incongruous note.

It wasn't only the cars which gave her pause, for even as she approached, an effigy of Father Christmas on a sleigh, complete with reindeer, was being hoisted into position on the front of the house. Three men were currently working to secure the installation, easing it into place with many a merry quip and yell of, 'Watch it!' and, 'Left hand down a bit!'

The decoration – if you could call it that – was dotted with hundreds of light bulbs which would dispense signs of seasonal cheer to the neighbourhood. In mid November.

Ellie consulted the piece of paper on which Evan had written the number of Freddie and Anita's house. Surprising as it might seem, this was definitely it. Ellie dived for shelter from the drizzle into a deep porch and located the doorbell.

The front door opened to a blast of warm air, some heavy rock music, and the whine of a vacuum cleaner. A woman in her forties, pretty enough in an insipid way, held the door open. She was talking into a mobile phone, complaining that someone had let her down. Was this really the right house?

Ellie hesitated.

'Yes?' The woman shut off her phone. 'We don't buy at the door.'

Ellie reddened. Did she look like someone selling dusters? 'I'd like to speak to—'

'He's not seeing any visitors at the moment.'

'Oh. Well, Evan Hooper asked me to drop in this photograph of—'

'I'll take it, shall I?' The woman reached for the packet.

'Who is it, May?' Freddie, the man of the house, appeared from the back of the hall; tubby, dark of hair, florid of countenance, genial in manner. Casually but expensively dressed. She recognized him from the old days and noted that he wasn't exhibiting any particular signs of grief. No wringing of hands or dishevelled appearance.

'Evan Hooper asked me to bring—'

'I know you, don't I? Of course. You're Mrs Quicke?' Shaking hands, drawing her inside. 'Long time no see, what with this and that. Hard times, your husband and now my wife . . . Come on in. Horrible day, isn't it?'

The insipid blonde looked annoyed. 'Yes, but Freddie! You agreed, no visitors.' She even went so far as to lay a hand on his arm. 'You need time to—'

'It's all right, May. Don't fuss so.' He stepped away from her, letting her hand slip off his arm. 'Do come on in, Mrs Quicke. You find us all at sixes and sevens, always the same when we have to put the lights up, wasn't sure whether or not to do so this year, was it lacking in respect, you know? I decided to go ahead when May said the neighbours would be so disappointed if we didn't. Everyone looks forward to it. Only now I'm wondering whether it was the right thing to do. Oh, this is May, my right-hand woman from the office, keeps me on the straight and narrow, ha ha.'

May held out her hand to be shaken, unwilling to be

dismissed. 'Pleased to meet you. I'm sure you understand, Mrs Quicke, that it's early days yet and he must take care not to overdo things.'

'Yes, yes,' said Freddie, sweeping Ellie into a sitting room occupying the depth of the house. A hothouse atmosphere, lilies wilting in a cut-glass vase, a Siamese cat giving Ellie a look of annoyance, a plump girl with a broad face – possibly Polish – wielding a vacuum cleaner.

'I can't stay,' said Ellie, trying to give him the photograph again. 'I just brought—'

'No, no. I insist. May; can we rustle up some coffee? And . . .' He struck his forehead, addressing the cleaner. 'Sorry, forgotten your name for the moment. Could you, do you think . . . somewhere else?'

The cleaner pinched in her lips, but removed herself and the hoover. May, however, was not so easy to dislodge. She said, 'Freddie, you promised me you would have a quiet time today and not rush about, but deal with some of the paperwork that—'

'Yes, yes. It's not really that important, is it? Mrs Quicke, do have a seat. The coffee will be up in a minute, won't it, May? Now, Mrs Quicke; I've been meaning to call on Evan, but, well, you know how it is, one's own life gets suspended somewhat when . . . Where does the time go, I ask myself? It was only yesterday that . . .' He heaved a great sigh, then turned on May, who had stubbornly refused to do as he'd asked. 'May, dear. Coffee, please?'

May's colour rose, but she admitted defeat and left the room.

'Now,' said Freddie, 'we can be comfortable. May is a treasure, an absolute blessing, I don't know what I'd have done without her, especially at the beginning when I couldn't seem to lace up my shoes properly, or tell you which day of the week it was. But now I'm sort of coming out of it, trying to pick up the pieces, ha ha. May's quite right, I'm not coping all that well, but it has been on my mind to get in touch with Evan. I must not lose touch with my old friends. So tell me; how is he?'

He seemed genuinely to care, and Ellie – who had written him off at first as a man who was recovering rather too fast from his wife's death – began to warm to him. She said, 'You two go back a long way.'

'I was best man at his first marriage. What a woman! Anita always said it wouldn't last, that she was too much of a man for him. His other wives came and went, so to speak. Serial monogamy, Anita said. She, my wife, was godmother to one of theirs, can't remember which one for the moment. Anita and I, we never had any offspring, more's the pity. I used to envy old Evan with all his . . . Not that we weren't happy, Anita and I, you get used to these things, and as I always say, what's meant to be, you've just got to cut your cloth and get on with it, right? So, how is he bearing up?'

'He's a bit down; it's a slow progress getting back on his feet and he's inclined to give up. He needs a lot of encouragement. If you could find time to visit, cheer him up, it might help. But I do understand that when someone dies, your own life is put on hold.'

He put out his hand to pat hers. 'Yes, you know all about that, don't you, with your first kicking the bucket as he did. Who'd have thought it, eh? I mean, he always seemed so fit but there it is, and we can never be sure what lies in store for us and all that. You remarried, I hear. A man of the cloth? Working out all right?'

She wasn't offended because he seemed sincere in his enquiries. 'Very much so.'

'Second time round,' he said, nodding. 'Not that I want another crack at it. Anita and I, we didn't always see eye to eye, how could it be otherwise, but we were good friends. Always.'

Ellie spared a thought for May, who might or might not have aspirations in Freddie's direction, but if she did have any such hopes she was doomed to fail. This man was still in the depths of grief, though on the surface he was coping well enough.

He wiped the heel of his hand across his face. 'Do you believe, Mrs Quicke? In life after death, I mean? I was brought up a Catholic, though Anita wasn't that way inclined, and . . . I can't help but worry about her, wherever she may be. Suicide is a sin, isn't it?'

'Are you sure that it was—'

'Oh yes. *Compos mentis* and all that, right to the end. It was the third time the cancer had come back, and it was the prospect of losing her hair again which did it. There was no hope, you know. Perhaps she'd have gained another month. At best. It would have been a miserable, long drawn-out death. She knew that, and so did I. I did wonder whether she might . . . But she didn't even hint . . . I must have had an inkling though, because I checked that she hadn't enough pills to do the job, before I left.'

Ellie nodded. She hoped such a thing would never happen to her. Suppose Thomas were suffering from terminal cancer, and he asked her to help him die? What would she do?

But no, that would not happen. His faith was so strong, he would never put her in that position.

Freddie's eyes were far away. 'The thing is, I've tried to fool myself but I can't. I did know what was at the back of her mind when she encouraged me to go to the old school reunion. She said it was to give her space, a bit of time to herself, but I didn't reckon on her getting hold of any more pills. Stupid of me. She was always the bright one. I don't know who supplied her with . . . But it doesn't matter, does it? The thing is, I knew what she intended to do, though I pretended I didn't. So I'm as guilty as she is.'

Ellie didn't know what to say. She didn't, in all honesty, know exactly what to think. If the pain got so bad . . . what was the right thing to do? Ask the doctors for more painkillers?

Dear Lord above, put the right words in my mouth.

She said, 'She loved you very much. She saw to it that you weren't involved.'

His eyes were shiny with tears, but he held them back. He patted her hand. 'I'll go to confession this weekend. Haven't been for years. Get it off my chest, what? Thanks for listening. There's not many people you can talk to about . . . well, anything of real importance, is there?'

The door opened and May bustled in, her mouth downturned with disapproval. She was carrying two mugs of milky coffee slopping over on to a tray. She put the tray down with a thud, saying, 'The man from the Co-op rang again. I said you'd ring him back when your visitor had gone. And the men who are putting up the lights want a word.'

'Co-op Funerals?' Ellie took a sip of the coffee – which was instant rather than ground and over-sugared – and tried not to pull a face. 'I believe they're very good.'

'Yes, her father and mother, also her aunt, I believe. The service will be at the church she used to attend on high days and holidays. I used to go with her, often as not. A good choir, decent preacher. Cremation. Family flowers only.' He picked up the envelope Ellie had brought and drew out the photograph. He smiled. 'Yes, that's a good one. She hated having her photograph taken recently, her hair, you know. She had such beautiful hair. Thank you, Mrs Quicke. Appreciated. You can tell my old friend that I won't be alone. I've got family, cousins and an old uncle of hers, all coming to stay for the funeral on Monday. My sister said she'd come earlier, which is a mixed blessing, but most of them will be here at the weekend some time. My sister's wonderful in a crisis. She'll see to making up beds and providing food and all that. I said I thought the family would probably all like to go to the Carvery afterwards, but she said they'd expect to come back here, and she'd arrange the food and drink. If Evan can make it, that would be good. But if not, tell him I'll pop in to see him as soon as I can find a moment.'

'I'll see you out,' said May, appearing at Ellie's elbow. 'You didn't have an umbrella, did you?'

May wanted Ellie to leave, and there was no need for her to stay, was there?

Freddie came to the door with her, rubbing his hands, looking around. 'You know, I'm not at all sure we should have the lights up this year.'

May overrode him. 'You know it had all been agreed before she did away with herself.'

Freddie winced. Ellie wondered if May realized how tactless she was being. Perhaps she did?

'Nasty day,' he said, waving Ellie off. 'Keep in touch, right?'

Ellie smiled and nodded, without committing herself. As she reached the pavement, it occurred to her that there was one person who might well have been interested in hastening Anita's demise, and it wasn't her husband. No.

If one had a nasty, suspicious mind – and Ellie had to admit that it was a failing of hers to think the worst of man and womankind – then you would look hard at the ever-helpful May, who might well have taken the opportunity to assist Anita into the next world.

It was true that the one-time cleaner Ruby and the middle-class golf club player Anita had both died of overdoses, and there was some question as to how they'd managed to obtain enough pills to do so. It was perhaps understandable that a friend might have helped both ladies to their deaths, but there was no connection between them. How could there be, coming from such different backgrounds?

Ellie turned her mind to mundane matters, such as what they should have for supper that night, and whether or not it would be a good idea to ring the doctor about Vera, although it was widely known that antibiotics didn't help with flu. You just had to keep taking painkillers and fluids.

Wednesday afternoon.

She got to the checkout point and couldn't remember her pin number. Eight five oh something. She tried what she thought it should be twice, and the assistant said if she got it wrong the third time the card would be blacklisted and she'd have to ring some helpline or other to reactivate it. She had to leave her groceries there as she hadn't enough cash to pay the bill.

She had it written down as a telephone number in her diary, but she couldn't find her diary. Perhaps it was in her brown handbag, the one that she could wear over her shoulder?

She remembered some things better than others. She remembered opening the door, nearly ten months ago it must have been, to find poor Dr Ben, his face twisted with pain, clutching at his heart. She hadn't been her husband's practice nurse all those years for nothing. She'd realized he was having a heart attack, helped him inside and searched his pockets for his medication. She couldn't find it, so she rang nine nine nine. He'd gone by the time the ambulance came.

That was a bad day. After her husband had died two years

earlier . . . another heart attack . . . What was it with these doctors that they ignored the symptoms? . . . Anyway, Ben was the only doctor in the practice to keep in touch. No waiting in the surgery for her while he was alive. He used to come to see her regular as clockwork, every other Friday afternoon. He made sure she always had enough painkillers and sleeping tablets, they'd have a small sherry and a gossip and off he'd go. He was a lovely man, and she missed him.

She didn't find his bag till later. Going out to close the gate after they'd taken him away, she spotted something brown under the laurel bush by the front door. He must have dropped his bag there when he felt the first pang.

It had started to rain, so she picked it up and took it inside, lest it get ruined. She took out her own tablets, of course, and anything else she thought might come in useful. She'd stopped needing sleeping pills some time ago but they did come in handy for other people.

She rang the surgery next morning and said she'd found his bag outside in the garden. They came to collect it and said some drug addict must have cleared out his bag of pills before she got to it. She didn't contradict them because having them made her feel much more secure. Insurance for a rainy day.

Eight four oh two sounded right. Or was it nine four oh two?

FIVE

Wednesday afternoon

E llie struggled to get her key into her front door. Hampered by the bag of dry cleaning which she'd picked up on the way home, she found it a tricky business. Thomas never had this trouble with the front door key, but for some reason Ellie did. Perhaps she should have a new one cut?

Finally, she was in and out of the rain but not free to sit down and have a rest, for there was Rose, their housekeeper, wringing her hands, bobbing up and down, in a terrible state. Her cheeks were flushed. Had she been crying?

'Oh, thank goodness you're back, I didn't know what to do, I tried ringing you, but my fingers are all thumbs and I couldn't seem to get the right number down so I asked the man who came to read the electricity, and he did it for me, but then he said you were switched off and weren't taking calls, so then I thought of trying Thomas but he's in a meeting and said he'd ring me back but he hasn't. I really didn't know what to do for the best so I rang your secretary but she's not at home and in any case it's not really her problem, is it?'

'What isn't?' Ellie said, dumping the dry cleaning and shedding her wet coat and umbrella. 'Has there been an accident?'

'No, no,' said Rose, wringing her hands again, trying to explain and making a poor fist of it. 'It's Vera. At least, it ought to be Vera, but she's so poorly that I don't think she's up to understanding what's going on, and indeed I didn't tell her, though perhaps I ought to have done, but she's running such a fever that I hadn't the heart.'

Ellie guided Rose down the corridor into the kitchen and sat her down. 'Cuppa, my dear? Now calm down and tell me what's been going on. From the beginning. I went off to see Evan and you . . . What did you do?'

Rose gulped, but tried to obey. 'I was going to make a steak and kidney pudding, and then I thought, oh dear! It's nearly ten and I'm sure Vera needs a hot drink, so up the stairs I went to the top—'

'Rose, you aren't supposed to climb stairs nowadays.'

'Well, needs must, and I'm all right if I take my time about it. Anyway, she was ever so hot and croaky and so I came down and got her some lemon and honey and took it upstairs again . . .'

Rose hadn't been managing the stairs for months. And she'd done it twice in one morning?

'Good for you,' said Ellie, making a pot of tea for them both. 'And then . . .?'

'I started the pastry and I'd got the steak and kidney on to cook when the phone went and it was Mikey's school. He's played truant. Again!'

'What! I delivered him to the school gates myself this morning.'

'I suppose he waited till you were out of sight and went off on his own business.'

'Just wait till I catch him.' Ellie got milk out of the fridge.

'That's just it,' said Rose, deep in misery. 'He got caught this time, good and proper.'

Ellie nearly dropped the milk bottle. 'He got caught? Doing what?'

'I couldn't quite make out. Anyway, straight after the school got off the phone, the police rang asking to speak to Vera because they'd got Mikey down at the station, and I told them it wasn't possible to get her to the phone, and they said it was important and I said however important it was, Vera couldn't manage it and I asked them what was wrong, and they said Mikey had been caught on the building site, red-handed, and they needed someone, I couldn't quite understand who they needed but I said you were out and so was Thomas and it was something to do with having a responsible adult on hand, and they said would I do, and I said I couldn't, not really, with the pastry half made and not understanding exactly what had gone wrong, and maybe it was the wrong thing to say and I ought to have gone down there as I don't like to think of the lad in the hands of the police because ten to one they'll jump to the wrong conclusion—'

'What is it that he's supposed to have done?'

Rose wrung her hands in misery. 'I don't know! All I know is he's down there all alone, and they said he was being unco-operative and they needed his mother to be there before they could talk to him. I suggested they get one of his teachers, and they took the number of the school and said they'd do that, but you know what Mikey's like and if he doesn't want to talk, they won't get a word out of him.'

Ellie told herself to keep calm. 'Vera really is bad?'

'I went up again to see if she was feeling better, but she wasn't, so I didn't say anything to her, which I'm not sure whether I was right or wrong to do so, but then I tried to ring you, and then Thomas, and then I rang your secretary but at last you're here and can sort it out now.'

Ellie sat down with care, trying to take in what was happening. Mikey down at the police station? Caught red-handed, doing what? All that talk of sabotage . . . No, no! It couldn't be! But that's what everyone always said, wasn't it? That their little darling couldn't possibly have been responsible for whatever it was they were supposed to have done.

Mikey was from a single parent family.

Mikey was a stubborn little cuss at the best of times.

What to do next? Ellie poured tea with a hand that trembled. She handed one of the mugs to Rose, saying, 'Drink up.'

'I'm so glad you're back.' Rose wiped her eyes and blew her nose.

'Yes,' said Ellie. Should she ring her solicitor and ask him to help? No, first she must find out exactly what was going on. She took her own mug of tea back into the hall and rang the local police station. With any luck, it would be DC Milburn – Lesley – in charge of the case, and she'd get a sympathetic ear.

Unfortunately, she landed up with a desk sergeant – probably a civilian nowadays? – who didn't have the time or the patience to discuss a simple case of vandalism by a lad who'd been truanting from school. Who was Ellie, and what relation was she to the lad in question? Mother or grandmother? Aunt, perhaps? Guardian?

'I'll be there in ten minutes,' said Ellie, crashing down the phone and wondering if it would be best to walk or wait for a cab to take her there.

Rose appeared in the doorway, blowing her nose again. Was Rose going to go down with flu, too? 'Is he going to be all right?'

'Of course he is,' said Ellie, mentally crossing fingers. 'You get on with the supper. If there isn't time to make a steak and kidney pudding we could have the pastry as individual dumplings in beef stew, as they only take half an hour. I'm going to check with Vera and then get down to the station.'

Up the stairs she went. How many times had Rose done it today? Poor dear, no wonder she was worn out. Into Vera's flat. Nice and tidy. Everything clean and neat.

Ellie knocked on the door to Vera's bedroom, and a hoarse voice bade her enter. Vera was in bed, the bedclothes disarranged. She looked flushed and her eyes were half closed, not focusing properly. A jug of lemonade was on the stand beside her bed, with some packs of painkiller, evidence of Rose's attentions.

Vera tried to sit up when she saw it was Ellie. 'Sorry. I'll be getting up soon. Can't leave everything to Rose. Aches and pains, that's all. Better soon.' She was also running a temperature, if Ellie were any judge of the matter. And the light from the window was bothering her.

Rose was right; Vera was in no condition to do anything at all. 'Everything's under control. Don't you try to get up till you feel better. I just popped in to see how you are.' Ellie drew the blinds halfway down at the window. 'Is there anything you need?'

'Mikey . . .?'

Ellie spoke the truth, if not the whole truth. 'I took him to school today.'

'He's up to something . . .'

'He usually is. I'll check. You have a nice sleep and I'll be up to see you again in a while.'

For various reasons Ellie never felt comfortable at the local nick. She did realize that members of the public weren't meant

to feel comfortable there. It was even possible that a firm of
architects had been employed to make sure the surroundings
were as stark and forbidding as possible.

There was another reason why Ellie avoided the place. She
hadn't intended to make an enemy of the Detective Inspector
whom she'd nicknamed Ears, but that is exactly what she had
done, and he was one who'd hold a grudge for ever.

As she entered the hallowed precincts, she imagined how
Ears would relish her appearance on behalf of a disadvantaged
lad of mixed race who'd been caught thieving – or whatever
it was Mikey was supposed to have done. Ellie cringed at
the thought. Perhaps he was out on a case somewhere. She
hoped.

Ellie fidgeted, waiting for the desk sergeant to notice her.
A civilian was doing the job nowadays. Chosen for brawn
rather than brains?

'I'm Mrs Ellie Quicke. I've come to collect the boy Mikey
Pryce.'

A stone face. 'You're the lad's mother or grandmother?'

'Neither. His mother is employed by me as a housekeeper.
She and her son occupy a flat at the top of my house. His
mother is in bed with flu. I suppose you could say I was a
sort of guardian. May I ask what's going on?'

'You are responsible for him?'

'In a way, yes.'

'Yes or no?'

'Then; yes. May I see him?'

'Take a seat.'

Ellie did so. More waiting. People came and went. Some
police, some members of the public. No Ears, thank goodness.
Eventually, Ellie went back to the desk. 'May I ask who is
handling this case, and why you have him here in the first
place?'

A different man behind the desk. The same stonewalling
attitude. 'What is your name?'

Ellie looked at her watch. 'Is DC Milburn around?'

'Take a seat.'

Ellie did so. And at last Lesley Milburn appeared. 'Mrs
Quicke, what are you doing here?'

'I was told my housekeeper's young son has been brought here. His mother's down with flu, and I'm trying to find out what's going on.'

Lesley Milburn conferred with the duty officer, looked thoughtful, asked Ellie to wait a moment, and disappeared. More time passed.

Finally, Lesley reappeared, accompanied by a large, sandy-haired woman. Lesley introduced them. 'This is my colleague, who has been dealing with Mikey – or trying to do so. DC Collins, Mrs Quicke.'

Ms Collins looked as if she'd be a nice, commonsensical girl under different circumstances. Today, however, she looked as if she'd run out of patience. 'Look, in my view this is just a bit of mischief that's gone too far. Ordinarily, we wouldn't want to waste police time over it. We'd give the lad a good talking to and send him home. But there's a complication. The man who brought him in insists the boy must be charged with criminal damage. He says it's not the first time he's been caught and warned, but that he keeps coming back and doing it again. He says the boy has got to be stopped.

'We've warned him that because of the boy's age, no magistrate would give him anything but a slap on the wrist, but the complainant insists that we must make an example of the boy, to discourage others. He says that if the juvenile courts won't deal with his vandalism, he'll complain to Social Services that the lad is out of control.'

'Ouch.'

Lesley nodded. 'Given the boy's background – single parent, truanting and so on – it's not impossible that he'd get his way. If the boy were to admit he'd been stupid and expressed regret . . .? But he's dumb.'

Ellie felt herself go pale. Mikey had been very fond of his stepfather, Edgar Pryce, and had become mute after his death. It had taken time and patience to get him talking again, but he'd been talking to her and Thomas last night, hadn't he? So why had he stopped talking now? Ellie said, 'His mother has flu. And I mean serious flu. Don't you need an adult to be with him before you can question him?'

'We asked for a teacher to come up from his school, but

they said there's no one available till after four o'clock. They were not surprised to hear he's been truanting again.'

'Give a dog a bad name,' said Ellie. 'May I see him?'

A shrug. 'If you can get him to understand the position he's in . . .'

An empty interview room. Mikey was led in, wavering on his feet. He didn't appear to know where he was. Ellie called his name, but he didn't react. Instead, he subsided on to the floor, first kneeling and then collapsing sideways till he was lying down. His eyes were half open, his clothing was in disarray and there was a nasty bruise on his jaw. Had he been in a fight?

Ellie was alarmed, and so was Lesley Milburn.

Ellie said, 'He's ill!'

Ms Collins looked uneasy. 'He was asleep when I went to fetch him. I suppose he's not yet woken up properly.'

Lesley wasn't pleased. 'Something's wrong.'

Ellie knelt down beside Mikey and pulled him into her arms. He was soft and pliable within her embrace. 'Get a doctor! Quickly!'

Lesley Milburn knew how to make things happen. She opened the door and yelled, 'Get the doctor!'

An echo returned. 'What, now?'

'At once!'

'Keep your hair on.'

Lesley knelt down on the other side of the boy to Ellie. 'Better not move him.'

The sandy-haired DC Collins had flushed unbecomingly. 'He was all right when I checked on him a while back.'

Ellie stroked the boy's cheek. 'He's been in a fight?'

'Not exactly, no. The workman said the lad fell down some stairs and banged his head when he was discovered. He said the lad was swearing something chronic on the way in, vowing to put his eyeballs out with a lighter or something. Kicking him in the shins. He said there was nothing wrong with the boy till he found himself in here and realized there are consequences to what he'd been doing. That's when he started acting stupid.'

'Looks like concussion to me.' Lesley Milburn was anxious. 'You didn't think to get him checked out?'

'He was all right, I tell you. Wouldn't talk, that's all. What was I supposed to do?'

Lesley looked grim. 'We'll have a word about that later.'

Ellie felt the boy stir within her arms. 'It's all right, Mikey. Keep still. I'm here.' She could feel his heart beat against hers. 'Do you hurt anywhere special?'

He half raised his hand to his head, then let it fall.

Ellie said, 'You're as bad as your mother, in bed with flu.'

Lesley clicked her tongue. 'Flu? You think the boy has got flu as well?'

'It would account for his sleepiness. Except . . . You say he got a knock on the head when he fell down the stairs?'

Ms Collins pushed out her jaw. 'The complainant said the lad was caught red-handed. I've got brothers myself, and I know what mischief they can get up to. They can do a lot of damage on a building site unless they're stopped, and it's no good saying that boys will be boys.'

Mikey was so hot, he was almost steaming. Ellie pulled off his jacket, discovering a cut in one sleeve. It was on the underside of the sleeve. The words 'a defensive wound' came into her mind. 'Someone attacked him with a knife?'

'What? No one mentioned a knife.'

Ellie lifted his arm so that they could see the damage. 'Look for yourself. When I left him this morning he was in good health, no bruises, his clothes were neat and tidy and his jacket didn't have a slash in it. He's been assaulted, hasn't he?'

'He fell down some stairs.'

'Before or after he was knifed? Look, his sweatshirt has also been cut . . . Can you help me move him so that we can see . . .? No, not much blood. Just a scratch. I don't think he needs stitches, but—'

'Kids do mess up their clothes and—'

Ellie was on the warpath. 'I don't think his injuries are consistent with the story you've been given. I agree that he shouldn't have been on the site, and that he was trespassing. But it's clear that someone hit him across the jaw, perhaps managing to knock him out, and if he did take a tumble down the stairs, did he fall or was he pushed? Concussion can be serious. It would account for his sleepiness and inability to talk.'

Lesley and the sandy-haired constable exchanged glances. It was obvious to Ellie that Lesley outranked Ms Collins and that there were going to be words spoken about the way Mikey's case had been handled.

Ellie probed further. 'One of the interesting things about this is that Mikey wasn't brought in by the site manager, whom I know very well and who would certainly not have beaten the lad up, taken a knife to him, or thrown him down the stairs. As you probably know, I have shares in the new hotel, and have been advising them about the way the site was to be developed. So, who brought the lad in?'

'It was someone called Preston,' said Ms Collins. 'He told me he was the man in charge of the site this morning.'

'Preston. Preston.' Ellie tried to remember. 'Ah. If I'm right, he's one of the older men, who's been with them for years. A plumber who also does tiling? Can turn his hand to almost anything? It's true that the plumbers have had some problems on the site. But Preston is not the foreman, nor the site manager.' She looked down at Mikey. 'How long is that doctor going to be? Should we take him to hospital?'

'I'll check.' Ms Collins removed herself.

The boy's lips moved but he didn't open his eyes. Ellie touched his forehead. 'He's running quite a temperature.'

Ms Collins returned with a little Indian woman bustling along behind her. Middle-aged, no nonsense, Western clothes. She was British from way back, probably born here.

She said, 'Let the dog have a sight of the bone, then.' Despite her diminutive stature, she lifted the boy on to the table with ease and set about examining him.

'Concussion?' said Lesley Milburn.

Ellie thought: Ambulance. Overnight obs. I'll have to stay in hospital with him, which means telling Rose . . . and Thomas . . . and what else am I supposed to be doing? Who's going to look after Vera? Ought we to tell her about this or not?

Ellie's anxiety mounted by the second. 'He does seem very sleepy.'

Lesley said, 'He's not talking. His jaw's not broken, is it?'

The doctor shook her head. 'His jaw is not broken, nor is it dislocated, but someone's given him an almighty whack on his chin. Someone's aimed a knife at him. You can see the boy lifted up his arm to fend it off.' She peeled back the sleeve of his sweatshirt. 'Ah, the knife cut through his shirt but there's only a scratch on his arm, and it's hardly bled at all. A defensive wound. He was fortunate, wasn't he?'

She looked up at the two policewomen to see that they had registered her words. They had. The doctor said, 'Help me off with the rest of his outer clothing.'

They did so in silence.

The doctor said, 'I see heavy bruising on his legs and shoulders. I observe that large hands have clutched the boy around his upper arms. Someone has used unnecessary force to restrain him.'

'Not I,' said DC Campbell hastily.

The doctor said, 'Better take photographs in case a civil case is brought against the police for assault.' She got out a pencil torch and aimed it at each of Mikey's eyes in turn. He winced, turned his head away. She took his temperature. His head lolled on his neck. He was only semi-conscious.

'I thought at first,' said Ellie, tentatively, 'that he'd got flu? His mother's gone down with it, and he's normally an active child. But it's more than that, isn't it?'

The doctor nodded. 'Flu? Yes, there's a lot of it about. It could be, but in addition, he's been beaten up and knifed. I'll put in a report on his injuries. I don't think he's concussed but someone will have to watch him through the night, in case he relapses. No need to hospitalize him. Send him home. Four-hourly painkillers, plenty of fluids. Don't forget to photograph his injuries.' She whisked herself out again.

The two policewomen looked at one another. Ellie fancied a bad-tempered exchange of thoughts. Well, one blaming the other wasn't going to get them anywhere.

She said, 'Here's a how-de-do. I'd better get him home soonest. Meanwhile, who's got a camera?'

Lesley muttered something which, if Ellie had heard it properly, was probably unprintable and left the room.

Ms Collins had flushed to her forehead. 'Well, how was I to know?'

'Of course you couldn't,' said Ellie, trying hard not to blame the woman for taking the word of a white adult against a lad of mixed-race who'd been caught trespassing . . . at the very least. Lesley returned with a camera, and pictures were taken of Mikey's bruises and the damage to his arm, his jacket and sweatshirt.

Ellie huddled Mikey back into his clothes. He was a dead weight in her arms, eyes half-closed, skin far too hot. She asked, 'What happens next?'

Lesley grimaced. 'An official complaint has been made and will have to be followed up. There's some paperwork . . .' She glanced at Ms Collins, and glanced away. 'You'll have to sign that you're taking responsibility for the boy. Meanwhile take him home and put him to bed.'

'Can you get me a taxi or find someone to give us a lift?'

'I'll see you home.'

Yes, thought Ellie, because you also want to pump me about the ladies who are dying in droves. All right, it's exaggerating to say they're dying in droves, and I ought not to do that, but I'm tired and fed up and worried about Mikey and if she tries to make out I ought to have done more for her in the case of the suicidal ladies, then I'll flip. Though I'm not quite sure what that means. Flip. Sounds like Flipper the dolphin.

'Sign here,' said Ms Collins, producing some paperwork.

Ellie did so, without reading it, which she knew very well she ought not to do, but she was beyond caring. And if anyone said she ought to have got her solicitor in on this, she'd slap them, because there hadn't been time to arrange it and boys needed their mothers at such a time.

She cradled Mikey, who seemed to have fallen into a restless sleep. Still far too hot. She put in a spot of praying while they waited.

Dear Lord, give me strength. I think I've probably handled this badly, but you know all about the broken and wounded and how you pick them up and make them better . . . And yes, of course I ought to have got hold of my solicitor. I'll get on to it in the morning. My back does ache, but I'm not going to put him down.

Please, dear Lord, help us to sort this out? I'm sure Mikey couldn't have done anything very awful but, if he has, then

he'll have to take the consequences. I'll stand by him, anyway.
As will Vera. Oh dear. Why can't life just potter along without
things going wrong?

Lesley took them out of a back door at the station and down
a ramp to a car park. She opened the back door of a Toyota
and helped Ellie put the boy in the back seat. He lay where
he'd been placed, limp as a rag doll. Ellie got in beside him.
She did up her own seat belt and took Mikey into her arms.
Perhaps he ought to be strapped in, too, but she was beyond
such niceties.

Lesley had barely turned into the main road before she
spoke. 'I know this is a bad time to ask, but did you discover
anything for me?'

Ellie tried to bring her mind back from wherever it had
gone, to answer the question. 'I'm not sure. There was another
death which might be regarded as an assisted suicide, but the
husband definitely didn't do it.'

'Names and dates.'

'Call round tomorrow and I'll give you what I have. This
business of Mikey trespassing. The police aren't going to take
it further, are they?'

'A formal complaint has been made. You must see that we
have to look into it. And it's clear he was trespassing at the
very least.'

'Yes, I know. He's always over there, and he has been told
not to, but . . . trespassing is such a minor offence.'

'Sabotage isn't.'

True. Ellie thought about that. 'I don't think the company
would want to prosecute a child, would they? I've some influence there. I could offer to pay for any damage he's done. If
any. The other thing; suppose I file a formal complaint against
Mr Preston for assaulting the boy?'

Did Lesley smile? Yes, probably. 'Why not? We can discuss
it when I call tomorrow.'

SIX

L esley parked in Ellie's driveway and helped her passengers out. Ellie, supporting Mikey, sought for and found her latch key, which for once behaved itself . . . but no sooner had she got the door open than she was confronted by an unwelcome guest.

'Mother, where have you been?'

Diana. More complications.

'In a minute, Diana. First things first,' said Ellie. Between them Lesley and Ellie half carried and half dragged Mikey into the hall. He didn't seem able to walk by himself.

'Where?' said Lesley.

'On the hall chair for the moment,' said Ellie, easing her back.

'Mother, what's going on!'

Rose arrived, letting out cries of distress. 'You found him, then? Oh, the poor boy. Has he eaten anything? Bring him through into the kitchen.'

'Mother!'

'In a minute, dear.' And to Lesley, 'Thank you, Lesley. See you tomorrow?'

'*Mother!*'

'Yes, yes. Rose, has Thomas returned yet?'

'Yes, he's had a bad day, though, and I don't think he's all that well. He's had his tea and gone to his quiet room. Shall I fetch him?'

Another problem. Mikey's bedroom was on the top floor, but how were they to get him up there if Thomas were not able to carry him? An alternative suggested itself: every now and then Mikey took his sleeping bag and made a nest for himself downstairs. His favoured haunts were the study at the end of the corridor, or the quiet room to which Thomas retired when he needed to think and to pray. No one had been able to break Mikey of this habit of wandering the house at night, and it would be easier to nurse him downstairs – perhaps in Rose's bed-sitting room next to the kitchen? – rather than having to carry him up to the top of the house.

Lesley said, 'See you, then.' She vanished into the dusk.

Ellie dithered. Yes, it would be sensible to have Mikey in bed downstairs, but if Mikey had flu and gave it to Rose then she might be seriously ill, and they couldn't risk that, could they? 'Rose, perhaps he can sleep in the spare room on the first floor tonight?'

The cat Midge stalked across the hall and disappeared down the corridor with a flick of his tail. Mikey and the cat were seldom apart.

So where was the boy? He wasn't where he'd been placed on the hall chair. Ellie followed the cat down the corridor past the dining room – which Ellie hardly used except for her weekly business meetings – and into Thomas's quiet room. It was a well-proportioned room which had had no obvious purpose in life until Thomas had decided to use it for reflection, meditation, prayer . . . whatever. It was simply furnished with a couple of chairs, an occasional table and a rug on the floor. The only ornament – if you could call it that – was the Victorian embroidered picture of the Good Shepherd carrying a stiff-looking sheep over his shoulders, which Ellie had rescued from the junk cupboard under the stairs.

Thomas's prayers were imprinted on the air of the room, so that anyone who entered felt their spirit quieten down. He used it night and morning and sometimes between whiles, especially if he had some difficult problem to solve.

Thomas was indeed there. He was sitting in his big chair, the curtains drawn against the darkening sky, and with a side light on. He was fast asleep.

Mikey had discarded his outer clothing in dribs and drabs as he entered the room and was now in his sleeping bag at Thomas's feet. His eyes were closed and his breathing regular. The cat was curled up on Mikey's feet.

Ellie bent to touch the boy's forehead. His temperature was almost normal. Now how had he managed that? One moment he was ill enough to think about taking him to hospital and the next he was on the mend. And fast asleep. No kidding. His breathing purred . . . as did Thomas's.

'Well, there's a sight for sore eyes,' said Rose. 'We'll let the men be for the time being, shall we?'

Ellie wasn't sure. Oughtn't she to wake Thomas and find out what had gone wrong with him that day? Oughtn't Mikey to be fed some food and drink?

On the other hand, perhaps sleep was the best medicine for both of them.

'Mother!' Diana was calling from the hall.

Ellie started. Diana needed attention. Of course. How many days till her baby was due?

'Yes, dear,' said Ellie, ushering Rose out and closing the door behind them. 'Rose, how about supper?'

'The beef stew, remember? With dumplings. Now don't you fuss about Vera. I've been up to see her, gave her some more lemonade and aspirin, and she's gone back to sleep again. She asked after the boy, I said he was with you, and she said that was all right.'

Well, it might or not be all right and Rose oughtn't to have to climb all those stairs, but for the moment everything seemed to be under control. Except for Diana.

Diana was restless, walking around, massaging her lower back. 'My back aches, and I'm so tired. However much longer can it be? I went to the hospital this afternoon and they said it would be a couple of days yet.'

'Babies come when they're ready and not before.' Ellie let herself down into her big, high-backed chair with a sigh. It had been a long day, and it wasn't over yet.

Diana twisted herself into a chair, but couldn't settle and got out of it again straight away. 'I can't get comfortable. I had a call from Evan and found him on the floor. He'd tried to switch the kettle on or something, and fallen. I had ever such a job to get him back into his chair, and he'd, well, wet himself.' She squeezed her eyes shut.

Was that really a tear? Ellie couldn't remember the last time she'd seen Diana cry. Mind you, her situation was pretty dire. 'Was he alone in the house?'

'He was. I do think you might have stayed till his daughter

got back from school. She was supposed to be back by then but she was late, some after-school club she helps out with, as if it isn't more important to look after her father than some brats who are truanting more often then not and who have no intention of doing anything with their lives but deal in drugs and get pregnant. Excuses, excuses. She's useless at looking after Evan. I did think she'd take her share of sitting with him, but no, it's all me, me, me!'

'She's a nice girl,' said Ellie, non-committal. 'It's good of her to volunteer for the after school club, you know she's working for her exams, and she does do the early morning shift with Evan.'

'It's not enough.' Diana tried another chair only to heave herself out of it again. 'I did think I could rely on you for more than the odd half hour.'

Ellie bit back some sharp words. She thought of all the things she ought to be doing at that very moment: finding out what had gone wrong for Thomas, seeing to supper, checking on Vera, sorting out what it was that Mikey had done . . . and then Lesley Milburn wanted news of the dodgy suicides . . . and there were all the usual problems arising from her charity work . . . she hadn't passed Edwina Pryce's latest missive on to her solicitor yet . . . And Diana wanted a babysitter!

She said, keeping calm, 'You'll have to pay someone. A professional. Perhaps a man who could help Evan with his walking? A man might be less embarrassing for him, don't you think?'

'I can't afford it. The business is not doing well enough. I'm juggling too many balls in the air. If I stay at home we lose customers.'

'Has the doctor any advice?'

'He suggested an agency in the Avenue which might be able to provide him with a full or part-time carer. The thing is, I don't like to use people who come without a recommendation. And the cost! I'm not made of money.'

'How about a volunteer? Ah, but would they know enough to be of any use in an emergency? What about a District Nurse, or whatever they're called nowadays. Surely the doctor can advise—'

'I was thinking more on the lines of someone he knows, someone whose company he'd enjoy.'

'Someone he could flirt with, you mean?'

That annoyed Diana. 'Certainly not! He wouldn't be interested. But he has been ringing around giving the old sob story to some of his old flames, and he did mention a couple of people, golf club members, who might be persuaded to spend time with him. I wondered if you might know them. There's Marcia something-double-barrelled, Rosemary, and someone called Polly or Pauline. I think I've met them in passing, but I don't know one from the other. All widows, all left comparatively well off, I think.'

Ellie shrugged. 'I never really got to know the golf club lot.'

Diana laid a piece of paper on the table. 'Here's their names and addresses. You could perhaps visit them, explain the situation—'

Ellie didn't know whether to laugh or to slap her daughter. 'You've got a nerve.'

'Yes, I have, haven't I?' Was that another tear on her cheek? 'But you see, I'm at my wits' end. I want to do the best I can by him, and I know my strengths and my weaknesses. I can run a business but I can't do the sympathetic, caring bit very well. You can. So, will you help me out?'

Against her better judgement, Ellie said, 'I'll see what I can do. I'll pop over to visit him tomorrow lunchtime, stay with him for a bit and try to see one of your lady visitors in the early afternoon. I'm not promising anything more than that, mind!'

Wednesday evening

She was terribly upset. She would have a little sit down, turn the telly on, put her feet up.

It wasn't her fault. She hadn't even touched the girl!

Ruby had said she didn't like the look of her sister's baby when she was born, and had she been right! Caught thieving from the shops before she was ten, cautioned so many times, no one could remember how many. Ruby had been upset about it, but there, the girl had taken after her father, hadn't she?

Thought the world owed him a living which, as Ruby said, it never had done and never would.

At least the girl hadn't started truanting till she was fourteen, after her first abortion, but after that it had all been downhill. She'd never seemed to understand about contraception. Three abortions, was it? Or four? Regular as clockwork.

How the girl had managed to hide that last pregnancy of hers nobody knew. She'd put on so much weight, maybe she hadn't even noticed it herself. No one was going to worry too much about what had happened to a girl like that now, were they?

Petra had been carting bags of shopping up the stairs, tripped over a child's scooter on the landing and fell. Clear as the nose on your face.

No one had touched her. Called out to her, yes. Petra had turned round to see who'd been calling her name, and that's when she fell over the scooter. Bump, bump, bump.

The stairs were in a quiet cul-de-sac at the back of the shops. There was no one else around. The older woman had thought at first she should call for help but she hadn't got her mobile phone on her. She did have one, but she wasn't sure where it was, and she didn't want to wait around in the rain, it made her hip ache. Someone would be bound to come along and see the girl in a minute.

She had got on the bus round the corner and had been in such a fluster she couldn't find her bus pass at first, but then she did find it, so that was all right. The whole thing had shaken her up, rather.

She was still all of a tremble. Perhaps she would have a shot of something to calm her nerves.

Wednesday evening

'Thomas, wake up! Supper!'

He groaned, and stirred.

Mikey slept on, oblivious. Ellie touched the boy's forehead. His skin seemed cool. Could he really have managed to produce a temperature in order to avoid questioning at the police station? She wouldn't put it past him.

But not speaking? The doctor didn't think the boy had concussion but wanted Ellie to keep an eye on him. Well, she would do that. His not speaking was an emotional thing, wasn't it? Nothing to do with his bang on the head. Or was it?

Thomas yawned, and stretched. 'What's the time? And –' as he tried to stand up – 'why is Mikey sleeping on my feet?'

'He's had a hard day. I'll tell you all about it later. Leave him be and come and have something to eat. You've had a difficult time too?'

'Urgh.' He shook himself. 'You could say so, yes. Plagiarism. I know students crib from the Internet and try to pass the stuff off as their own unaided efforts, but you don't expect it from a colleague.' Still yawning, he followed her out to the kitchen.

'No one you know and like, I hope?'

'Far from it, but I only just spotted the problem in time. Another day and it would have been too late. We'd have gone to press and then what a furore there would have been! He's an important man – at least in his own estimation – and he's not best pleased that I pulled his article. I had to go and see him to explain why I did so, and what he might do to produce something I could accept in the future. Luckily, I'd got another article in hand which I'd put by for the next edition.' Thomas chuckled, regaining his usual composure.

Rose served up a good, rib-sticking supper of beef stew with dumplings and they all felt better when they'd cleared their plates. Rose put some aside for Mikey to eat when he surfaced, and told Ellie and Thomas to leave her to clear up as they'd only be under her feet if they stayed in the kitchen. Rose was rising to the occasion. Ellie only hoped she wouldn't pay for it later on.

Mikey appeared, dragging his sleeping bag and with the cat in tow, as Thomas made himself a cup of good coffee and Ellie prepared to move out of the kitchen.

'Are you all right, Mikey?'

He hunched his shoulders and didn't reply. Midge settled himself on the chair next to Mikey and prepared to receive a portion of the boy's supper.

Ellie turned the boy's head to her. His eyes looked all right to her. She didn't think he'd got concussion.

Now, how was Vera? Ellie toiled up the stairs to the top of the house to make sure the girl didn't need anything and found her fast asleep. Good. Then down to the sitting room to have a chat with Thomas.

'So, tell me what's been happening,' he said, subsiding into his big La-Z-Boy chair with his cup of coffee. 'When I got home Rose was flapping around but not making much sense. I gather Vera's gone down with flu, Mikey's been caught doing something he shouldn't, that you went to babysit for Evan, and then rescued the boy from somewhere.'

'I really don't know what to do about Mikey. Sometimes I think he's a lot cleverer than I am, and that it's no good second-guessing what he's up to. A workman at the hotel site hauled Mikey off to the police station, saying the boy had been sabotaging the work on a regular basis. He laid a formal complaint, emphasizing that Mikey was truanting from school and was from a single parent family. He said the boy had fallen down the stairs and bumped his head when he'd been caught, which explained why his clothing was in a mess. The police took this at face value, and in a way I don't blame them for doing so, because Mikey didn't defend himself in any way or even bother to speak.'

Thomas was concerned. 'Not speaking?'

'I know. I'm worried about it, too. The boy had been roughly treated to put it mildly, but it was only when I arrived and started asking awkward questions that they called in a doctor and had him properly examined. The doctor noted various bruises which didn't tally with the workman's story and, worst of all, a defensive knife wound on his forearm—'

'What?' Thomas shot upright in his chair. 'The boy was knifed?'

'Don't be alarmed. It's only a scratch. His jacket took the brunt of it. But if he hadn't been wearing a couple of layers of clothing, his arm would have caught it. And yes, he was knocked about. He was also running a high temperature. I thought that in addition to everything else, he might have flu and indeed he still might have, because how he could produce such a high temperature on demand I do not know. I brought him home, I turned my back on him for a second, he made his way to your quiet room and ended up at your feet, asleep . . . and his temperature now seems normal. Work that one out.'

Thomas relaxed, laughing, stroking his beard. 'The young imp. But, a knife?'

'Definitely a knife. But, if he really has been sabotaging the work at the hotel—'

'It's his playground. He feels proprietorially towards it. He wouldn't damage it. Why would he?'

'Yes, he does love the place. For that very reason I wondered if he'd resented the fact that the work there is nearly finished and tried to delay it. Hugh has banned him from the site, but—'

'It didn't stop him going there again today.'

Ellie raised her hands in the air. 'Tell me about it. I delivered him to school this morning. I saw him walk through the school gates. What else could I have done? Now, it's too late to phone Hugh tonight but I'll have words with him tomorrow, see what I can sort out. If I offer to pay for the damage, I'm sure Hugh won't press charges. The big worry is if the police involve Social Services they might start poking around, wanting to take Mikey into care. It would kill Vera.'

'We won't let that happen.'

She was comforted. If Thomas was on the warpath, who could withstand him?

'And that's all that's troubling you?'

Ah, he knew her so well. 'I spent some time with Evan, who is about the dreariest of companions you could imagine, all doom and gloom. Diana wants me to sort out an official companion for him from among his circle. Well, I can't vet them all, but I could sound one or two of them out to see if they are sympathetic and sensible.'

'Hmph!' said Thomas. 'Isn't it up to Diana to soothe his fractious brow?'

'Possibly, but that's not one of her talents.'

'I don't see why you should have to run around after her, or him. I do worry about you, you know.'

Ellie tried to explain. 'I like people and I like to be of use to them. Yes, it's tiring and sometimes it's tiresome but I do feel I'm being of use when I'm helping other people.'

He laid his hands over hers. 'Aren't your days busy enough as it is?'

'I inherited all that money. I didn't earn it and I didn't ask for it. I don't feel that I have a talent for handling it, but it's been dumped in my lap and I have to look after it as best I can. Looking after it is not enjoyable. I prefer dealing with people. I'm interested in them, what they think and do, and how they cope with their lives. I feel I understand them, and sometimes I do feel that I can help them. I infinitely prefer talking to someone to reading the minutes of meetings or rubber-stamping paperwork.'

He held her hand, then patted it.

She blinked. It was all the world to her that Thomas understood. He hadn't married her for her money. That had never been of interest to him. He loved her because she was right for him, and he was right for her.

She said, 'Oh, and the oddest things can happen. Detective Constable Milburn – who's asked me to call her Lesley, by the way – wants to know if I'd heard anything about the untimely deaths of some elderly ladies in the vicinity. According to her, we are surrounded not by ladies who lunch, but by ladies who pass away prematurely, possibly assisted by their friends or relations. Now, Evan asked me to drop something into a friend of his called Freddie, whose wife's recent death is a possible case in point—'

'Do we know him?'

'Sort of. Golf club acquaintances. Freddie and his wife were friends of Evan's, and she took an overdose recently. Thomas, gossip drifts your way from all quarters. Have you heard of anything like that?'

Silence. Thomas stroked his beard. She could feel the intensity of his thinking. He put out his hand to riffle through the *Radio Times*, checking what might be on the box. Then laid the magazine down again. More frowning.

'Mm?' she said.

A shake of the head. 'Dunno.'

'Lesley also mentioned someone else, a former cleaning lady whose niece seems to think she was pushed into the void in untimely fashion; the aunt was afraid she was about to be moved to an old people's home. I've met the niece and was not impressed. I'm not sure what to think of her story. Freddie's wife was threatened with a return of cancer. Both took an overdose. In both cases there was a query as to how they'd managed to collect so many pills, and Lesley wants to be quite sure that nobody helped them.'

'Ah. Older people can get confused, take their nightly medication, go to sleep, wake up and mistakenly take another dose.'

'Especially if they're dreading the future. Especially if they've managed to stockpile not just one but quite a few extra doses . . . which in both cases is denied by the relatives.'

'Relatives are usually understanding and sympathetic if the sufferer is in intense pain and wants to end it. They may not actually connive to supply extra pills, although I think that over the years I've been asked to conduct a funeral for several people whose misery has been cut short unexpectedly.'

'What is your position on that?'

He pulled a face. 'I pray about it and ask for forgiveness if I've overlooked some way that I might have eased their pain.'

'You turn a blind eye.'

'I hope and trust I haven't misread any signals. How about you?'

She sighed. 'I've been trying to think of anyone I knew who might have gone down that road and I can't, except that my mother did say once . . . but it was years ago, and I didn't know them. It was some couple she'd known for ever who died within days of one another. I mean, one died in hospital and the other was found dead in her bed at home the next morning. I have no idea how I'd act if I were faced with such a situation. I hope it never happens.'

She shuddered. 'Someone just walked over my grave.'

Wednesday evening

It was lovely to hear from old friends. She'd been half hoping and half fearing that he'd contact her, because she'd heard he was in a bad way.

Dear Evan. They'd known one another for ever. The great thing about old friends was that you never needed to explain anything. Mind you, his choice of wives . . . Well, least said the better. Her husband had always said some men were ruled by impulse, and he wasn't referring to their choice of shoes, was he?

Evan said he was desperate for company so of course she agreed to visit. He said he'd ring her back when he knew exactly when he'd be free, which was a bit of a facer if he really was so much alone. But there, perhaps someone had come into the room and he didn't want her to know that he was contacting such an old friend. Yes, that would be it. Diana must have come in, and he'd not wanted her to hear. Well, well. Concealing the truth from his new wife so soon?

Or really desperate.

If he didn't ring back, she'd have to find some way of getting to see him.

SEVEN

A nasty, wet, windy morning. Also, a business morning. Ellie usually wore comfortable casual clothes around the house but on business meeting mornings she felt obliged to make an effort. Even if no one else was impressed, dressing formally made her feel better able to play the part of the head of her charitable trust. True, others would make all the necessary decisions, and only occasionally was she called upon to do more than dispense coffee and, even more rarely, to adjudicate. Thomas said she was an excellent captain because could have steered the good ship *Lollipop* with one finger on the helm while her crew worked their socks off to earn her approval. Ellie thought he exaggerated.

The meeting would start at ten, but before that . . . Oh dear, it was going to be a busy day, wasn't it? Thomas had risen early and by now must be down in his quiet room, saying the office for the day. Rose might or might not be up and about. Ellie pulled on a good white blouse and a navy skirt. That outfit wasn't quite warm enough, but she found a blue and white woollen waistcoat to go over it. She slipped on some dark-blue brogues, which were comfortable and still new enough to look smart, and climbed the stairs to the top floor to check on the invalid.

Vera was blearily awake, eyes at half mast, temperature still far too high. Ellie cajoled her into taking a shower while she herself changed the bedlinen and found a clean pair of pyjamas for the invalid. Mikey was – thank goodness – sprawled across his own bed, fast asleep. Still too warm for comfort. Did he have flu, was he going down with it? Mindful of the doctor's words about concussion, Ellie shook the boy awake and made him open his eyes. He yawned in her face, curled himself into a ball and retreated from the day. Ellie lifted his arm and inspected the scratch on it. Healing nicely. No need for stitches or a bandage. She moved him into a more comfortable position and pulled the duvet over him. He still didn't wake up.

Should she leave him in bed, or try to make him go to school?

Best be on the safe side. She'd ring the school and tell them he was sick.

Down to the ground floor. Rose was up and about but not dressed. Rose had filled the dishwasher but not set it running. Was there enough other crockery and cutlery for breakfast? Well, it didn't matter if plates didn't match, did it?

Thomas came bustling in, rubbing his hands. He'd been out to check on his car, parked in the drive outside. 'There was a frost last night, but the car's all right. I must remember to renew the antifreeze. Shall I cook breakfast?'

The phone rang. Diana. 'Just ringing to check. You can sit with Evan this morning, can't you?'

'No, dear. Thursday is my business morning. Remember?'

'But I'm relying on you to—'

'Sorry, Diana. I really can't. It takes all morning. I've got a pile of other work to see to but I said I'd pop in to see him at lunchtime, and I will.'

'You'll check on those other women as well?'

'I'll try.'

Ellie put the phone down, and it rang again. This time it was Hugh, the project manager from the hotel site. 'Mrs Quicke, I was up at Head Office all day yesterday, and I've only just heard about the boy being taken to the police station. Is he all right? I'd like to come round and talk about it.'

She looked at her watch. Bother, she'd forgotten to put it on this morning. 'I was going to ring you. Can you come straight away? I've a meeting at ten.'

Thomas, pulling on his car coat, carrying a Thermos of hot coffee, kissed her ear. 'Won't be late. Hopefully. Is Vera all right? And the boy?'

She nodded at Thomas and said to Hugh, 'See you in a minute.'

As she put the phone down, it rang again. Lesley Milburn. 'Sorry to ring so early but there's been a development which you need to know about. Not good news, I'm afraid. May I come round?'

What could it possibly be? Could they prove that Mikey really had done some damage at the hotel site? Were they going to charge him with it? Her brain went into spasm. The business meeting . . . She couldn't cancel. Vera was still too poorly to be asked to do anything. Mikey was asleep. Rose was up and about. Evan must be visited.

Ellie stilled her breathing. Surely nothing bad could happen if she put off talking to Lesley for a few hours? 'I'm tied up all morning and early afternoon. What about teatime? Half three, say?'

'Can't you make it any earlier?'

Ellie suppressed panic. Could she rearrange everything? 'No, I really can't.'

'Oh. Well, I suppose it won't make much difference. By the way, did that girl Petra come to see you about a job?'

'I gave her some advice, but I don't think she was prepared to take it.'

It was going to be a difficult day.

Ellie phoned Mikey's school and got the secretary, a frosty personage whose function was to intimidate all parents and prevent them, if possible, from speaking to the genial head teacher. Ellie foresaw a difficult interview with the head at some point, but for now she simply reported that Mikey had gone down with flu and wouldn't be in that day. She did not try to explain about the police involvement. No doubt the subject would come up later.

Hugh rang the doorbell as she replaced the phone. He shed his coat, making no attempt at small talk.

'Tea, coffee?'

He shook his head.

She led the way into the sitting room, wishing she'd had time to tidy up before he came.

He said, 'I'm heartsick over this. I wouldn't have got the police involved if I'd been there, but it's gone too far for me to stop it. Normally, I'm on site all day and every day but first there was this meeting at Head Office, which was bad enough, and then they phoned me from the site to say there was a problem. Someone had underestimated the number of tiles needed for the bathrooms and we need another two hundred but our accounts people have unaccountably failed to pay their last invoice so the supplier refused to play ball. I had to spend hours trying to sort that out, and by the time I got back to the site it was too late. In fact, it took a while to find out why the men were so edgy, and when they said . . . I couldn't believe it. I rang the police station, and they said you'd taken the boy away.'

'Eventually, yes.'

A heavy sigh. 'I couldn't get a straight explanation out of the men. They said to ask Preston, but he'd gone home after he'd taken the boy to the station, so I went over to his house to talk to him about it. He's a good workman, or has been, can turn his hand to most things, probably retiring after this job's finished. I've never had cause to question his integrity before. He says he caught the boy red-handed under one of the baths, with a wrench, trying to undo a nut. If he'd succeeded, there'd have been a slow drip of water, not easy to trace . . . and the damage . . .'

'And the damage to the boy?'

He stared. 'What damage?'

'In his statement to the police, Preston says the boy tumbled down some stairs when he was caught. This was supposed to explain why he'd been clouted on the jaw, had massive bruises on his upper arms, and oh, yes, don't let me forget it, a knife cut which slashed through his jacket and sweatshirt. Luckily, it only scratched his forearm.'

Hugh stared into space. Then focused back on Ellie. 'Mikey doesn't carry a knife?' He made it a query, but he knew the answer really.

She said, 'Of course he doesn't. Workmen often carry knives, don't they?'

Hugh licked his lips. 'You're saying . . . No, no. Why would Preston . . .?'

'Unless . . .?'

Hugh didn't want to consider the prospect of one of his own men turning traitor on him. 'Preston said the boy acted sullen when he realized he'd been caught. I suppose he might have hit his head when he tumbled down the stairs.'

'Possibly. He'd certainly been clouted on his jaw. The doctor at the police station checked him out for concussion and said it probably wasn't, but organized photographs to be taken of his injuries. His mother had gone down with flu earlier that day. The boy was running a high temperature. He's been asleep more or less ever since. I'm hoping it's only flu.'

Hugh passed a big hand over his face. 'What a mess.'

'Suppose we turn the scenario around? Mikey came across one of your men in the act of sabotage, and whoever it was reacted by lashing out at the boy.'

'Not Preston.'

'If it wasn't Preston, then why did he take it upon himself to haul the boy off to the police?'

He stared at her, and she stared back.

'No, no. I can't believe it.' He didn't *want* to believe it. 'Suppose . . . suppose Preston found Mikey looking at a leak which had been started by someone else? Preston jumped to the wrong conclusion and overreacted.'

'I'd like it, too . . . if it weren't for the knife. Preston – or someone – went for Mikey with a knife.'

Hugh kneaded his cheek. 'I don't like that.'

'You can't ignore it. Mikey has a knife slash through his jacket and his sweatshirt. It's a defensive wound. He'd held up his forearm to ward off a blow. The thickness of his clothing saved him from a nasty cut down his forearm. He's scratched, and will need a new jacket and sweat shirt, but that's all.'

'I can't see Preston lashing out with a knife. He's a family man. He wouldn't.'

'Then . . . who?'

'Preston wouldn't have used a knife on a boy. I'll have another chat to him. Perhaps he did overreact when he found the boy where he ought not to have been, but I'm sure he wasn't responsible for the boy's injuries.'

Ellie had a feeling that Hugh was waltzing around the issue, concealing some information, hiding something? But why? And what?

He said, 'I'll go down to the station and say we are not going to press charges.'

That was fine as far as it went. 'And I'll see to it that Mikey pays no more visits to the site – when he's recovered.'

He shifted uneasily. 'I must remember to get that rope cut that Mikey uses to get over the wall. What with this and that, I forgot about it this morning.' He scratched the back of his neck. 'You must understand that Preston is one of the old guard. He's worked for me full time on a number of projects over the years, and I've never known him overstep the line. It's uncharacteristic. I'm sure we'll find there's some perfectly simple explanation for what happened. Preston and Mikey may have stumbled across the damage at the same moment. Or perhaps the boy tumbled down the stairs and hurt himself on his own. Preston picked him up and—'

'And knocked six bells out of him? Again, I say, if not Preston, then who?'

'I don't like to think that any of my men . . . You say you've got evidence? What sort of evidence?'

She hadn't really got anything, had she? 'Photographs of the boy's injuries were taken by the police at the station.'

'You can't prove Preston did it.'

'Agreed. I suppose it depends exactly what Preston accused the boy of doing, when he made his statement to the police.'

'What does the boy say?'

'Nothing. He's too ill to talk.' Crossing her fingers.

Hugh shook his head. 'I'll ask if anyone else witnessed the incident. I'll get Preston to write out a full account of what happened. The worst of it is that it's thrown us behind schedule again, so there's going to be even more questions asked at Head Office.'

The front doorbell rang. There was a bustle out in the hall; voices were raised, doors were opened and shut. The business meeting was about to start in the dining room. Ellie looked at the door, wondering whether to make her excuses to Hugh or to her fellow trustees.

Hugh made up her mind for her. He stood up, holding out his hand. 'Tell the boy . . . I don't know what you can tell him, except that I wish him well. All right?'

'Thank you, Hugh.' She shook his hand, helped him on with his coat, and saw him off the premises.

What next? The answerphone light was winking again. What was it Lesley Milburn wanted to say to her? Did Preston's formal complaint accuse the boy of an offence so serious that Hugh would be unable to stop things going any further?

Well, she couldn't think about that now. She had a business meeting to attend. She put her head round the dining room door, saw everyone was there but that no coffee had yet appeared. 'I won't be a moment.'

Where was Rose, who was always ready to feed and water visitors? Not in the kitchen. Ellie returned to the hall, to see Rose halfway up the stairs, panting and holding on to the banister. 'Sorry, Ellie. Long way up. I thought I heard the boy cry out but my legs gave way. Old age is a terror, isn't it?'

Ellie managed to pull Rose to her feet and helped her down into the hall with an arm around her waist. 'Go and have a rest in your own room, my dear. I'll see to everything.'

'Just like you.' Rose creaked her way along. 'You think you're Superwoman. Come to think of it, a nice little lie down would be just the ticket. I'll be back on my feet again in no time.'

Ellie eased Rose on to her bed, switched on the telly with the sound turned low, and almost ran back into the kitchen. The breakfast things were still on the table but the dishwasher had run its course. She put the kettle on to make a cafetière of coffee, while throwing cups and saucers on to a tray.

Stewart, who had once been married to Diana but was now thankfully and happily remarried with a new family to look after and love, came in to see if he could help. Much to Diana's disgust, Stewart was now the highly valued general manager of the trust. 'Rose said there was some kind of crisis? Is there anything I can do?'

Ellie was fond of Stewart. 'Find the sugar and the milk jug. Crisis? Yes, you could call it that. Stewart, could you make the coffee and take it in? Vera and Mikey are down with the flu and I need to check on them before I do anything else.'

Ever practical, Stewart buckled to, while Ellie started up the stairs, slowing down and breathing hard before she got to the top of the first flight. If she was finding it hard to cope, she wasn't surprised that Rose had given up.

Vera was still in bed and, if possible, looked worse than before. Her temperature was still high, and the sandwich someone had made and put beside her bed was uneaten and going stale. She half opened her eyes to give Ellie an approximation of a smile, and said, 'Mikey all right?'

'He's down with flu as well. I'm looking after him. Don't you worry about anything except getting well. Have you taken some aspirin? Have you enough to drink?'

Vera nodded and drifted off into sleep again. Best thing for her.

Next door, Mikey was lying in bed, eyes open, not moving. The cat Midge was lying, curled up, on his tummy. Ellie touched his forehead. Warm, but not hot. He hadn't got flu, had he? Or had he?

'Are you well enough to get up?'

He shook his head a fraction.

'I told the school you'd got flu, but I don't think you have. Mikey, I know you're in trouble and I want to help. Hugh's been round, anxious for you. We need to talk about what happened. I haven't told your mother anything, she's too poorly to be bothered, but at some point I do need to hear your side of events.'

He shook his head again and closed his eyes. He had his own small television set and computer. What was the betting he'd be out of bed and switching them on, the moment she left the room? She wasn't a betting woman.

'Are you hungry?'

No. Well, Vera kept her freezer and fridge well stocked, and there was a microwave as well as a conventional oven in their kitchen. The boy wouldn't starve.

Ellie descended the two flights of stairs, trying to clear her mind of everything that had been happening recently in order to concentrate on the business of the trust.

Ellie had never been particularly interested in luxury for herself, but had inherited sizeable estates from her first husband, from his aunt and, latterly, from her good neighbour Mrs Pryce. She had set up the charitable trust to deal with these bequests.

This morning's meeting ought to be routine but she was the chair and must keep her wits about her. It wasn't fair to the others to have a chair whose mind was occupied with thoughts of sabotage and/or how many painkillers you could take for flu in any twenty-four hour period.

Today there were only three other people at the meeting: Stewart himself, who had overall responsibility for the administration of the trust; Kate, their financial guru; and Pat, Ellie's part-time secretary, who took notes and saw that everyone did what they'd promised to do from one week to the next. All three were well on top of their jobs and zipped through the agenda with ease.

Despite her best intentions, Ellie let most of the meeting pass by in a daze. She was pretty sure she hadn't missed anything . . . until Stewart uttered the name of that time-wasting spend-thrift, Ms Edwina Pryce.

He passed a letter on headed notepaper to Ellie. 'The Pryce woman has got a new solicitor who's alleging that you are behind the series of 'accidents' which have caused the work at the hotel to fall behind schedule. He claims that you are acting against the best interests of the hotel and have placed the Pryce family's future in jeopardy.'

'What? Wait a minute! I had a letter from her solicitor the other day but—'

'She proposes that you resign from the board and transfer your shares in the hotel to her by way of compensation. What's going on, Ellie?'

Ellie flushed. What a tiresome woman Edwina was! Whatever would she think of next? And what did she mean by saying Ellie was behind the sabotage at the hotel? As for asking for 'compensation', the idea was ridiculous! 'The woman is impossible!'

'Tell me about it,' said Kate, shuffling papers. Kate had the responsibility of passing Edwina's outstanding bills for payment by the trust.

Stewart gave Ellie a reassuring smile. 'I haven't had any dealings with the woman, personally, though I've heard you say she's difficult.'

'Difficult?' said Ellie, trying to think of a more appropriate word to describe Edwina – and failing. 'When Mrs Pryce died and left me her estate it was with the proviso that I kept the surviving members of the Pryce family out of the bankruptcy court. Mrs Pryce knew the bequest was a poisoned chalice since it was unlikely Edwina would change the habits of a lifetime and live within her means. And she hasn't. Far from it. She's a bottomless pit, and I can't cut her off, no matter how much I'd like to do so. Still she's not satisfied. Does she really think I'd hand over our shares in the hotel to her? I don't understand her.'

Stewart looked worried. 'She seems to have sent a copy of this letter to a director of the hotel chain whom she addresses in first-name terms. If he decides there's even the shadow of a case to answer, their solicitors will swing into action. They've invested a lot of money in the rebuild and refurbishment and are not going to be happy about this development. Can't you reason with Edwina?'

Ellie was annoyed. 'She sent me a similar letter, and she's been in touch with Evan Hooper about it as well. It's all pie in the sky. She's threatening this and that so that we'll pay her off to keep her quiet. I'm not playing. Thomas said I'd better pass the letter on to my solicitor, and I will do so as soon as I've a minute to spare. Let him deal with her.'

Then she stared into the distance. What did Edwina Pryce mean by saying that Ellie had been responsible for the recent problems at the hotel site? That was too ridiculous for words. It was far more likely that she herself . . . No, no. How could she? Or, indeed, why should she?

Ellie shook her head at herself and returned to the matter in hand. 'It's annoying enough that she's trying to draw Head Office into the argument, but what's even more annoying is that we'll have to pay *our* solicitor a fee to counter *her* solicitor's claim. Now that *is* what I call annoying. More coffee, anyone?'

'Yes,' said Kate. 'I expect you're right. She's a past master at getting us to pay for whatever it is that she wants.' She flicked through a pile of bills. 'Talk about biting the hand that feeds her . . .! I'll get you to sign a cheque for her last month's expenditure before I go, Ellie.'

'Oh well,' said Stewart, 'let the solicitors fight it out.'

Thursday afternoon

After the meeting broke up, Ellie did another scurry around the house.

Up to the top: Mikey was not in his room, and his computer screen was dark. Oh.

He wasn't in their sitting room, either.

Ellie stood at the window which overlooked not only their own back garden, but also, beyond that, the garden of Pryce house.

The scaffolding had come down from the back of the house, and over the past couple of weeks there'd been men toiling away to create a patio there. They had finished laying paths and were now putting down turves to make a lawn. The designer preferred by Ellie and accepted by Hugh had envisaged guests having drinks outside in good weather. There was even a children's play area with brightly coloured equipment in one corner.

The dilapidated greenhouses had long ago disappeared, but an enchanting Japanese-style gazebo had been placed where guests might admire the rambler roses which had been Mrs Pryce's favourite, and which once again adorned the ochre-coloured London brick of the century-old walls. The bedding was mostly easy-to-maintain shrubs, but today a man was planting bulbs in giant stoneware containers on the patio.

Ellie was soothed by the sight. It wasn't going to be the cheapest of gardens to maintain. They could have covered the whole of the back garden with tarmac and made it into a car park, but this was to be a very special hotel, offering far more than overnight motel facilities.

Ellie told herself not to stand there daydreaming. She pulled herself away from the window and went to check on Vera, who was deeply asleep, but woke when Ellie called her name.

'Let me take your temperature.' It was not quite as high as it had been, but still well over the arrow.

'I must get up.' Vera's voice was a croak.

'No, you mustn't. Pamper yourself for once. We can cope. Now I'll fetch you some more drinks and fruit. Anything else you fancy?'

'Mikey . . .?'

'I'll look after Mikey. Relax and enjoy a good rest. Do you want me to ring the college, tell them you're down with flu?'

'If you would.'

Down the stairs Ellie went. Hadn't the cleaners been due today? What day of the week was it, anyway? Thursday? Then . . . Where was her watch? She'd put it down somewhere, but . . . No time to look for it now.

She rang the college and reported that Vera was off sick. They said a lot of their other students were off sick, too.

Now where was Mikey? Not in the quiet room, which was where she'd thought he might be. It was lunchtime. Well, nearly half past twelve, and that was lunchtime for Ellie.

Rose put her finger to her lips as Ellie arrived in the kitchen. Mikey was flat out in the big chair, asleep. He was warm but not hot. His flu – if that was what it was – was abating. He didn't stir when Ellie touched him. Midge the cat was on the floor at his feet eating . . . a biscuit? It might not be a biscuit. It might be something the cat had filched from somewhere. Best not enquire.

Rose looked ragged, her hair in wisps and her cardigan buttoned awry. 'The boy's all right in here, isn't he? He says he got some more drink for his mum and she's asleep and for me not to bother her. Then he had three scrambled eggs on toast and a pint of orange juice, and fell asleep. I didn't like to disturb him.'

Three eggs and a pint of juice? His appetite had returned, then. Perhaps he didn't have flu after all? Yes, but he hadn't eaten much yesterday, had he? Maybe he was just making up for lost time?

Rose gestured to Vera's laptop open on the table in front of her. 'I'm trying to do the weekly order from the supermarket. Vera's shown me how I don't know how many times, but I can't make head nor tail of it. I think I've ordered fifty packs of peas. Or that's what it says, and I can't remember how we get to pay the bill.'

Ellie tried to concentrate, but couldn't. There are people who can organize their lives through the medium of computers, and there are those who can't. She couldn't. Full stop.

'Tell you what, Rose; cancel it. I've got to go and spend an hour with Mr Hooper, see that he eats something for lunch. I'll probably do him scrambled eggs, too. Quick and easy. I'm supposed to be making a couple of calls on the way back, errands for Diana, and then I'll pop into the Avenue and get some food at the shops on my way back. If there's too much for me to carry, I'll get a cab. Have we anything in for supper?'

'Veg we have, if you count stuff in the freezer. Potatoes we have. There's a lasagne Vera made the other day, double portion. I'll get it out of the freezer to defrost. We could do with some more fruit, though. Let me make a list . . .'

EIGHT

Thursday afternoon

It was raining. Or it had just stopped and was about to start again. Ellie rang for a cab, and while she waited for it she tidied up the sitting room and rescued the piece of paper Diana had given her with the names on it of possible Evan-sitters. She looked for her watch, but it was nowhere to be found. She did find her mobile phone, though it looked as if the battery was getting low. No time to do it now. Into the cab and off we go.

It would have been a help if Diana had thought to give Ellie a key to their house. Evan's daughter would be at school, and he would take his time getting to the front door. Did Ellie have time to ring home to see how Mikey and Vera were? She fumbled in her bag, found her mobile, remembered just in time that the battery was low and decided not to risk it.

At last the door opened. Evan was in his wheelchair, and it didn't look as if he'd bothered to shave that morning. A bad sign. 'Where have you been? I've been worried sick, thinking you'd forgotten all about me.'

'No, no.' Let's be cheerful, shall we? 'A busy morning, business meeting.'

'It's all right for some. That's what I ought to be doing, not stuck here all by myself with nobody to talk to and nobody to care whether I live or die.'

'Now, you know I care. What do you say to some scrambled eggs?'

'Can't you do better than that?'

Ellie held on to her patience with an effort. Hadn't she boasted only last night to Thomas that she liked dealing with people? 'Unless there's something in the freezer which I can cook for you quickly, it'll have to be scrambled eggs.'

Scrambled eggs it was, as both the fridge and the freezer were almost empty. Now, how was she going to deal with that problem? Diana ought to . . . Well, don't let's start on that. Diana couldn't. She couldn't be expected to. Well, you might expect, but you wouldn't get.

Patience, she told herself. You'll think of something.

She cleared away the dirty dishes that had accumulated in the kitchen and started the dishwasher. Evan hung around, getting in her way.

She said, 'Diana says some of your old flames might be wanting to visit you. How do you feel about that?'

He looked dodgy. 'Hrrrm. Yes, I suppose so.'

Now what did he mean by that? Ah. 'They've been in touch already, wanting to soothe your troubled brow?'

Almost, he blushed. 'Why shouldn't I ring round some old friends, see if they can spare an hour to keep me company?' Turning aggressive. 'What's it to do with you, anyway?'

She despaired. Why bother with such a boor? 'Diana is worried about you. She worries about leaving you alone, and she worries about not being at the office. She wants to do the best she possibly can for you, but she's not sure how. She asked me to help out, and I'll do what I can even though I've a lot on my plate at the moment. Now, tell me about this harem of yours. Old friends, you say?'

'Flutter-byes,' he said, with a cross between a grin and a grimace. 'Good for a gin and tonic and not bad partners for a round of golf.'

'Pleasant enough for an afternoon's entertainment?'

'Too long in the tooth for that.'

Did he mean what she thought he meant? Dirty old man! She tried again. 'I wonder if any of them play bridge? Perhaps you could find another couple, make up a foursome.'

'Bridge! Hah!' He gave her a sly look. 'Poker, now?'

Did he mean strip poker? She wouldn't put it past him, the randy old goat. Him in a wheelchair, too. 'Bridge,' she said, as firmly as she could. 'A gentleman's game.'

'Meaning that poker isn't?'

She laughed, because she'd meant exactly that. Or half meant it. 'Evan Hooper, you are winding me up.'

He laughed. 'Nice to see you with some colour in your cheeks.'

She twisted round to see the clock. 'I've got to go. I'm supposed to vet one of your ladies this afternoon, and I'm expecting a visit from a policewoman later on.'

'What have you been poking your nose into now?'

She said, without thinking, 'Ladies who die before their time, and Edwina Pryce.'

'Ah.' He massaged his chin. 'Edwina. Nasty piece of work. She's been ringing me almost every day. First she said she wanted me to find her a better flat to move into so that she could rent out her present one. I told her to ask Diana. Then she offered me the sale of Pryce House, which I told her straight she has no right to do. Wrapped up in all this was a lot of guff about how appallingly badly you've treated her, and that she believes you're behind some dark dealings at the hotel, which I couldn't make head nor tail of. Total garbage. She wants me to make you "see sense". I told her you were impervious to threats. You take care, now.'

'Thank you, Evan.' She bent over and kissed his cheek. Much to her own surprise, and possibly to his, too.

'See yourself out.' Back to his surly self.

First on Diana's list for a visit was Marcia something-double-barrelled. Ellie used her mobile on the way, to check that the lady was in and would agree to see her. Marcia lived in a large Edwardian house but, according to the rank of bell-pushes in the porch, this one had been divided into flats. Ellie shivered. There was what some people called a brisk wind, and she was feeling the cold today. She hoped she wasn't going down with flu.

She fidgeted, worrying about how long this would take before she could get back home and find out what was happening there. Mikey . . .

A tinny voice through an entryphone. 'Yes?'

'Ellie Quicke. Evan Hooper's mother-in-law.' That sounded grand and also a bit off since Evan was almost her own age. The front door clicked open, and Ellie stepped into a dark hall with a tiled floor. Substantial doors led off to right and left, and one of these stood open to reveal a well-dressed, well-preserved woman with impeccably groomed grey hair and a good if slightly heavy figure. An advertisement for Burberry, Harvey Nichols, and the cream that's supposed to rejuvenate your skin. This woman had been handsome in her time. She was also accustomed to exerting authority. An ex-councillor? Possibly still active in the field of politics? Tory, of course. No, perhaps independent.

A hand with many rings on it was extended to be shaken. 'Do come in. We've met before, I think, at the golf club? Your husband used to partner me now and then. He died young, didn't he? You never took to the game, did you? I seem to remember his saying you had no talent in that direction.'

Well, that was a good start, wasn't it? Ellie forced a smile. 'Yes, he loved his game of golf. My second husband doesn't play at all, though perhaps he should, to keep his weight down, you know?'

Eyebrows were lifted at that, indicating disapproval. The sitting room was furnished by Harrods with a preponderance of brocade, velvet curtains, tassels and orchids in pseudo-Chinese pots. There was a huge flat screen above the fireplace and below it a carriage clock which now chimed the hour. Ellie started. Three o'clock already?

There were four silver-framed family-style photographs on a side table.

Marcia saw Ellie looking at them and said, 'Son; plus second wife and children. The others are ex-husbands.' She counted them off on her fingers. 'Number one died of cancer. I divorced number two after he ran off with his secretary, who was half my age. She didn't last long, went off with someone who had more money to spend on her. He came whining back to me but by that time I was on to number three . . . only, he had a heart attack and died within the year. I'm not on the lookout for number four. How about you?'

Ellie blinked. 'I'm still on my second.'

The furniture in the room was arranged in an unusual way. All the overstuffed chairs and settees – of which there were plenty – had been moved so that there was a sort of corridor of carpet leading from the fireplace to a strange contraption under the windows.

Marcia was holding something . . . a putting iron? Was that the right term for it?

'Do sit down. You're in the way. I need to practice my putting.' She dropped a golf ball on to the floor, measured distances with her eye, and swung the putting iron, sending the ball skimming across the carpet and plop! into the plastic container under the window. Ah, an improvised practice 'hole'.

'Not bad,' pronounced Marcia, laying her club – if that was the name of it – down and hovering in front of a lacquered Chinese cabinet. 'One for the road?'

Meaning what? A sherry? At that time of the afternoon?

Ellie told herself not to be so judgemental. 'I still have a lot to do today, I'm afraid.'

Marcia shrugged and poured some orangey liquid. 'Carrot juice. I'm not fond of it but it's supposed to help you live longer. It looks better from a decanter, don't you think? So, who asked you to come? Evan or the darling little wifey? Not that she's either a darling or little, come to think of it. She doesn't resemble you, does she?'

Ho hum. One of those women who thought 'speaking her mind' wasn't bad manners but was 'making her position clear'.

'Diana is very worried about Evan.'

'So she should be. Isn't it her job to look after him in his hour of need?'

Ellie set her teeth. 'She also has to keep the business going. Plus the baby is due any day now. She's at her wits' end to know how to juggle her priorities.'

'I've known him a long time. She'll lose him if she's not careful.'

Ellie decided to ignore the insinuation that Evan might discard Diana for another woman. 'Oh, I don't think he's that poorly.'

'I didn't mean that, and you know I didn't.'

Ellie felt her colour rise. 'The prognosis is excellent but it will take time for him to get back on to his feet and into the office. Meanwhile he has much to look forward to.'

Marcia cracked out a laugh. 'Oh well, if that's your position. I suppose you can't allow yourself to think otherwise.

Take it from me, if he doesn't get the attention he thinks he deserves, he'll be looking for wife number five any day now.'

'Not with a longed-for son about to be born.'

Marcia shrugged. 'Don't say I didn't warn you.'

'It's a difficult position for everyone. I agree he needs diversion. A companion or series of them. Someone up to his weight, if you see what I mean.'

Marcia sipped her carrot juice, laid it down again. 'I keep telling myself this is good for me. I used to get through a bottle of wine a day. Had to stop that. I won't have my second husband outliving me.'

Ellie began to like the woman. 'Could you bear to sit with Evan for a couple of afternoons a week? Perhaps you could get him to practice his putts, even while he's in his wheelchair.'

'You think I'm up to his weight?' Sardonic.

'Oh yes. You know you are, too.'

'Mm. Are you sure you won't have a small one to keep the cold out? I can break my rule of not drinking if a visitor would like one.'

'Wish I could, but I've got a policewoman coming round to see me later on today and I have to keep my wits about me.'

'Really? Someone told me that you fancied yourself as a private detective.'

Ellie grinned. 'No more than you fancy yourself as Evan's fifth wife.'

Marcia barked out a laugh. 'That's true. Not my scene. I like him, of course. Known him for ever. Good drinking companion. Not a bad golf player, successful in business but . . .' She shook her head. 'Dunno about the future of the estate agency. Perhaps the dreaded Diana is right to concentrate on keeping it afloat. Thank the Lord I've a portfolio of shares that hasn't sunk too low. I'll drop in to see him, find out what days might suit. I can do Mondays and Wednesdays, two to four, no cooking or cleaning and I'm not helping him to the toilet and back. Suit you?'

'Thank you, yes.'

'He has a daughter, hasn't he? Schoolgirl, comes home at

four or thereabouts, so she can take over then. Who's doing morning and lunchtime?'

'I've done a couple or hours here and there but can't commit to more. He's suggested a couple of other women as well.'

'Pauline, perhaps?' A furrow appeared between the eyebrows. 'She's a bit past it, if you ask me. Pleasant enough. At least she could phone for help if there was an emergency.'

'Not the type to divert him from his problems?'

'She used to be sharp enough – a good bridge player if my memory serves me right – but her husband's death took it out of her. It seems to me that the death of a loved one either stiffens you up or rots your backbone. I used to know her quite well, we were both on some committee or other . . . raising funds for the new library at the school, I think. Then she went on to take up some lost cause or other. I'm not into lost causes, as you might gather. I won't waste time and energy on something which hasn't a chance of succeeding. Haven't seen her for some time, heard she'd let herself go, fancies she needs a hip replacement but the doctors say she isn't bad enough, but there . . . *Tempus fugit* and all that rot. Not sure she's got it in her to stand up to Evan, but any port in a storm. Sure you won't join me in a small one?'

She took another gulp of her carrot juice, shook her head, said 'Grrrr!' and set it down again.

'No, thank you. I really must go.' Ellie, worrying about Mikey and, well, everything, made as if to get up.

'Don't go yet. There's nothing on the telly, and I'm not in the mood to be by myself. Tell me about the visit you're expecting from the police. What have you done to deserve that, eh?'

'Not me.' Would it be indiscreet to mention the ladies who'd left life unexpectedly? Possibly. But Marcia probably knew at least one of them. 'I expect you know Freddie and his wife Anita?'

Marcia concentrated. Her intelligence was formidable. 'I do. I did. He didn't murder her, though.'

'Who said anything about murder?'

'You said the police are involved.'

'Not in that way, no.'

'Then why did you mention them?'

Ellie grimaced. 'I have a much younger friend in the police force. She has a nose for, what shall we call them, irregularities? A woman went to the police to report her aunt had died unexpectedly—'

'Not Anita. No nephews or nieces.'

'No, indeed.'

'Her husband was distraught.'

'So I've observed.'

'If anyone were going to knock Anita off, it would be his little PA, whiny-faced May.'

Ellie laughed. 'Agreed, but I don't think she did it. I liked Freddie. He's feeling guilty, thinks he ought to have prevented Anita from killing herself.'

A sideways glance. 'No one's going around saying that, are they?'

'Only me. And only to you.'

'Not to the police?'

Ellie sighed. 'Do you think Anita killed herself?'

A nod.

'Do you think she saved up her tablets till she had enough to do the deed?'

A long silence while they both thought about this.

Finally, Marcia said, 'I'll see you out, shall I? Tell Evan I'll ring him, pop round to see him, suggest we play the putting game. And let him win. Well, some of the time, anyway.'

She extended her hand, and Ellie shook it. 'Thank you, Marcia. Do call me Ellie.'

'Till we meet again. As I'm pretty sure we will, now we've made one another's acquaintance.'

'You'll let me know if you hear anything about another untimely death?'

'So long as you rule out Anita.'

'Do you fancy Freddie for your fourth?'

Marcia was amused. 'It would never work. He loved Anita dearly, and I'm a better golf player than he is. He's a social player. It would gnaw away at him, knowing I could beat him any day if I wanted to.' She opened the front door. 'A nasty evening. Did you park in the road outside?'

'I don't drive. I have my umbrella, and it's not far.'

Marcia cracked out a laugh. 'Take care not to run into any murderers on the way home.'

Thursday afternoon

Evan had rung her again, wanting her to . . . She couldn't make out exactly what it was that he wanted. She'd been so worried about him; the prognosis wasn't good, was it? If he'd only get himself up out of his chair and get around on crutches, doing his exercises, he'd be well on the way to recovery . . . or if not complete recovery, at least on the road to it.

He said he wanted company. He might just want to talk about himself. In her experience, that's all most men wanted.

If he wanted more than that, if he really was as miserable as he said, then she supposed she'd have to help him, but it did take it out of her.

She'd better visit him as soon as possible. She'd nothing else on, and Diana wouldn't be back till late. She really didn't have anything else on that day, did she? She did wish she could find her diary. She felt lost without it.

Ellie scurried through the rain, round one corner, across a busy road . . . whoops . . . a white van went through a large puddle and she only just drew back in time . . . along another road and up what couldn't really be called a hill but did get her to slow down a bit, and then into her own road at last.

Oops! She just realized she'd promised to do some food shopping on the way back, and it had completely slipped her mind. Oh well, she'd sort something out later.

Detective Constable Lesley Milburn's car was already parked in front of the house and the driver's seat was empty, so Rose must have let her in.

All day Ellie had been trying not to think what bad news it was that Lesley had to impart, and her imagination had run away with her. She'd decided that she really did not want to hear what it was that Lesley had to say but she couldn't avoid it, except perhaps by emigrating to another country, or . . . how about going down with flu? No, perhaps best not.

After the usual struggle with her key, she let herself into

the house. It was getting dark. She switched on the lights in the hall. There were no lights showing down the corridor which led to Thomas's study and quiet room, so he couldn't be back yet.

Rose materialized from the kitchen, muting her voice to deliver gobbets of news. 'I've put that nice policewoman in the sitting room and given her a cuppa. No doubt you'd like one too, such a nasty day as it is. Oh, and the washing machine's ground to a halt again.'

Rose always overloaded the machine. Ellie gave the usual advice. 'Try running a Rinse and Spin programme.' That usually did the trick. 'How is Vera? I do hope you haven't been going up and down the stairs to look after her?'

'Mikey perked up a bit this afternoon and went up to see her. He said she was a little better. He made her a cup of tea, would you believe? Though I don't think she drank it, because he came down later for some lemons for her. I sent him up with a jug of my lemonade which he said she was getting through like nobody's business. I put up some sandwiches for her, too, and he said she did eat one though I think he had the rest, the little devil. Then he came down and went off to sleep again in the big chair in my sitting room with the telly on, and I haven't liked to disturb him because he's not well, the little angel.'

'So he really is ill?'

Rose looked as worried as Ellie felt. 'It seems to come and go with him. You go and deal with that policewoman, who is a nice enough person but you can tell she's sitting on some bad news, she's got ants in her pants as they say.'

NINE

L esley Milburn was standing by the window, looking out on to the sodden garden. 'Thanks for seeing me at such short notice. Rose looked after me beautifully.'

'Sorry I'm late. There's a lot going on at the moment.'

'I know how busy you are.'

'I saw Hugh this morning. He's the project manager from the hotel site. He says they won't be pressing charges against Mikey.'

'Good.' Lesley sighed, rubbed her forehead. 'Except that it's gone too far. The thing is that my colleague, the one who took Preston's statement and looked after Mikey, well, she was not entirely happy about it.'

'You mean she knew she ought to have had Mikey examined and his injuries noted before I arrived and made a fuss, so she took it to a higher authority to get her own version of events in first?'

'I wouldn't put it like that.'

'Well, no. She's your colleague, and you have to stand up for her. I suppose she'll get an official reprimand for what she did. Or rather, for what she didn't do.'

'She is a conscientious officer and . . . This is so difficult. I've been trying to work out how to tell you, and there's no way to put it that you're going to like.' She took a deep breath. 'She did take the case to the boss, and he instructed her to get Social Services involved at once. Not next week, or in due course, but immediately. He says the boy must be removed from an environment in which he truants and commits criminal damage. He says his mother has let him get out of hand and is clearly unable to exercise any kind of control.'

Ellie groped for the nearest chair. In her head she heard Lesley's voice repeat 'out of hand . . . out of control'.

Lesley looked anxious. 'Are you all right?'

Ellie cleared her throat. 'Don't tell me Ears is doing this out of a respect for law and order. He's doesn't give a damn about the boy. He's doing this to get back at me.'

Lesley looked as if she were going to cry. 'Of course not. He's concerned. It's his job to, well, see the bigger picture.'

Ellie thought of saying a rude word, but restrained herself. They both knew that Ears had long wanted to humiliate Ellie and had seized on this chance to get at her through her protégé. Ellie said, giving every word due weight, 'Ears is a small-minded, pettifogging person who has been promoted beyond his abilities. If that's slander I'm prepared to back up my words with chapter and verse.'

Lesley was unconvincing in his defence. 'You know I can't see it like that. And I'm never quite sure what "pettifogging" means.'

Ellie tried to smile. 'Neither am I. It sounds right, though.'

Lesley nodded.

Silence.

Ellie said, 'Of course the boy needs a good talking to. Of course he shouldn't have been truanting, and he shouldn't have been at the hotel site. But until he recovers from the beating he was given and the loss of his voice, there's no way we can find out what really happened. Hugh said he'd investigate. He doesn't want to think that one of his workforce is lying. I can see his point of view. Preston is no fly-by-night, and he's due to retire any day now. It would be easy just to forget the whole thing. I'd agree, if it weren't for one thing—'

'The knife.'

'Yes. The knife. That puts an entirely different view on the matter, doesn't it? Hugh doesn't think Preston would use a knife on a child, and I'm inclined to accept his judgement. Also there has been some sabotage at the site which may well affect the date for the opening of the hotel. This means that people at Head Office are getting involved, so even if Hugh refuses to prosecute, there's going to be repercussions.'

'A refusal to prosecute won't stop Ears taking action. He says Preston made a formal statement, and that we have to act on that.'

'When you say that Ears is getting Social Services involved, what sort of timescale are we thinking of? I mean, Mikey and his mother are both ill. Neither can be interviewed at the moment. Thomas and I can guarantee the boy's good behaviour in future, can't we?'

'You are not his legal guardians. I don't know exactly how Social Services would respond, but . . .'

The door creaked open, and in stalked Midge, tail erect. He ignored both women to plod to the fireplace, where he lay down and began to give himself a thorough grooming.

Ellie and Lesley looked at the door through which the cat had come. Mikey and Midge were almost always together. Was Mikey lurking just outside the door? Had he been listening to their conversation? And if so, what would he do about it?

'Excuse me,' said Ellie, and went to the door to look out into the hall. There was no sign of Mikey but there were plenty of doors nearby behind which he could hide, including the dining room, the cloakroom and the big junk cupboard in the hall.

The door to the kitchen quarters was open, as usual. Ellie could hear Rose's telly from where she stood . . . also, the washing machine swishing away. Well, at least that was working properly now. She hoped.

She returned to the sitting room, shutting the door carefully behind her. 'How long do you think we've got before they come asking questions?'

A shrug. 'A couple of days? Normally, it would take longer, but the pressure's on. Your solicitor can advise you.'

'I'll get him on to it. Meanwhile, let's see what Hugh can discover. Will you give us warning of any visitation?'

'I will if I can but I may not hear. I'm not in the loop on that one.' Lesley got to her feet, brushing herself down. 'You didn't by any chance have an opportunity to look into the untimely deaths we spoke about?'

Ellie tried to put Mikey out of her mind. 'Um, that girl Petra came to see me. I think she imagined I'd give her a job at the hotel just like that, but she isn't qualified for anything she wants to do and she isn't interested in training for it. To tell the truth, I wasn't impressed, though I must admit she did make me feel uneasy about Auntie's death.'

'Oh, her. Well, she's out of it for the moment, anyway. Tumbled down some stairs outside her flat and wasn't found for a few hours. Concussion and a badly sprained ankle. They're keeping her in hospital overnight and then sending her home. She's way off her rocker, in my opinion. You won't believe this, but she rang the police from her hospital bed, wanting us to charge her cousin with causing her to fall down the stairs.'

'Really? And had she?'

'Of course not. Ears told me to check her out, so I went to the hospital and took her statement. Then I went to call on the cousin, which was a nice waste of my time, as she had a solid alibi for the whole day, out shopping with a friend who's getting married. Social Services have taken Petra's boy into care until she can cope again.'

'Really? How come she laid it at her cousin's door, apart from the fact that she thinks the cousin is the Wicked Witch of the North and responsible for everything from global warning to the milk going off?'

A shrug. 'She says her cousin was lying in wait for her on her return from the shops, and that she'd booby-trapped the stairs with her child's scooter, causing her to lose her balance and crash down the stairs. Sheer clumsiness, if you ask me.'

Ellie said, 'Petra told me she had a live-in boyfriend, but I must admit he didn't sound the type to step in and take care of her or the boy.' Ellie allowed herself a flicker of amusement. 'Two single parent families in trouble. Petra's child is taken into care, and Vera's is threatened with the same fate. If I know anything about Petra, she'd be bound to say there's one law for the rich and another for the poor. I can afford to fight for Mikey – who has certainly strayed from the straight and narrow – while Petra's boy has done nothing wrong as far as I know, and his life is going to be at the mercy of officialdom for months to come.'

'Yours may be, too,' warned Lesley. 'Once they think a boy is at risk—'

'Understood.'

'You didn't hear of any other doubtful deaths?'

Ellie hesitated. 'Yes, I did, but I can't see what good it would do to dig up someone who took an overdose when she was facing a recurrence of cancer. Oh, I don't mean that you ought, physically, to dig someone up. That was a figure of speech. Best let sleeping dogs lie.' She laughed at herself. 'There I go again, misusing words.'

'You must tell me if you've heard of anything suspicious. What about the elderly woman who lived in a house over-looking the park?'

'Nothing there. The only death I've heard about is . . . You know, I can't see what earthly good it would do to tell you about it. It would only cause a great deal of distress to the family, who are already deep in grief.'

'I can't afford to overlook anything. You must let me be the judge of what is or is not important.'

Ellie held her gaze. 'If your mother was dying a painful death, and she asked you to fetch her some strong sleeping pills from the chemist, would you do so?'

'That's not the point.'

'Yes, it is. If Petra's aunt and this other woman that I've heard about, if they committed suicide, surely there's nothing you can do about it?'

'If she was helped to commit suicide . . .?'

'Did someone put a gun to their heads? Or hold pillows over their faces? No. The most you can say is that someone, when asked to do so, provided them with extra pills. No one is saying that the women who committed suicide were forced to take them, were they?'

'They might have taken them by mistake, thinking them to be harmless.'

'I grant you that would be murder.'

Lesley grimaced. 'Murder with mercy? Names, Ellie. Please.'

'I'll think about it and let you know.'

Once she'd seen Lesley off the premises, Ellie searched for Mikey. He was not in the kitchen, but the washing machine was doing what it ought to, and Rose was happily peeling potatoes for the night's meal. Wait a minute, weren't they having a lasagne? With *potatoes*?

Oh well. There'd be some frozen green vegetables in the freezer, and they could easily be cooked at the last minute. And for pudding? They'd have cheese or fruit and lump it. Or maybe ice cream.

Mikey wasn't in Rose's bed-sitting room and neither – she checked – was his sleeping bag. He wasn't in Thomas's quiet room, nor in his study at the end of the corridor. He wasn't anywhere on the ground floor.

Ah. She knew where he'd be. Upstairs in bed with his mother, which would ensure he couldn't be questioned. Yes, there he was. Asleep. Or pretending to be asleep. In his own sleeping bag, on top of his mother's bed.

Vera was still in the grip of flu. She opened bleary eyes, tried to smile at Ellie and made as if to get up . . . and fell back with a grimace, hand to head.

'Don't worry about anything,' said Ellie. 'Is it time for you to take some more painkillers? And I'll bring you up another jug of lemonade. You concentrate on getting well again.'

Mikey slept through it all.

Well, he didn't open his eyes, even when Ellie laid her hand on his forehead. She thought he was warm but not feverish. She stood over him, wondering what was best to do. He was an imp and an angel and deserved a good telling off, but she suspected he was going to run rings round her if she tried. Perhaps Thomas would have more luck when he returned from setting the world to rights.

She went downstairs to make some more lemonade and carried it back up to the top of the house for Vera. Neither Mikey nor his mother seemed to have moved while she was away. Midge the cat was now sitting in a sort of hollow between mother and son. Oh well.

So many trips up and down the stairs. It would have been easier if Vera and Mikey had been put to bed in the guest rooms at the end of the first floor corridor, but Ellie hadn't anticipated the problems of having to look after people in the attic, had she?

The landline phone was ringing as Ellie reached the hall, and she sank on to the hall chair to take the call.

'Hugh here. I know it's a bit late, but would you like to come over to the site? The men are working overtime to catch up so they're still around.'

He wasn't asking a question, but issuing a summons. Ellie winced, hearing rain beat against the front of the house. Hadn't she done enough for one day? Rose needed help in the kitchen, or who knew what would be on the table for supper? Mikey needed watching twenty-four seven, and Thomas would be home soon, needing the consolations of the fireside. Plus it was still raining.

She held back a sigh. 'I'll get a cab and be with you in fifteen minutes.' If she could find her old mac, and perhaps some strong boots? Where had she left her umbrella?

Dusk had fallen with a heavy hand. Street lights hardly alleviated the gloom. Traffic swished through the rain, gutters overflowed. Tempers didn't just fray, they disintegrated.

The site was not looking its best under these conditions, but security lights illuminated the scene to some extent. Ellie followed a lorry through the gap in the fencing which protected the site from vandals and petty theft. The forecourt was water-logged, with piles of unidentifiable but no doubt essential components stacked around. Men in hard hats scampered here and there, shouting incomprehensible directions to one another. Polish? Ah, but there was an Indian, a Sikh by his turban . . . which headgear was now sensibly covered with a blue bath cap.

Hugh's site office was in what had once been the mansion's garage. The strip lights in there were so bright that they made her blink. Hugh himself was on the phone, but brought the conversation to a close when he spotted Ellie. No smiles today.

'Like to visit the scene of the crime?'

Ellie couldn't think of anything she'd like less, but she nodded and followed him across the covered courtyard – in the process of being reglazed – and into what had once been the kitchen quarters of the old house and had been transformed into communal sitting rooms for the guests who would soon grace the premises. The kitchens themselves, plus the laundry and maintenance rooms, were all now to be found in the basement. Painters and decorators were everywhere. So many, in fact, that it seemed they would be falling over one another in their haste to get the job done. Where the painters had finished, carpets were being laid. Where the carpets were down, curtains and blinds were being fitted and furniture unpacked.

The lift was not working, so Hugh led the way up the grand staircase to the first floor . . . and then to the second . . . and on to the top floor with its pretty dormer windows . . . one of which overlooked Ellie's own garden in the next road. Hugh paused to let Ellie catch him up on the top landing. She was breathing heavily by the time she reached his side. Too many stairs to climb in one day. All right, she knew she ought to do something about her weight, but really . . .!

Through open doors she could see electricians attending to light and power fittings in a number of newly furnished bedrooms, while their en suites next door were being cleaned by a couple of heavily muscled young women in skimpy vests and jeans. Polish cleaners?

The landing was littered with boxes of tiles and discarded cardboard. Mirrors, bathroom cabinets, light fittings and glass shelves stood around, partially unpacked. Through a newly decorated bedroom they went into a small en suite beyond. Bath, washbasin, toilet, bidet and heated towel rails had already been plumbed in, but the walls were only now being tiled, the floor hadn't yet been dealt with and the cladding for the bath leaned against the wall.

A burly man in his early sixties, wearing a peaked cap instead of the regulation hard hat, was rapidly and efficiently tiling the walls over the bath. He was being assisted by a gormless-looking younger man with a prominent Adam's apple and a sniff, whose only function appeared to be handing over materials to the man actually doing the work. The younger man's jeans were worn so low that Ellie wondered how on earth they were kept up. Both workmen suspended operations when Ellie and Hugh stepped through the doorway.

'Mrs Quicke, this is Preston and his apprentice, Dave,' said Hugh. 'Preston's already told me what happened yesterday, but I said you'd like to hear it yourself.'

'All these interruptions. I'm falling behind,' said Preston in a toneless voice which grated. The voice of one severely deaf? Ah, yes. He wore hearing aids in both ears. He might be working on a bathroom but he himself didn't look all that clean.

Sniff, went his assistant.

'If you please,' said Hugh, in a mild tone which nevertheless brooked no argument.

'What?' said Preston.

Hugh repeated himself, in a loud, clear tone.

Preston turned on Dave. 'You carry on. I'm watching you, mind!' He addressed a point above Ellie's shoulder. 'I can't see what good this will do. We caught him red-handed, using a wrench to loosen that nut down there.' He gestured to a fitment on the wall under the bath. 'If he'd not been stopped, he'd have flooded the place. I shouted. He shot out of the door and took a tumble down the stairs. I never laid a finger on him. He's a liar if he says I did.'

Sniff. 'That's the truth, innit!' echoed the gormless-looking assistant.

Ellie measured distances with her eye. She hadn't realized there were two people involved. But, if there were, then it was easier to see how Mikey sustained his various injuries. She told herself to tread carefully.

She said, 'Do you two always work together?'

'What?'

She repeated the question, a little louder.

Preston nodded. 'My nephew. I'm learning him the trade.'

Ah. Hugh had once mentioned that there were some family members on the workforce, which made it necessary to use tact if he had to deal with minor infractions of rules.

'You travel together to work?'

'What?'

She repeated the question, louder and enunciating clearly.

'He lives next door but one. Some days I gives him a lift, some days he comes on his own. Yesterday he come in with me.'

'So you arrived together. You came up the stairs together?'

He leaned towards her, frowning. Had he understood? Yes, for he nodded. 'We come up together.'

'You'd been working in here the day before?'

'What?'

Sniff.

Ellie redirected the question to the gormless Dave, who said, 'We finished tiling next door, see, then started in here. But there weren't enough tiles. Behindhand, we were.'

Preston grinned, catching on. 'And you not helping, holding us up.' Still that monotone.

She tried a smile. 'A good workman is careful to pack up his tools at the end of a day's work, and to take them home with him. I'm sure you do that, don't you? Dave?'

'A course.'

'You'd never leave your tools behind overnight, would you?'

Preston looked bewildered. He was not following this.

'What? A course not.'

'Of course not. So where did Mikey find a wrench first thing in the morning, before you two got here?'

Dave blinked. Chewed on his lip. 'Dunno. I suppose someone was careless.'

'More than careless. Criminally negligent. I think perhaps some questions ought to be asked as to who was responsible for leaving a wrench around? A wrench that might have been picked up and used by any vandal who walked on to the site.'

Shifted feet. Sideways looks.

Hugh was taking it all in. Not interfering. Good.

Preston's tone was aggressive. 'We found him with a wrench, interfering. Then, as the boss weren't around, I took him down the station and handed him over.'

Try a different tack.

Ellie turned on the sniffing assistant. 'Do you both carry knives?'

Preston didn't react, but the lad's hand went to his jeans pocket, wavered, and returned to duty.

Ellie said, 'I expect you both do, for work. That's right, isn't it, Dave?'

The lad shot a look at his uncle and nearly dropped the tile he was holding. 'I suppose.'

Ellie pointed. 'That last tile you put on is crooked.'

Preston understood that all right. He inspected his nephew's work. 'Stupid git. What did I tell you about keeping the lines straight?'

'Which of you hit the boy first?' said Ellie.

A tinge of colour came into Preston's sallow cheeks. 'Fecking nuisance, underfoot, poking and prying. Got what he came for, didn't he? Dave! Out the way. Let me do the job or we'll not be done this fortnight.'

Hugh indicated to Ellie that they should retreat. Back through the bedroom, and the landing, and down the stairs they went. Both preoccupied. When Ellie opened her mouth to speak, Hugh hushed her. 'Wait till we're in my office.'

Yes, of course. There were workmen everywhere. Most glanced sideways at Ellie. Normally, she'd be greeted with smiles and a nod because they knew her position with relation to the hotel and many of them had been involved in carrying out suggestions she'd made about this and that. So why the sideways looks? They must know Hugh had invited her to talk to Preston and Dave. They would all know what Mikey had been said to have done. How did they feel about it? Difficult to tell but, at a guess, they were closing ranks behind Preston and Dave. Understandable, if unhelpful.

Back in his office, Hugh closed the door behind them and offered a cup of tea and a seat, both of which Ellie declined.

She said, 'In my opinion, Mikey caught them using their wrench to loosen the nut on that fitment under the bath. They were startled. Hadn't expected to see him. They reacted without thinking. One of them struck out with his knife, a reflex action more likely to come from the lad Dave than from his older, more experienced uncle. Mikey put up his arm to protect himself, and the knife sliced through his clothing but fortunately did hardly any more damage than that. It was probably Preston who clouted the boy on his jaw, picked him up in a bear hug and threw him down the stairs.'

Hugh propped himself against the back of a chair. 'I agree, although I can't see why they should turn saboteur.'

Ellie couldn't, either. It was a puzzle.

Hugh rubbed his chin. 'The men are getting restless; every delay jeopardizes the bonus they have every right to expect at the end of the contract.'

'I understand what you're saying, and I don't envy you, trying to sort that out. Has Preston always been that deaf?'

'It's got a good deal worse this last few months, which was one of the reasons why we were letting him go when this job finishes. We're taking the nephew on the strength instead.'

She was getting angry. 'Dave will be a liability, not an asset, won't he? You know perfectly well that they were in it together, and even if you can get rid of Preston, you'll still have a rotten apple in the workforce. What Dave did once, he'll do again.'

He spread his hands. 'I'm aware of it. Give me some proof . . .?'

She couldn't.

TEN

'I'm home!' Ellie had passed Thomas's car in the drive on the way in. She'd been afraid her front door key would play up again, but it had behaved itself for once. Good. She expected to hear Thomas's cheerful voice as she disposed of her umbrella and mac. She was dying to tell him all about her day, and she desperately needed to ask his advice. How disappointing it was that Hugh had been unable to get the truth out of Preston! Ellie wasn't sure what to do next. Meanwhile, Mikey's future looked grim.

The house seemed quiet. Unnaturally so?

Ellie found Rose dozing in her big chair in her room, with the telly on but muted.

The lasagne was bubbling away in the oven, and a big pot of potatoes ditto on the hob. No green vegetables? Thomas would eat lasagne with potatoes, of course, but must not be encouraged to do so. She could get some beans from the freezer at the last minute to go with the lasagne. As for the potatoes? Well, potato and leek soup could be made tomorrow. Good winter food.

So, where was Thomas? Not in the sitting room, where he sometimes fell asleep in his La-Z-Boy chair in front of the television while waiting for the six o'clock news. He was not in his quiet room, nor in his study.

Stairs. Again. She pulled herself up the first flight. Thomas was sitting on their bed, fully dressed, staring into space. He was frowning and barely registered her presence when she touched his forehead. A high temperature. A headache.

'Be all right in a minute,' he mumbled.

Flu. Thomas didn't like to give in to minor ailments but he did get fearsome colds, which sometimes went to his chest. She'd have to order him to bed, or he'd try to keep going and make himself really ill.

'Into bed with you. Have you taken any painkillers?'

His frown deepened. 'I think so. I came over with the shivers, driving back. Lucky I didn't have an accident. Are you all right?'

'Fine. There, now. Undress, get into bed and relax. I'll fetch you something to drink and look in on you later, when you've had a nap.'

'Someone phoned.' A deeper frown. 'Can't remember. Wrote it down. I think.' He began to undress. She left him to it.

More stairs. Vera had got as far as shrugging herself into her dressing gown and was with Mikey in her sitting room on the top floor watching television. Vera looked dreadful, Mikey looked half asleep.

Vera tried to smile. 'Isn't it silly? I keep falling asleep. But I'm much better. I'll be up and about tomorrow. Just a bit shaky, still. Mikey's been looking after me beautifully, but I'm afraid he's going down with it, too. Says he doesn't want any supper.'

'Take your time.'

Mikey looked at Ellie from under heavy eyelids and didn't respond when she asked how he was feeling. Maybe he had flu, too. Maybe he was just pretending to be ill. Or maybe he really did have concussion and ought to be in hospital.

What to do for the best? The doctors were all busy with flu victims, but Mikey's injuries were something else. If Ellie did nothing and he got worse, she'd never forgive herself. Vera wouldn't forgive her, either. Ellie decided that it would be better to be safe than sorry, and to call for help. If the doctors thought she was a silly old woman fussing unnecessarily, then so be it.

She phoned the helpline for the NHS.

The anonymous voice on the other end of the line listened to the symptoms displayed by Thomas and Vera, and said in a sing-song voice that Ellie was doing the right thing, but to contact them again if she noticed any worsening of their condition. When it came to a description of Mikey's injuries, the sing-song voice changed its tune. Someone would be with her as soon as possible, taking into consideration all the many calls on their time at the moment.

Ellie made more lemonade. Double quantity. Some for

Thomas, some for Vera and some for Mikey. Suppose Rose were to go down with it, too? Ellie shuddered. It didn't bear thinking about. *Please, Lord. Let us keep fit. Please?*

Up the stairs we go. Take it easy. More haste, less speed, and she'd drop one of the jugs of lemonade if she went too fast. Oh, but her legs were getting so tired. Maybe all this climbing of stairs might make her lose weight. In her dreams!

As she descended the stairs again, the doorbell rang. Two paramedics, efficient if weary. This was just another routine visit to them. Up the stairs. Check on Thomas. 'No, missus. Everything's fine. Not to worry. Yes, if his cough turns nasty, contact your doctor for some antibiotics.'

Up the stairs to the top. Vera was back in her own bed and clearly feverish. Temperature checked, etcetera, etcetera. Same verdict. 'You're doing the right thing. Now, there was a boy . , ?'

There was indeed. He was lying full length on the settee in their sitting room, looking fragile and somehow older than his years.

The tired faces of the paramedics sharpened to attention. 'What has happened here?'

'He was in the wrong place at the wrong time. He was punched on the jaw, knifed, beaten up and thrown down some stairs. The police know about it.'

The paramedics were thorough. Mikey's 'obs' were taken. He had to show all his bruises all over again. The scar on his arm had to be inspected. 'Healing nicely.'

Lights were shone into the boy's eyes. The very slightest of frowns indicated that yes, it was a good thing that they'd been called in.

'We think he'll be just fine. Boys of this age, they usually bounce back pretty quickly, although he does seem to have been roughly handled. You should wake him every hour on the hour throughout the night, make sure he's responsive. Give us another ring if you can't wake him or he develops any new symptoms, right?'

Notes were written up and the paramedics departed, gearing themselves up for another visit to another patient on their long, long list.

Back in the sitting room, Ellie collapsed into her big chair, feeling her age. Did they think she was Superwoman? It was all very well saying she had to check on Mikey every hour through the night, but she wasn't sure she was capable of doing so.

She decided not to tell Rose, who would want to share the nursing and must not, repeat NOT, do any more climbing up and down stairs at her age.

Ellie closed her eyes for five minutes. There was something she ought to have done, some action she ought to have taken, but she couldn't think what it was. Perhaps a little nap before supper would do her good.

Thursday night to Friday morning

Thomas was so restless in the night that Ellie removed herself to sleep in the guest bedroom next door. At eleven she checked on Mikey. He was fine. She went back to bed and reset the alarm for an hour's time, but couldn't seem to drop off to sleep. She tossed and turned. At midnight she dragged herself out of bed and climbed the stairs again to the top of the house to check on Mikey. Again, he was fine.

She staggered back to bed and set the alarm again. If she didn't get to sleep soon, she'd be good for nothing the next day. She hoped she wasn't going to be the next one to go down with flu, but if it happened, it did, and that was that. Worse things happen at sea, or so her mother had always said. Ellie was disinclined to believe that. She thought drowning must be the most awful death, though when she came to think of it, perhaps fire might be worse.

She shook her head at herself. What were all these morbid thoughts doing in her head? She sent up an arrow prayer. *Give me love in my heart, keep me praying . . . and please look after all those I know who are in trouble.*

Oh dear. She was getting depressed.

She roused herself at one, checked on Mikey. He was not pleased at being woken up, but neither was Ellie at having to wake him.

She tumbled back into bed, and though she thought she'd

set the alarm for two o'clock, she hadn't, for the next thing she knew it was time to get up. She couldn't think at first what was happening. It was another dark morning. Then she remembered she ought to have checked on Mikey every hour – and hadn't. Suppose . . .?

Oh, dear Lord. Let him be all right.

And he was. Grumpy. Disinclined to get up, but all right.

Praise be.

How could she have been so remiss?

She pulled on any old clothes, checked on Thomas – no worse – and Vera, heavily asleep and still too warm for health.

It was only when Ellie entered the sitting room and noticed the dust on the mahogany furniture that it struck her the cleaners hadn't been round that week. Or had they? Possibly they'd been round during her business meeting? No, she didn't think they had. She had a slight headache. Perhaps she was going down with flu? She'd ring the agency in a minute and ask if they could send someone to help Rose out while Vera was incapacitated.

Rose was having a lie in.

Ellie didn't disturb her. She got herself some breakfast and prepared some more lemonade for the invalids. She was running short of jugs in which to put the lemonade. Up the first flight of stairs we go . . .

A ring at the front door. What, at this time of morning?

She put the jugs down and descended the stairs to open the front door. Two unsmiling faces, one male and one female. Acne for the male and dyed hair for the female. Umbrellas and macs and briefcases.

Briefcases? Officialdom? Oh. How to handle this?

'Ms Vera Pryce?' A card was thrust at Ellie.

Social Services. The woman was clearly in charge, older and authoritative. The man was in his thirties, possibly a failed teacher? The droopy sort.

Ellie wasn't fooled. These two couldn't be fobbed off with any old story. They were backed by the Might of the Law and would be obstructed at her peril. 'I'm Mrs Quicke,' said Ellie. 'I own this house, and Vera is my part-time housekeeper. Do come in.'

They entered, stamping water off their shoes, shedding outer clothing but retaining the briefcases. Ellie did not lead them through to the sitting room, but ushered them instead into the room which she used for business meetings, which was still in disarray following the meeting earlier that week . . .

'Do take a seat.'

They sat, eyes everywhere. Briefcases were set upon the table, forms produced and laid out.

Ellie waited. She knew why they'd come, and she wasn't sure how to handle it. Mikey was a young rogue and deserved a spanking . . . except that one was not allowed to spank children nowadays, was one? Children at risk could be wrenched away from their families and friends and school, and put into care perhaps at a considerable distance away, where they would learn a whole raft of new tricks from unsuitable new 'friends'. A good spanking might hurt at the time but would certainly drive the point home that transgressions met with instant punishment . . . But no. Not allowed.

Yet at that very moment, Ellie, grinding her teeth in annoyance at finding herself in this position, would dearly have liked to box the lad's ears, or worse! She, who had never lifted a finger to her own daughter . . . But that was another story, and she mustn't think about Diana now.

'Yes?' she said, deciding not to offer coffee.

'We wish to speak with Ms Vera Pryce, about her son . . . Michael.'

'She's in bed with flu. So is he, which is why he hasn't been to school this week.'

That was almost not a fib. Almost.

'Really?' The older woman was definitely the one in charge. Papers were consulted. 'We understand his attendance at school has been unsatisfactory. We have the figures here.'

The man spoke up: 'And you are what relation to him? Grandmother?'

'He is no relation of mine, but under the terms of Vera's late husband's will, I am responsible for . . . Well, it's difficult to explain exactly, but I have a duty to look after the boy and his mother.'

'We understand that she has no husband, and that the boy's father is also conspicuous by his absence?'

'She was bringing the boy up by herself, working as a cleaner to support them both, when she met Edgar Pryce and she became his carer. They got married, and Mr Pryce adopted Mikey before he died. He asked me to keep an eye on them afterwards.'

'Ah. She has a new boyfriend, I assume? A live-in boyfriend?'

'No. Certainly not.' Ellie felt her blood pressure rise. 'Has someone suggested that she has and that she's been neglecting her son? If so, that's slander. Or do I mean libel?'

'Calm down. We have to make these enquiries, you know. Now, you state there is no boyfriend, living in or otherwise?'

'No.' Ellie told herself that losing her temper was not going to help matters.

'Very well. We have noted what you say.' A piece of paper was slid across the table to Ellie. 'Now, this is his school record of attendance for the current term. It doesn't look as if you've kept much of an eye on him, does it?'

Ellie looked and found her earlier inclination to box Mikey's ears fell far short of what she'd like to do to him now. Tarring and feathering? Hanging, drawing and quartering?

She said, inadequately, 'The little devil! How on earth has he managed to keep up with his school homework, if he's been absent so much?'

'By being there part of each morning or afternoon session.'

'Ah.' Ellie leaned back in her chair, frowning. 'He's a bright lad, you know. Says school's boring. I've been wondering if he ought to try for a private school, somewhere that he'd be stretched.'

'Can Ms Pryce afford that?' Cynical.

'No, but under the terms of his adopted father's will, I'd be responsible for the fees.'

Another piece of paper was scrutinized. 'I suppose that will be up to the courts to decide. It appears he has been charged with various offences in connection with sabotage at the Pryce Hotel.'

'The hotel consortium will not be pressing charges.'

Eyebrows were raised. 'A statement has been made, and

unless it is withdrawn, it is not up to the hotel to decide whether or not he should be prosecuted. Even if it is withdrawn, the Crown Prosecution Service may still decide to act.'

What could Ellie say, except that she was going to have a long talk with Mikey at the earliest possible opportunity? They'd warned him what might happen . . . after the event.

'So the question is,' said the woman, 'whether or not to remove him from his present unsatisfactory surroundings, in which he plays truant at will and spends his time performing acts of vandalism amounting to thousands of pounds worth of damage.'

Ellie managed to say, 'The case against Mikey is not proven,' and knew she'd failed to convince.

Arched eyebrows again. 'We have sufficient concerns about the boy to take the matter very seriously indeed.'

'What about his injuries? You can't ignore them.'

The woman was forgiving, patience itself. 'I understand he tumbled down the stairs when he was caught.'

'That's not what the doctor at the station said. And what about the knife wound?'

Startled. Notes were consulted. 'There's nothing here about a knife. We take a poor view of children carrying knives.'

'It was used *on* him, not *by* him.'

A smooth smile. 'No doubt all will be made clear in due course. But if he was carrying a knife . . .' A doleful shake of the head.

Ellie set her teeth. 'He wasn't. He was attacked with a knife. The doctor can confirm it.'

'I'm afraid we don't have the doctor's report here.'

No, they wouldn't have it, would they? Ellie wondered, uncharitably, whether Ears had directed it to be 'misfiled' or 'mislaid'. Oh, surely not. He wouldn't go as far as that, would he? Or would he? She said, 'Fortunately, there is another way you can check. I was so worried about him that I called the paramedics in to look at him last night, and they took notes of his injuries: suspected concussion; bruised ribs; a punch on the jaw. And they were concerned about sepsis on the knife wound.' She might as well pile it on.

They looked annoyed. This interview was not going to plan.

Ellie said, 'Look, I realize he's been a naughty boy bunking off school, and I can assure you he's going to get a right royal rollocking about it, but he has a stable home here, looked after by his mother, by me and by my husband – who is a minister of the church – and by our housekeeper. We are all sensible adults who care for him. Can't you leave it at that?'

'I'm afraid we don't see it quite that way.' The woman gathered her papers together. 'It's no good your pretending that his circumstances are acceptable, because clearly they are not. Now, we'd like to see Ms Pryce and inspect the accommodation she is currently occupying in this house.'

Problem, thought Ellie. Mikey might be up and bright-eyed, watching the telly or on his computer. Or he might be in bed, feeling poorly. On his past form, you couldn't guess which it might be. If they found him up and dressed, watching telly . . .? That would not be good.

What could she do about it?

Well, how about some delaying tactics?

She led the way back to the hall and gestured towards the kitchen quarters. 'Our elderly housekeeper has a bedsit and bathroom facilities along here. You wish to see them?'

Without waiting for their answer she led the way into the kitchen.

Rose squawked. She was dressed, sort of, in a mismatched Fair Isle jumper and plaid skirt, and was making herself a pot of tea.

Ellie was soothing. 'It's all right, dear. They're not burglars. Just a couple of social workers come to see where Mikey lives, what sort of accommodation he and his mother have, and how he's doing. I've told them he's in bed with flu but they have to see him for themselves.' She introduced her visitors. 'This is Rose, an old family friend who is also our housekeeper.'

Rose didn't know the worst of what they had on Mikey but she knew enough to respond with a bright nod.

'Now, Rose, don't you disturb yourself,' said Ellie. 'I was on my way up to see to our invalids when our visitors came, with some more lemonade for them. Thomas – that's my husband – is down with it, too, I'm afraid.' She turned to the social workers. 'Lemonade is about all they've been able to get down themselves this last couple of days. Do you need to see Rose's accommodation? She has her own bed-sitting room here, shower room, toilet and so on. And this way we have the larder and laundry room.'

She opened doors for them to have a peep in and indicated the door to the back stairs. 'We don't use those much nowadays. Now back to the hall . . .' She led them down the corridor opposite. 'Here we have the dining room, which is the room where we met . . . We really only use it for business purposes nowadays. On the left is my study, to the right there's my husband's quiet room, and this is my husband's study at the end.'

She threw open doors, urged them to look into each room and waited for them to do so. Time counted here. Rose wasn't good with stairs at the moment. It was probably wrong to hope that she'd taken the hint and . . . Well, on with the job.

'Now, back to the hall. As you can see, there is the conservatory ahead while to the right at the back of the house we have our sitting room. Mikey is welcome to visit all of these, and does so.'

The social workers exhibited impatience. 'But where does . . .?'

Ellie started up the first flight of stairs, stopping where she'd abandoned the two jugs of lemonade. 'Could you carry one of these for me, do you think? I'm not as young as I was.' She handed one of the jugs to the man, who accepted it with an air of bewilderment.

They reached the landing. Ellie said, 'Now when I first asked Vera to move in to help Rose, she and Mikey occupied rooms at the end of this corridor, but—'

It was the social workers' turn to squawk as a shambling, bear-like figure wobbled out of the master bedroom, holding on to his head.

'My husband, the Reverend Thomas,' said Ellie. 'He's also gone down with flu, so I wouldn't get too close, if I were you.'

They both took a step backwards.

Ellie said, 'Thomas, my dear; I've brought you up some lemonade. You should be in bed. What's the matter?'

He peered at the visitors with half-closed eyes. 'Visitors?'

'Some people who want to see what's up with Mikey. Nothing for you to worry about.' She steered him back into their bedroom, leaving the door open so that the social workers could see for themselves what she was doing. She deposited her jug of lemonade on the bedside table. 'Shall I pour you out some more lemonade? When did you last have some painkillers?'

'Got to get up . . . Can't take time off!'

Ellie took his arm and pushed him gently back on to the bed. 'You're not fit. It won't hurt if the magazine is a day late. What do you pay an assistant for, if not to do the things you can't, anyway? I'll have words with her, and we'll decide what ought to be done and what we can leave till you're better.'

'Grrrr!' But Thomas allowed the duvet to be drawn over himself.

Ellie shut the door on him and said to the social workers, 'He really cares for Mikey, you know. They spend a lot of time together. Now, as I was saying, along the corridor here is the guest bedroom, en suite, and the room I keep for my grandson when he has a sleepover . . . and at the end are the rooms which Mikey and Vera occupied before their flat upstairs was ready.' She led the way down the corridor, opening doors and waiting for them to inspect the rooms, which they did without comment.

'Now,' said Ellie, turning back to the stairs. 'One last flight to the top floor, where Vera and Mikey have a self-contained flat all to themselves; that is, if you except the cat Midge, who goes wherever he wishes. Watch that he doesn't trip you up, won't you?'

As the two visitors laboured up the last flight of stairs, the woman said, 'Don't they have a separate entrance?'

'Unfortunately, the council keep turning down my application for an outside staircase. Something to do with the parking, although Vera doesn't have a car. If you can do something about it for them, I'd be grateful.'

'You allow them part of the garden for their own use?'

'We designated a part for them, but Mikey doesn't like

boundaries and goes where he wishes. We don't object.' Oh, perhaps she shouldn't have said that about boundaries. Had she made enough noise down below, to tell Mikey what to do? Would Rose have managed to get up the back stairs in time, to warn them what to expect?

ELEVEN

They reached the top landing at last. It was light and airy up here in Vera's flat, even on a day when it was spitting hail outside. Ellie opened doors in turn. 'Kitchen. Bathroom.' Neither were quite as immaculate as usual. 'Normally, Vera looks after them beautifully, but she's been confined to bed for the last few days.'

The two social workers opened the fridge and checked the contents of the freezer. Vera kept them well-stocked, so they couldn't find fault there. They poked and pried into cupboards. Ellie seethed. She wanted to hit them, but told herself that would be counterproductive.

Ellie said, 'Vera's an excellent cook. We usually eat all together downstairs in the big kitchen in the evenings, but of course she cooks for herself and Mikey as well.'

The man deposited the jug of lemonade on the counter and washed his hands at the sink. Had the jug been sticky? Ellie rather hoped that it had.

Once they'd finished there, she led them to the next door. 'This is their sitting room.' No sign of Vera or Mikey. Disarranged cushions on the settee. The television was probably still warm, but not on at the moment. Some books had been strewn around. Midge the cat was curled up asleep on the biggest chair.

Ellie let out a slow sigh of relief as she stood back to let the social workers enter. 'As you can see, it's a nice big room with windows overlooking the garden.'

Surprise! They didn't look happy about it.

'Doesn't the boy have a room of his own?'

'Of course he does.' Ellie proceeded down the landing, throwing more doors open so that they could take a peep inside before she shut them again. 'All mod cons. Central heating. Utility room. Cupboard for vacuum cleaner, study for Vera – she's doing a part-time business course, as you probably know . . .'

Apparently, they didn't know, for they looked both surprised and annoyed.

Ellie opened the door at the end and stepped inside, holding on to it so that they could follow her in if they wished. She made it clear by her body language that she was fed up with this, that their search was unnecessary and a complete waste of time. This time they glanced in, but didn't actually enter the room.

Ellie said, 'This is Mikey's bedroom. Not all that tidy, but what can you expect for a child of that age?'

'So where is he?' asked the woman, going on to the offensive.

'In bed with his mother, of course. Where else?' Ellie paused outside Vera's bedroom, tapped on the door, and said, 'May we come in for a moment, Vera? Some people have come to see if you're all right.'

'Sure. Just let me get up and—' A weak voice.

'No worries, my dear,' said Ellie. 'If you're not fit to talk, my visitors will quite understand.'

Vera's voice wavered. 'I'm afraid we're hardly up to having visitors.'

Ellie opened the door and went in. Satisfactory. As pretty a tableau as you could expect. Vera was in bed. She was heavy-lidded, just about awake and very pale. Mikey's dark head was on the pillow at her side.

'I think he's asleep again,' said Vera, stifling a cough and reaching for a nearly empty glass of lemonade. 'He wakes and sleeps and tries to look after me, even though he's not too good himself. He even tried to boil me an egg this morning, would you believe? Not that I could eat it.' She tried to sit up, but Ellie pressed her back on to the pillows.

'Don't try to get up too soon.'

Vera let herself drop back on to the pillows. 'My head goes round whenever I try to stand. Mikey had to steer me to the toilet this morning. Who are these people?'

The woman peered at Mikey. 'This is the boy?'

Ellie soothed Vera back on to the pillows. 'The school sent someone round to make sure Mikey was all right. Now, my lad.' She gently prised Mikey out from under the covers. 'I'm sure you need to go to the toilet, don't you? Let me help you, now I'm here. No need to worry your mother.'

No one could accuse Mikey of being slow on the uptake. He responded like a sleepwalker, eyes half open. Ellie walked him out to the bathroom and invited the social workers to step in there with them.

'No need to worry his mother about this, but you'll need to verify the report of his injuries. Mikey, dear? Can you wake up for a moment? Let the kind visitors see what the bad men did to you . . . You see the bruise on his chin? The knife barely scratched his arm, as you can see. Thank heaven he was wearing a jacket and a sweatshirt, or he'd have had to have stitches. And, yes, Mikey . . . could you just pull up your pyjama top for a moment, to let us check how your bruises are getting on . . .? Nasty, aren't they? Never mind, soon be gone. We'll step outside while you do your duty, and then I'll get you back to bed again.'

She almost pushed the social workers out on to the landing, frowning. 'I suppose you are now going to ask if his mother inflicted those injuries on him. Well, she didn't. As you can see, she's hardly capable of swatting a fly at the moment. The boy was struck and knifed on the site, by the very people who reported him to the police. The doctor who saw him at the police station – do try to find her report, it's informative – anyway, she warned me he might have concussion, due to being thrown down the stairs at the building site. So, as I said, I called in the paramedics last night to look at him. Please check with them, too. I had to keep waking him up every hour in the night to make sure he wasn't going into a coma. I think he's all right, but it's all a bit worrying.'

'His injuries were not inflicted by a boyfriend of his mother's?'

'Oh, really!' said Ellie. 'Have you seen any evidence of a boyfriend? Haven't you looked in every room? Have you seen anything to support your theory? No, of course you haven't.'

She looked at her watch . . . or where her watch was supposed to be. Where had she left it? 'I suppose I ought to take his temperature again. Would one of you like to take it for me . . . rectally, perhaps? My eyesight, these new thermometers, the old ones were a lot easier to read, weren't they?'

'No, no,' said the woman, retreating a step, as did her side-kick. 'No need for that.'

The boy came out of the bathroom, wavering on his feet, looking half awake. Ellie helped him back into bed next to his mother. 'There, now. I've brought you up some more lemonade, which I seem to have left somewhere. Perhaps the kind gentleman will fetch it for you from the kitchen?'

The man shot an indignant look at Ellie but did as he was bid.

Ellie smiled at him as he handed the jug over. 'Thank you. So kind. There now, Mikey. Drink as much as you like, must keep up the fluids, and back to sleep you go. Soon be better.'

The social workers looked as if they were sucking acid drops.

Ellie ushered them out, saying, 'Well, I think you've seen everything now, haven't you? I'll be up to see the invalids again later, make sure they take some aspirin or whatever. I don't think Vera's going to be back to work for a while yet. I hope it doesn't go to Mikey's chest. Or Thomas's. He gets terrible chest colds in the winter, makes him quite poorly. Is there anything else?'

'Not for the moment.'

They descended one flight. Then two. Into the hall.

Ellie helped them with their macs and handed them their umbrellas. 'Do you think I ought to get a nurse in to look after them all? I could try the agency I use for cleaning the house . . . But you don't want to know about that. It's just that I'm a bit worried what might happen if I go down with flu, too.'

The woman said, 'We'll be in touch.' Ice in her voice.

'Of course,' said Ellie. 'Mind how you go, now. This horrid rain makes driving so difficult, don't you think?'

Ellie watched her visitors drive away before, moving with care, she let herself down on to the hall chair, leaned back and breathed out. What a relief.

Rose crept down the stairs, taking her time about it, and collapsed on to the bottom step, holding on to the newel post. They smiled at one another.

'Well done, Rose. I couldn't think how to warn him.'

'That young limb! Oh, if I never have to climb those stairs again, it'll be too soon, but I managed it all right while you were showing them around down here. Mikey was dressed, watching the telly and munching biscuits when I got to the top. I was panting fit to burst, but I told him what was happening and he caught on, quick as a flash. Then I hid behind the door to his bedroom while you showed them round, the interfering, no good busybodies. Vera hasn't a clue what he's been up to, has she, poor girl?'

'He needs a good whacking.'

'My dad used to put us across his knee. I don't know as it did much good, though it did make us remember not to do it again if he could catch us at it.'

'I know. I'm just so frustrated, don't know what to do for the best.'

Rose hauled herself to her feet. 'Well, all this sitting around won't get the baby his bottle, will it? We'll be eating the lasagne again this evening, won't we? And if you're going out, we could do with some more lemons and maybe some ice cream for the invalids?'

What to do next? A thousand things.

Thomas; it was always a worry when he caught a cold. He might be a big, strong man, but he could be felled by a simple virus, and if it got on to his chest he'd need antibiotics. As for Mikey! It was more than time that that young man came clean about what he'd seen and done, and about what had been done to him.

Ellie snapped her fingers. She knew she'd forgotten something! She ought to have got her solicitor on to Edwina's case straight away, not to mention getting him to fend off Social Services. She dithered. Yes, that was important. There were probably lots more things she ought to be doing, but perhaps most immediate of all, she must get Rose to slow down or she'd make herself ill and then where would they be?

The answerphone light was winking. Messages. Wait a minute, hadn't Thomas said something about a message? Yes, he'd scrawled something on the pad by the phone, but she couldn't make head nor tail of it. 'Tunnel'? No, that couldn't be it. Perhaps the answerphone held a clue?

Message number one, which had been left early the previous day. 'Ellie, so sorry.' A woman's voice. 'The agency here. Everyone's down with flu. Two of the girls started work in your kitchen quarters on Tuesday as I expect you noticed but then one collapsed, so they had to call it a day. I'm at my wits' end. I'll call you back as soon as I can sort something else out.'

Ellie sighed and deleted the message.

Message number two, also left the previous day. Lesley Milburn. 'Sorry to convey more bad news, Ellie, but I've just been told that Social Services are going to call on you tomorrow . . .'

Ellie deleted that message, too. The bureaucrats had come and gone, and for the moment boarders had been repelled.

Message number three. They were still on Thursday. Diana. Of course. 'Mother, have you been able to fix up someone to sit with Evan on a permanent basis yet, because I simply—?' Ellie deleted the message without hearing it all the way through.

Message number four. Evan. We were on to Friday, at last. What on earth could he be ringing her about? 'Ellie, you there? Are you coming round later today?'

That would be today, would it? Friday? Ellie was getting confused.

Evan continued, 'I was so down in the dumps after you left yesterday, I was ready to put my head in the gas oven. But then . . .' He laughed. 'An old friend came round, what a surprise! We had a noggin or two and put the world to rights. I felt a lot better. She would have stayed on, but my daughter came back and cooked us a good meal. The first I've been able to enjoy for a long time. And Diana wasn't too late.

'Then, you'll never guess, that old rogue Freddie turned up this morning. He's on the biggest guilt trip you can think of, stupid fellow! Fixated on Anita's death and who could have helped her into the next world. Told him to pull himself together and advised him not to let that whiny little secretary bird of his to get a stranglehold on him, because anyone can see what she's after, he he! He should be so lucky, eh? I told him, if in doubt, get some Viagra. So, give me a ring. Let me know when you're coming round, eh?'

Ellie grinned. The old devil. She was beginning to be more amused than annoyed with her son-in-law. She didn't think she'd be able to leave the house today, what with so many invalids to cope with, but perhaps she could ring him later. Delete.

The last message. Thomas's secretary bird, coughing and sniffling. 'Sorry, so sorry. Can't make it. Dreadful headache. Will you tell him I'll have to take a few days off?' Today's date.

Oh. Now that was too bad. Should she tell Thomas or not? No. Best leave the invalids in peace. Delete.

Rose arrived in the doorway, with her mouth turned down. 'You'd best take it easy today, Ellie, or we'll both be down with it, and then what will we do? Paint a cross on the door and hope some charitable person will be good enough to phone the undertakers if we snuff it?'

'It's not as bad as that. Vera will be up and about soon.'

'Thomas won't be up and about soon, take my word for it. You know what he's like when it gets on to his chest.'

'I know. I'll pop up and see that he takes—'

The phone rang. Diana. 'Mother, I rang you yesterday but you haven't had the courtesy to—'

'Flu, Diana. Vera. Then Mikey. And now Thomas. Also, I've got Social Services on my back, threatening to take Mikey into care.' Greatly daring, she added, 'I don't suppose you could spare the time to help me nurse them?'

Squawk. Horror, horror! Indignation! 'Whatever in the world . . .'

Ellie grinned and put the phone down. She muted the ring tone. If anyone rang now, she wouldn't hear it. The caller could leave a message, and she'd deal with it when she could.

Rose applauded. 'That's sensible. How about we both have a coffee and a biscuit, and put our feet up for a bit? Do us the world of good. After that, you'll be better able to cope.'

Ellie gave Rose a hug. 'Rose, I adore you. Your advice, as always, is excellent. Has Mikey eaten all the chocolate biscuits, or are there any left?'

The front doorbell rang. Ellie looked at Rose, and Rose looked at Ellie. Who could it possibly be? Could they pretend to be out?

The bell rang again. Ellie shrugged and went to open the door.

Surprise! It was the new widower, Freddie, all by himself with no attendant May hanging on his arm. Freddie was wet and miserable and, as Evan had hinted, too distressed to know what he was doing. He'd parked his car skew-whiff in the drive, so close to Thomas's that he wasn't going to find it easy to leave without a lot of manoeuvring.

Ellie said, 'Do come in.' She didn't think he'd slept the previous night. There were brownish stains around his eyes, and his hair hadn't been brushed that day.

'Can you spare a minute?' He stepped into the hall but made no move to take off his car coat. 'It's just that I couldn't wait, couldn't sleep last night, and then this morning . . . It's no use saying that I should go to the police because I couldn't bear to have it all over the papers and . . . You do understand, don't you? Evan said you would. He said that if anyone could sort it, you could.'

Ellie felt as if she'd like to go back to bed with the electric blanket full on, thank you, to be waited on by a team of sympathetic women with hushed voices and soft hands, who wouldn't allow any visitors or phone calls.

She said, 'I'm just going to have a cup of coffee. Would you like one?'

'Coffee?' He stared at her as if she'd suggested a cup of hemlock.

'Have you had any breakfast?'

'Breakfast?' He repeated the word. Clearly, it had no meaning for him.

Ellie rolled her eyes at Rose, who rolled them back. 'Can you manage some coffee for us, Rose? Then you must have a nice rest. I'll deal with the invalids later.'

'Invalids?' Freddie repeated that word, too. 'You mean Evan?'

'No. Members of my family are down with flu. Which reminds me, weren't you expecting some relatives of your own?'

'My sister arrived early. My older sister. She took charge. Do you have an older sister? Bossy. Very. Anita couldn't stand her. She's rearranged everything, food for the wake, the Order of Service. She's taken over the job of phoning people to tell them about the funeral, ordered May to go back to work, driven me mad. So I got in my car and went to see Evan. When I got back, she'd started taking Anita's clothes out of the wardrobe and was putting them into black plastic bags for the charity shop and I . . .'

Ellie divested him of his wet coat and led him into the sitting room, which was beginning to look neglected, with newspapers littered around the place, dying flowers on the table near the window, and more dust on the mahogany. She consoled herself by saying that Freddie wouldn't notice. He didn't.

'Couldn't get her to stop. We had a row. We always row. Ever since we were children, whenever we meet, we row. I put the bags in my car, thinking I'd take them to the office and keep them there till she'd gone. Then I remembered May would be there, and I couldn't face her. I didn't know what to do.'

Ellie indicated he take a seat. He did so, but jumped up again immediately and began to stride about the room. He hadn't shaved that morning, and he had odd socks on. Oh well.

'What Evan said . . . I mean, he wouldn't say it if other people weren't saying it too, would he? I can't stop thinking about it, now. That's what happens, isn't it? You wish you'd not heard the words, but once you have, you can't push them away and pretend you haven't been told. If everyone is saying it . . . What am I to do? You can see why I need your help, can't you? He said you don't charge because you don't have to, but I'd be prepared, honestly, it would be well worth it if I could only be sure . . . But then, if it's true, I can't let it go on, and yet . . . To tell the police . . . What good would that do?'

Rose brought in some coffee and a plate of biscuits. No chocolate ones, Ellie noticed.

She handed a cup of coffee to Freddie, who stared at it as if he'd never seen the like before. His hand trembled. He was going to drop the cup. Before he could do so, Ellie took it off him and put it on the table beside him.

Was that a faint cry from upstairs? She was needed up there, looking after the invalids, having it out with Mikey and getting on with things. She did not, repeat not, want to listen to this man drivelling on about something in the past which he couldn't have prevented, anyway.

She said, 'Now, Freddie; calm down. Sit down and explain yourself in words of one syllable.'

This worked, in as much as he sat down for two seconds, but sprang up again almost immediately. 'Evan said everyone thinks May gave Anita the pills that killed her. He thinks May worked on Anita to commit suicide because I'd got fed up with . . . and she thought I was giving her encouragement to . . . to . . .' He gagged.

Was he going to be sick? Oh dear! Understandable, but difficult to clean the carpet afterwards, and the smell did tend to linger. 'Dear Freddie, please sit down. Count to twenty, very slowly. Backwards. Twenty . . . nineteen . . .'

He sat, nodded his head as he counted. At least that had shut him up for a moment.

She said, 'Now, drink your coffee and eat a biscuit. That's what I'm going to do, too. After we've drunk our coffee and eaten our biscuits, we will be calm enough to discuss the matter in rational fashion.'

She wondered at herself, giving orders like this, but it seemed to work. He took a sip or two of coffee. Ate a corner of a biscuit. A slurp of coffee. The whole of one biscuit. He took another. Sat back in his chair.

'You're right,' he said. 'I was hungry. I didn't fancy having any breakfast. I told the workmen to stop work on the lights. I said I'd pay them for their time, but that I didn't want . . . Not now. It's not right.'

Ellie felt like patting him on the head and saying, 'Good boy.' She said, 'Perhaps you could switch them on just for Christmas Eve and Christmas Day.'

He was hanging on her every word. 'Yes. You're right. That would be the thing to do. Anita would like that.' A shuddering sigh. 'Would have liked that. So, you don't think I encouraged May to help Anita kill herself, do you? Because it never crossed my mind.'

'No, of course not.'

He bowed his head over his cup.

Silence.

Ellie worked it out. Should she speak the words, or pretend she didn't know what he was thinking? Correction, what he had thought?

Dear Lord, tell me what to do. If I'm mistaken and I mention my suspicion, he'll be even more distressed than he is now. Is it better to pretend I don't know? Because I really don't know for sure, do I?

She said, as gently as she could, 'Anita was the strong one, wasn't she?'

He nodded.

'When you heard that the cancer had returned, you must have felt dreadful, for her and for yourself. Watching someone you love gradually slipping away is a terrible thing. I know, because I had to watch my first husband die.'

His lips moved, but he did not speak.

'The bad news must have crashed in on you like a giant wave. A tsunami. You must have wondered how you were going to cope, how you could support her through it all, knowing there was no hope. Then practical issues had to raise their head. How long was it going to take? Did you need to alter the household arrangements? Get in Macmillan nurses?'

He nodded.

'Of course you thought first of her; but you also had to think of yourself. How to keep cheerful, how to make things easier for her, and how to keep going yourself. And yes, at some point you must have wondered what the future was going to be like without her.'

He put his head in his hands. 'Yes.'

'Did you know how long it was likely to be?'

'The doctors said that if she refused more treatment, it might only be a matter of weeks. If she had accepted the treatment, it would have prolonged her life for, maybe, six months.'

'How did you feel about that?'

'She said straight away that she didn't want any more treatment. She even laughed when she said it. She wasn't afraid to die. I didn't know what I felt about it. I backed her up. Whatever she wanted was all right by me.'

'You didn't think of asking for help with the extra nursing, from May, from your sister, from anybody?'

'We could have had the Macmillan nurses come in at night, but she said she didn't want them yet. I asked her if she wanted anyone else during the day, but she said she didn't. Just me. We knew it wouldn't be long, and I could cope. I thought, take it day by day. Every time I thought of the future without her, I went blank. And then I'd say to myself, "Time enough to think about that later."'

'Anita, on the other hand, looked at the situation and, rightly or wrongly, did something about it.'

'I did suspect . . . or not exactly suspect . . . But, at the back of my mind, we knew one another so well, you see, that I thought . . . Which was why I checked her medication before I went off for the weekend.'

'What more could you have done?'

TWELVE

Freddie looked at Ellie in despair. 'I should have had it out in the open. I should have got her antidepressants.' He straightened up. 'I should have got the sleeping pills for her.'

'She didn't ask you to do so, did she?'

He shook his head.

'She didn't want you to bear any guilt in this. She arranged that you would be away.'

He was silent for a while. Eventually, he nodded. 'I hear what you're saying, and of course you're right. I still wonder if May helped her, thinking that perhaps I'd turn to her when Anita had gone.'

'I don't think it's so much a question of your turning to her, as of her trying to . . .' Ellie hesitated. It had just occurred to her that it might never have entered May's head that Freddie would turn to her on the rebound. Perhaps she was only being kind-hearted and helpful.

Freddie said, 'You should hear what my sister called May. "Avaricious, man-eating, husband-stealing whore." I didn't know what to say.'

'Did she say all that on the phone to May? Or to her face?'

A reluctant grin. 'May came round to see that I'd eaten my breakfast, but I was hardly up and in my right mind. Must confess, had a tot or two of spirits when visiting Evan, and then had one or two more last night, what with my sister going on at me and, well, everything. I ought to have told my sister to shut up and not talk to May like that, but I didn't. I'm ashamed that I didn't. May didn't deserve that. At least, I don't think she did. What I mean is, if she did help Anita to die . . . I've asked myself how I'd feel about it if she did, and it's odd. I don't feel anything. Nothing at all.'

Shock? Yes.

Ellie said, 'Your sister is a harridan. Evan has a fertile imagination. It may well have crossed May's mind that you could do with a shoulder to cry on, but it may be no more than kindness on her part. It's up to you to decide whether or not you want her to step further into your life.'

'No, I don't. She's a nice enough woman in her way but I've never thought of her like that. She's not my type. And what's more . . .' He looked pleadingly at Ellie.

She sighed. 'What's more, you now find her embarrassing and wonder how you can get rid of her. You'd like to give her the sack, but what reason could you give? Unless, of course, you find out that it was she who provided your wife with the means to end her life.'

He reddened. 'Yes.'

'That's why you want me to discover what happened.'

'Yes. Will you?'

Ellie didn't know how to refuse him, for refuse him she must. She turned her head to the door. Was that Thomas calling for her? Rose must not go climbing those stairs again. Then she must get Mikey on his own and shake the truth out of him and . . . Well, she didn't really want to shake Mikey . . . Well, actually she did want to do just that, but . . .

She got to her feet, thinking this would be a good enough hint to Freddie to get himself moving. But he didn't. She picked up the daily papers which lay around and tidied them into a heap. She put the dirty cups and saucers – including one left over from the previous day which was on the floor by Thomas's big chair – and put them on the tray.

The flowers in the vase on the table by the window had had it. She put the vase on the tray, too. She said, 'Back in a minute,' and took the lot out to the kitchen. Rose was crooning along to the radio, while sitting in her big chair and reading the local paper.

Ellie dumped the dead flowers and put the vase and dirty cups into the dishwasher.

Rose said, 'The weather forecast's not good. This rain's with us for the rest of the week.'

'Mm,' said Ellie. 'Don't try those stairs again, Rose.'

'Trust me.'

Ellie returned to the sitting room. Freddie was making no move to leave. Should she start dusting around him? Bring out the vacuum cleaner? He was the sort who'd probably lift his feet and let her hoover around him.

He said, 'I'm sorry to take up so much of your time. I realize I'm procrastinating. The funeral's on Monday, at noon at the church, and then on to the crematorium. Will you come? An ancient uncle arrived this morning, and there's a cousin to be picked up at the airport this afternoon. My sister tries to marshal us all as if we were squaddies and she's the sergeant major. I'll have to go back, try to keep the peace.'

He tried on a smile. It looked as if it hurt. 'I'm not usually like this, you know. I run a successful business. I make decisions, snap, snap, snap. I think ahead, I plan. I choose my staff with care, and I've assembled a good team. We're weathering the economic storm, more than holding our own. I don't usually go to pieces.'

'No,' said Ellie, pleased to see another side of him.

He squared his shoulders. 'The only thing I have to reproach myself with . . . No, I don't think I did encourage May in any way. I really don't think I did. But I'm wondering if she misinterpreted, if I was in any way to blame for her actions. I would find that hard to live with.'

Handle with care. 'It is possible she may have misinterpreted something you said or did, but that doesn't mean she acted upon it. She may be as innocent as you.'

'How innocent am I, who did let the thought cross my mind that I hoped Anita wouldn't last too long, not for her sake but for my own?'

'Don't beat yourself up. If that thought did cross your mind, then you dismissed it.'

'Sensible little woman, aren't you?' He blinked. 'You're right, of course. Have to tie a knot and move on, as my mother always used to say when we fell from grace. I think you're right. I'll pop in to the Abbey, make my confession. Then back to work!'

The door slithered open, and in marched Midge. He made straight for Ellie, sat down in front of her and treated her to a giant yawn.

'Feeding time,' said Ellie, looking at the door and wondering if Midge had opened it by himself or not. He was capable of opening any door with a proper handle rather than a knob. But Midge and Mikey were inseparable nowadays. Suppose Mikey had come downstairs looking for help for Vera, but had stopped short of entering the room when he heard Freddie's voice?

She looked at her wrist. Where on earth had her watch got to? She really must look for it when she'd a spare minute. She got to her feet. 'Your coat's in the hall.'

That got him moving.

Mikey was not in the hall. A whisper of air as the door to the kitchen quarters closed.

That door was always kept open nowadays. Had he gone to look for Rose?

She said, 'Did Anita leave a message for you?'

'She did. "Sorry" and "I love you". A typical suicide note, apparently.'

'I wondered, have you looked to see if there might be an empty box in the waste-paper bin with a pharmacist's name on it? Or the name of the person who bought the sleeping tablets?'

He brightened up. 'That's an idea. I'll look. Thank you,' said Freddie, offering his hand to shake. 'I feel so much better after talking to you. Evan said you're good with people, and he's right.' He swung on his car coat and, passing the mirror over the hall table, exclaimed, 'I need a shower and a change of clothes. Wish me luck with my sister.'

He opened the front door and vanished into the rain.

The door to the kitchen quarters opened. Mikey, wearing a sweater, jeans and unlaced trainers. Fully awake and with the heel of a loaf in his hand. No temperature.

His mouth full, he gestured her to follow him up the stairs. So who was in need of her services? Into the master bedroom he went, still chewing. He pointed to the bed, which lacked an occupant. Thomas had spilt his lemonade all over it. Thomas was in the bathroom; she could hear him growling to himself as he showered.

'Are you all right, Thomas?'

'I'm a clumsy brute. Spilt the lemonade all over myself. Is there any more where that came from?'

'I'll see what I can do.' Bother. 'I'll change the bed. Throw your dirty pyjamas out, will you?'

She looked around for Mikey to see if he'd help her, but he'd vanished. Of course. She stripped the bed, took the linen down the stairs to dump in the washing machine, turned it on, and rousted out some clean sheets. She'd look for Mikey after she'd got Thomas back into bed again.

Friday noon

There wasn't anything in the local paper about Petra falling down the stairs and killing herself. You'd have thought it would have been given a couple of inches of space. Single parent mother of . . , whatever it was the child was called . . . long-term partner of . . .? Names escaped her nowadays.

Perhaps it had happened before the paper was put to bed – if that was the right word for it – and it would be in next week's edition. An upsetting episode, but the girl had brought it on herself, hadn't she?

Evan, now. She'd felt quite annoyed with him because he'd a lot to live for, what with a new wife, who was capable of looking after the office for him while he stopped at home, and a baby boy coming. But no, all he could do was whine about his aches and pains.

He never gave a thought to her problems. Wasn't that just like a man?

To think how Evan used to stride around the place, telling everyone what to do, boasting about his successes . . . Yes, he'd been a bit of a braggart, even her own dear husband had used to say so.

She did wonder if he were hitting the bottle a little too hard, because almost the first thing he asked her to do was to pour him out a whisky, no ice, no water. He'd sworn it was his first drink of the day, and he did calm down a lot afterwards. He'd even told her a joke or two, admittedly not in good taste.

If he asked her to help him she supposed she would have

to do so, but this must be the last time. She was getting too old and tired for it, nowadays.

Friday noon

Housebound, that's what she was. Invalids here, invalids there. Everywhere she looked were invalids. Well, to be accurate, there were only two of them, but neither was fit to get out of bed, and Thomas – although contrite about his accident with the lemonade – was going to need some serious nursing if she were any judge of the matter.

Vera was over the worst of it, but as weak as the proverbial kitten. She couldn't stand for more than two seconds without folding back on to her bed.

Mikey was like a silverfish. One moment he was in plain sight, and the next he'd whisked himself away. She supposed it was a good thing that he hadn't got flu, but when she laid hands on him, she'd . . . Well, she wasn't sure what she was going to do, but he'd be sorry he ever missed school.

Now, should she ring his teacher to see if there were any worksheets he could be doing while he was at home, or should she send him back to school? Back to school. Definitely. She'd make him go back. Tomorrow.

No, wait a minute, tomorrow was Saturday.

Saturday meant the weekend. She needed to do a serious shop for the weekend. She really would have to go online and do it as soon as she had a free moment. She didn't like shopping online. She was sure to make a mistake.

Perhaps Mikey would do it for her? If she could catch him.

Up and down the stairs we go. There were no lemons left for the invalids' drinks, and she couldn't really leave the house long enough to get some. If she ordered them online, they wouldn't come till tomorrow. Who could she get to run to the shops for her?

And the rain came down, and the floods came up . . . Well, almost. There were puddles on the lawn, and puddles in the drive. Passing cars in the road went swishing through yet more puddles. Anyone for Noah's Ark?

Passing through the hall, she heard the phone ring in a

muted, desperate way. She ignored it. Into the kitchen she went to check on Rose and root around in the freezer for some oranges, for any kind of fruit. Mikey was sitting at the table, eating an apple and using his mother's laptop.

Rose said, 'I'm telling him what we need and he's ordering it for us online. I've got fruit and spreadable butter and some greens; two lots of frozen would be best. We need tomatoes, not in tins. Cereals, his kind and ours. Oh, and tomatoes in tins. Now, from the bakery section, what about two wholemeal loaves, sliced if they have them? Some biscuits, chocolate and shortbread. Put down some iced buns or chocolate muffins for yourself, Mikey. We're out of balsamic vinegar and cooking oil, too. Meat next. What shall we have, Ellie?'

'A large chicken, some mince, some lamb chops and some sliced ham for the weekend.' Ellie tried to remember what they usually ordered. More meat, veg and fruit. More of everything. She did her best to make up the list for Mikey, concluding, 'We also need two packets of throat pastilles, some aspirin and a couple of big boxes of tissues, man size. Let me see what you've ordered, Mikey.'

He showed her, crunching away at his apple. It looked all right to her. She was pleased to see he'd added basics like potatoes and cat food. Mikey was even better at this than Vera.

'Fine. Press send.' She straightened up. 'The only problem is that it won't come till tomorrow. We'll need some fish for tonight. Salmon steaks, perhaps, and fruit.' She dithered, looking out on to the rain which was sheeting down. 'I'd better take a cab and get some.'

Mikey raised his hand, still munching.

'You want to go? Certainly not! If you're fit to go to the shops, you're fit to be in school. Oh, Mikey; what a mess you're in! We're going to have to have a long talk about this with your mother very soon, because she doesn't know the half of it, does she? But I don't want you bothering her with it now she's so poorly, understood?'

He nodded, stuffed the apple core into his mouth and dived into the larder where they kept Rose's basket on wheels. Rose hadn't been out of the house for weeks, and she certainly wasn't strong enough to trek to the shops and back.

'Mikey, if you're fit to go to the shops, you're fit to go back to school.'

He shook his head, grinning. Then he rubbed his thumb against his fingers in the age-old request for money.

Rose gave in first. 'Mikey, I'm not at all sure you should be allowed out after what you've been up to, but I don't suppose you'll come to any harm going to the shops and back, and it would save Ellie a peck of trouble.' She gave him a hug. 'Be careful, now. And make sure the waterproof cover is on the basket so the things you buy don't get wet. Get yourself some of your favourite chocolate biscuits while you're out. Do you want my umbrella?'

He shook his head.

Ellie turned him to face her. 'Dear Mikey. We're both so worried about you. I don't know that you ought to go out, but it's true we do need these things. You must promise me you won't go on to the building site? Cross your heart and hope to die promise?'

He nodded, serious. The bruise on his face was pretty bad, and the skin around his eye was still puffy. But if Mikey promised he wouldn't do something, he probably wouldn't. Probably.

Ellie fetched her handbag and counted out some money for him to take. She saw him dressed in sensible wet weather clothing and sent him out into the rain.

Well, a spot of rain wouldn't do him any harm.

As Ellie watched the boy disappear into the gloomy day, Diana drew up in her car with a squelch, manoeuvred herself out from under the steering wheel and waddled up the step and into the hall.

'Other people,' said Diana, in a savage tone, 'can rely on their mothers to help them when they're in trouble. I tried and tried to ring you this morning so that you could go to the hospital with me, but you didn't pick up.'

Ellie shot a glance at the phone. She remembered muting the tone so she'd get a bit of peace. She hadn't turned it up again, had she?

Diana was in full flow. 'I've been having back pains all night. Evan said it was no more than to be expected . . .'

Diana was Evan's fourth wife and he'd sired a fair number of children over the years, so he probably knew what he was talking about.

'. . . so, even though I didn't get a wink of sleep, I dragged myself off to work. But then it got worse so I had to take myself off to the hospital, only to be told that I was having Brampton Apples or something, and that the baby wasn't nearly ready to come.'

'Braxton Hicks. False contractions. I remember them,' said Ellie. 'Surely you had them during your first pregnancy?'

'I was younger, then.' Diana led the way into the sitting room and let herself down on to the big, high-backed chair in front of the fireplace. Ellie's chair. Diana sniffed. Was she really going to burst into tears? 'Evan can't think about anything but his own problems. He thinks I should be as concerned about them as he is. Also, he's drinking too much.' Diana rubbed the small of her back. 'The house is a mess. He's been having visitors, but never bothers to put the dirty glasses in the dishwasher. I counted six! Six! I did ask you to vet his callers. I thought you might at least do that for me. I don't want him dying of liver poisoning before the baby's born.'

On the defensive again, Ellie said, 'I did try. Six glasses? Did he give himself a clean glass each time? If so, there'd have been three callers. I know of two. Freddie—'

'Oh, him! Drinking himself into his grave because his wife had had enough of him.'

'Oh, come on, Diana. He's grief-stricken. Then there's Marcia. Is she a drinker?'

'She never refuses a snifter. Or Pauline.'

Ellie had forgotten she was supposed to visit someone called Pauline. She couldn't even remember whether she was a widow or not. Probably. Where did she live? Locally? 'Sorry, I haven't had time to get round to her.'

'I've only ever asked you to do one little thing for me, and you say you can't find "time to get round to her"? I need to have people visiting Evan who won't encourage him to drink. Mother, I despair of you! Don't you care what happens to me?'

'Don't talk nonsense, Diana.' Ellie bit her lip, because Diana did look deathly pale. 'You're not fit to go into work. Why don't you go home and lie down for a bit?'

Diana moaned, shifting on her chair. 'I can't get comfortable whatever I do. And who is to bring home the pennies, if I don't supervise everything at the agency?'

'You'll be suggesting next that I take over your desk at work.'

Diana was silent. 'I've been thinking about it, yes.'

'I was joking! No, Diana. No. I can't. Won't. I've enough on my plate already. Both Thomas and Vera have gone down with flu, and young Mikey's in trouble with the law.'

'I've always said that boy's no good.'

Actually, no: she hadn't.

Diana rubbed her forehead. 'I can't be expected to work when the baby's due at any minute but the staff are hopeless, running around like headless chickens.'

She only had herself to blame for that because she'd sacked an excellent second-in-command because he wouldn't cut corners.

Diana said, 'You run your charitable trust all right. You could easily help me out at the office, if you wanted to.'

Ellie's patience had worn out. 'No, I couldn't. It's not my scene, and you know it. Why don't you arrange for Evan to go in to work every day? He could direct operations from his wheelchair, because there's nothing wrong with his head. Get a taxi to collect him in the mornings and bring him back in the evenings.'

'He says he's not well enough. All he wants to do is to sit drinking with his old pals, and you haven't helped me at all in that direction.'

'I didn't realize you wanted his visitors to be teetotal. You should have said.'

Diana burst into angry, noisy tears. 'You never loved me.'

Ellie wondered for one awful moment whether this were true. But, no. Of course it wasn't true. She made herself calm down. In a reasonably convincing tone she said, 'I have always loved you. From the moment you were born, you were the centre of my life. I don't think you noticed me much, though, because you were always your father's little girl, weren't you? He loved you to distraction. He gave you everything you asked for, sometimes even before you asked for it.'

'*You* didn't. You were always saying "no" to me.'

'He handed me the hard part of parenting. It was always I who had to tell you that too much sugar was bad for your teeth, or that you couldn't have two pairs of very expensive shoes when there wasn't enough money to pay for them. He always wanted everything to be sunny side up when he talked to you, and he left it to me to warn you when your temper got out of control.'

'Whose fault was that? If you'd given me what I asked for—'

'When it was bad for you? Is that the right way to show love to your child?'

'You were always too busy or too tired to take me to ballet classes. I had to go on my own.'

Ellie set her teeth. 'I arranged for you to go with a friend, didn't I? I hardly stopped from morning to night, looking after you and your father. Oh, what's the use? I did my best by you and by him.'

'Not good enough.'

That was one word too many. 'Listen to me, my girl. I've put up with your nonsense from the day you were born because I loved you, and worried about you, and agonized how best to bring you up. But you weren't the only person I had to think about. There was your father, and your great-aunt, and then, I don't suppose you knew about them, but—'

'Oh, grant me patience! You're not going to go on about "the little children who were not meant to be", are you? Daddy would tell me every now and then that I was going to get a little brother or sister, but they never arrived, did they?'

'No. I lost three early. One I nearly carried to term, but . . .' She stopped. She'd lost that one because Diana, in a rage, had given Ellie a push at the top of the stairs and she'd tumbled down them and lost the six-month foetus. She said, 'Only one nearly made it. That sort of thing takes it out of you.'

'Well, you had me.'

'Yes,' said Ellie, feeling weary enough to weep, 'Yes, we

had you. And we loved you, even if we couldn't give you everything you wanted.'

'And you're still letting me down.'

Ellie closed her eyes for a moment. 'You are old enough to know better, Diana. Now, if you don't mind, I've got two invalids in the house who need me far more than you do. If you're well enough to go in to work, then I suggest you appoint one of your staff to look after the office while you take some leave. After all, you can't mean to work for a while after you've had the baby.'

'I don't plan to be away for more than a week.'

'Are you planning to take the baby into work with you?'

'Heavens, no. I shan't breastfeed. Evan will have to get a nurse in for it.'

Ellie blinked. Yet, what had she expected? Diana hadn't breastfed her first, either. Diana hauled herself out of the big chair and processed to the hall. She picked up her big coat with an effort and shrugged herself into it. 'I suppose that you'll be free to accompany me to the hospital when the baby decides to come? Evan can't, and I shall need someone with me.'

Ellie's mind zigzagged between Diana, her two invalids and Mikey, in trouble up to his eyeballs. 'If you can last out a couple of days, I'm sure Thomas will be over the worst of it. Vera is on the mend, too.'

'As usual, you put everyone else before me.'

Ellie didn't reply to that.

THIRTEEN

As soon as Diana had gone, Ellie corrected the volume of the bell on the telephone. She saw the answerphone light was winking, decided to ignore it and zipped into the kitchen. Rose was stirring something in a big pan. Soup for lunch, hopefully. Rose was singing along to something on the radio. She waved to Ellie, but didn't suspend operations. The washing machine was churning away. No Mikey as yet.

There were no more lemons to make into lemonade. Ellie found a bottle of elderflower cordial in the larder which was just about in date and made up a jugful to take upstairs.

Thomas was back in bed. Snoring gently. He was restless and far too hot. She put the jug on the table in the window, poured him out a glassful and left it by his bedside.

Up the next flight. Vera was relaxed, still in bed, awake but drowsy. She'd almost finished the jug of lemonade which Ellie had made earlier.

'You shouldn't have bothered to come up again. I can make myself a cuppa when I need it, and my headache's almost gone. Where's Mikey?'

'Gone for some more fruit. Back soon.'

'Who were those people this morning?'

Ellie grimaced. 'Mikey's been missing school. He needs a good talking-to. Don't you bother about it for now. The weekend's coming up, and he's going to turn over a new leaf next week.' Fingers crossed.

Vera was on the verge of tears. 'He is naughty. I've told him and told him, but I thought he'd mended his ways. I didn't want to worry you, because I thought I could deal with it. I've had two notes from school about his being away for the odd afternoon, but he's been keeping up with his homework. I've checked. So what is he up to now?'

Ellie sat on the bed, patting Vera's hand. 'He's bored at

school and wants to try his wings. Yes, we have to put a stop to it, but perhaps we might think about getting him into a school where the teachers would stretch him. He's bright enough to sit for scholarships in a private school.'

Vera blew her nose. 'But with his record from his current school—'

'Money talks. If necessary I'll cover his fees. For now, my dear, the best thing you can do is put his naughtiness out of your mind and rest. Get well. Would you like me to bring in the television from next door?'

As fast as tears ran down her pale cheeks, Vera wiped them away. 'No thanks. I'll get up soon and sit next door for a while, if my head lets me. At the moment, every time I stand up, I feel faint. I knew something awful had happened to Mikey when I saw those bruises of his, but he said he'd fallen down the stairs here, chasing Midge. Was that true?'

He'd actually used his voice to speak to his mother? Or had he mimed his 'accident'? Either way, Ellie wasn't going to add to Vera's worries by telling her about the problems at the building site. She'd have to know sooner or later, but in this case, later would be best. 'He fell down some stairs, yes. He's been checked over by a doctor, and it's just bruises.'

There was some truth there and some papering over the cracks. Vera seemed to accept what Ellie said. She sighed deeply and lay back, closing her eyes. 'Oh, Mikey.'

'Take it easy.' Ellie lowered the blind at the window and left. When she was halfway down the stairs, the front doorbell rang. A prolonged, insistent, demanding peal.

Trouble. Definitely.

Ellie opened the front door, and in came Hugh, carrying Mikey in his arms. Mikey's eyes were shut, and he was either asleep or had fainted.

'He was knocked down,' said Hugh. 'Crossing the road opposite the site. I don't think anything's broken. Where shall I put him?'

Mikey opened his eyes and began to struggle free.

Ellie sat on the hall chair. 'Give him to me.'

Hugh deposited the boy in her lap, and she held him tightly. His body melded into hers; his breath was warm against her neck. She rocked him to and fro. He sobbed a couple of times and then was quiet, nestling against her.

How she loved him!

Ellie thought of Diana, and of how her daughter had never sat on her lap to be loved and soothed like this. When Ellie had picked Diana up in the old days she'd stiffened and demanded to be put down. Perhaps you needed to be loved in return, in order to keep on loving?

No, that wasn't right. She still loved her daughter, but with a weariness that made her wonder, sometimes, how much longer she could go on doing so.

She asked Hugh, 'What happened? He went to the shops for me. He promised he wouldn't go on to the site.'

Hugh sighed, shaking his head. 'I was up top at the back when one of the electricians called to me to have a look. He was in one of the rooms at the front and had spotted the lad walking along on the opposite side of the road. None of us want the boy on site now, as you can imagine. I saw the boy, too. He was looking up at us. I shook my head to indicate he shouldn't try to come in. He turned away to walk on up the road. He was wearing that bright yellow mac of his, with the hood up. Easy to spot.

'It was still raining, but not as hard as it had been. Not bouncing off the road. I was concerned he might double back and try to get into the site, so I went on watching him. I knew he'd have to cross the road at some point, to get back home. He went on about twenty yards and looked both ways, to see if it were all right to cross over. There wasn't much traffic about. This vehicle came along, slowed right down. Mikey must have thought he'd plenty of time to cross and started off, but he misjudged it. The driver kept on going. Mikey jumped back but the wing of the car clipped him, sending him sprawling.'

Ellie clutched Mikey even harder. 'Intentionally? The driver meant to run the boy down?'

'No, no. The rain, the early dusk, he probably didn't realize . . . Anyway, we both, the electrician and I, ran for the stairs, and when we reached him, the boy was sitting on the pavement, trembling all over. There was no sign of the car, which hadn't stopped. We carried him into my office, checked him over. There's nothing broken. A bad bruise on his right side. We talked about taking him to hospital but he kept shaking his head, tried to walk off by himself, so I offered to bring him home. I hope we did the right thing.'

'I'm sure you did.' Ellie held the boy away from her. 'Mikey, is everything in working order? Nothing broken?'

He shook his head, dived back to hide his face in her shoulder.

'Did you get the licence number of the car, Hugh?'

'From that angle on the second floor? In the rain? No. It was all over so quickly. I mean, you don't expect . . . And for a minute after it happened we didn't react, standing there with our mouths open. Afterwards, we couldn't even agree on the make of the car.' He shot her a look from under his eyebrows. A look she couldn't read. 'I think it was a Toyota, four door, probably black. Dark colour, anyway. Not silver or red.'

Ellie didn't know anything about cars. 'You called the police?'

'We thought about it, but because the boy's in trouble with the police already and there was no harm done except for a bruise, we decided not to. What could we say? A hit and run. Ten a penny. I've got his mac in my car. He was trailing a basket on wheels. I've got that in the car, too.'

'He went shopping for me. I've got two members of the household down with flu and couldn't leave, so he offered. Now I wish . . . Mikey, I could shake you! Why weren't you more careful?'

He clung more closely to her by way of reply.

Hugh shook his head. 'A good night's sleep, that's what he needs.'

Ellie had a nasty thought. 'Were Preston and his mate Dave working on site today?'

He stared at her, not pleased. 'Of course they were there, finishing off that bathroom at the top. I tell you, it was an inexperienced driver hitting the wrong pedal. Or Mikey misinterpreting a signal from the driver to cross.'

Mikey shook his head.

Silence.

Hugh fidgeted. 'I really must get back.'

There was a stir behind them. Rose was standing there, listening. In some distress.

Ellie felt hot tears on her neck. Mikey was crying, too.

Ellie tried to stand up with the boy in her arms. Couldn't manage it.

'Hugh, would you be a dear and carry Mikey upstairs for me? I don't want his mother bothered because she's in bed with flu. I'll put the boy into the bedroom opposite mine on the first floor, the one which my grandson uses when he has a sleepover. We always keep the bed made up, and there's a bathroom next door that he can use.'

She led the way upstairs. Hugh followed, carrying the child, whose eyes were closed but who had tears on his cheeks.

Ellie opened the door to the bedroom. 'Here we are. Mikey, how about a shower to deal with those bruises? Yes? Can you manage by yourself?'

They watched the boy walk unsteadily to the bathroom. Then they heard the shower running.

Hugh fidgeted. 'I really ought to get back.' Yet he didn't go.

Ellie said, 'Dear Hugh. You've been wonderful. Thank you.'

'Why won't the boy speak?'

'It's an emotional thing. Mikey was very fond of his step-father and couldn't seem to talk for a while after he died. I suppose the doctors have a word for it. Gradually, it went away. Now it's back, and I'm inclined to blame the rough treatment he received from your men.'

'You can't prove that. Look, I don't want to be alarmist. I like the boy and I'm concerned for him. First he pokes his nose in where he's not wanted, is caught red-handed, and tumbles down the stairs when he tries to escape. Then he mistakes the signal from a car on the road and nearly gets run over. You need to keep an eye on him or something worse might happen.'

She didn't think she'd heard aright. Was that a threat? From Hugh, of all people?

He said, 'I'll fetch his raincoat and the basket on wheels, and leave them in the hall.'

'Thank you.' What else could she say?

She saw Hugh drive off and set off up the stairs, again. She could hear Vera calling out, 'Mikey, is that you?'

Ellie diverted to climb the stairs to the top, paused to press her side where she'd got a stitch, and tried to think what she could say to Vera. Not the truth. No, not yet.

She put on a bright voice. 'Well, the bad penny's turned up again. Wouldn't you know he's got thoroughly chilled going out in the rain, so he's having a hot shower. He's decided to sleep downstairs, so I'll just collect his pyjamas, pop him into bed in the guest room and get him a mug of hot milk.'

Vera might be unwell, but her instincts told her something was wrong. 'Let me see him.' She threw back the covers.

Ellie soothed Vera back on to the pillows, producing a smile that felt fake. 'Nothing to worry about, Vera. He'll be right as rain in the morning.' She collected his pyjamas to take downstairs, followed by Midge the cat.

She couldn't think what she needed to do next. Yes, she could. She was desperate for a cup of tea, and that must be her number one priority.

Down she went, to deliver Mikey his pyjamas, and to check on Thomas. She now had three invalids to look after, plus Rose, and no help in the house.

Rose appeared in the doorway to the kitchen quarters. Rose had her arms crossed and was standing with her feet apart. Rose was going on the attack. 'What's going on?'

'I wish I knew. If we could get Mikey to talk . . .'

Rose shook her head. 'He'll snap out of it when he's ready. One thing, he did bring the shopping back. Fish cutlets, biscuits and plenty of lemons, plus aspirin and throat stuff. I'll set about making some more drinks, shall I? We can keep some in the fridge.'

Cough, cough, from upstairs. Thomas must have woken up.

The phone rang.

Ellie wanted to say she wasn't there, but she knew that wouldn't help. She picked the phone up.

'I've found something.' A man's voice. Now who . . .? He said, 'I just wanted to be sure you were in. I'll bring it round. See what you think.' He cut off the call.

Ellie shrugged. She said to Rose, 'Someone says he's coming round. It can't be Evan, so it must be Freddie.'

'I'll put the kettle on.' Rose vanished.

Ellie pressed the button on the answerphone.

Message one, recorded that morning, Diana. 'Mother, are you there? I need you to come to the hospital with me. Pick up the phone, for heavens' sake! I can't wait around for ever. Ring me on my mobile.' Delete.

Message two, from the agency. 'So sorry, Ellie. We're still not able to field enough people to cover everyone. If you're desperate, ring me back, and I'll see if I can get someone to come over after the weekend.' Delete.

Message three was one of those automated ones which, if you didn't pick up, would go away. Hopefully. 'My name is Darren and I am pleased to inform you that you have won a hundred thousand pounds . , , press five to give us your bank details . . .' Delete. Scam number two thousand and two.

Message four, a woman's voice. 'Marcia here. I called on His Highness yesterday, had a tot or two with him. He seemed quite cheerful, said Freddie had been round. I've challenged Evan to a duel, see who can sink the most shots with our putting irons. I'll try to pop over there later today after my hair appointment, or maybe at the weekend . . . No, best not at the weekend. Diana wouldn't approve. Anyway, just to say I'm in touch. Bye.'

Message five? No, the front door. And it *was* Freddie, looking excited and much more alive than before. 'I found it in the drawer of her bedside table. Not with the rest of her medicines, which were in the bathroom cabinet and which my sister was in the process of clearing out, anyway, though I did ask her to stop. Anyway, she's so busy rearranging everything, I slid out of the house without her finding something for me to do. I really ought to be at the office, but they understand.'

He went straight through into the sitting room, and Ellie followed, switching on lights and drawing the curtains against the early dusk.

He held out a plastic bag with a small, empty cardboard box in it. The ends had been pulled outwards, and the box had been pressed flat. It had a label on it, from one of the pharmacies in the Avenue. Ellie took the plastic bag from him.

'Don't touch the box. That's why I put it in the plastic bag. Fingerprints.'

She nodded. She could read the pharmacist's label well enough. It was from Temple Pharmacy, which was the one both she and Thomas used. The contents had been sleeping pills. Yes. But where there ought to have been a label giving the name of the person who had been prescribed the pills, there was a blank. A label had been affixed at one time, but had later been torn off.

'You see? That's not where we get our medicines. We go down to Ealing Broadway to Boots, or get them at the supermarket. We don't use that pharmacy. Anita didn't get those pills from our doctor.'

'She might have got them elsewhere, so you wouldn't guess what she planned to do.'

'In that case, she wouldn't have torn off the label with her name on it.'

That was true.

Freddie did his pacing act again. She did wish he'd keep still for a moment. Was that more coughing from Thomas upstairs? She couldn't concentrate.

'What I want you to do,' said Freddie, 'is to find out where May gets her medicine. If it's from Temple Pharmacy, then we've got her and can go to the police.'

Ellie wasn't so sure. 'Even if May does get her medicines here, that doesn't prove anything.'

Freddie was dancing up and down with impatience. 'Fingerprints! I can easily find something she's handled, something from the office, her coffee mug, a piece of paper. They can match them up, can't they? I'll get on to it tomorrow. No, tomorrow's Saturday, isn't it? I keep forgetting, which is strange, really . . . But next week.'

Ellie let herself sink down into her chair. This day seemed endless. 'Even if what you suspect is true, even if there are May's fingerprints on the box, I'm not sure that the police would want to charge her with anything.'

'Then why did she tear her name off the box?'

'We can't be sure that she did.'

Now he was getting angry. 'I thought you were going to help me.'

'By proving that someone in your wife's circle provided the means for her to take her own life?'

He hesitated. She could see that he wanted to hit someone or something. She felt for him. 'Freddie, do sit down. Would you like a cup of tea?'

'I want . . . I want . . .' He sat, covered his face with his hands, and gave way to sobs.

Ellie let him be. A good cry was supposed to do you good, though personally she'd never found it did anything but give her a headache.

Rose came in with the tea tray. Rose obviously thought this visitor deserved more than a mug, because she'd used the good china. There were also some chocolate biscuits, thanks to Mikey's shopping expedition.

Oh, bliss. She poured out two cups of tea. She would take some up to Thomas in a minute. She took a mouthful. Wonderful . . .! And another. She drank half the cup off, even though it was really too hot to do so safely. Freddie hadn't touched his. She poured herself a second cup.

'Freddie, I realize you want answers, and you've been brilliant, turning up this important piece of evidence. Now, I happen to know that the police have been looking at one or two cases similar to your wife's even though it's unlikely that any charges would ever be brought against anyone who did some shopping for a person who wanted to commit suicide. You do understand that, don't you?'

A snuffle. A reluctant nod.

'I could ask my contact at the police station if she would talk to you about Anita's death. She may or may not have time to do so, but I think she is curious enough about what's been happening to want to speak to you about it. Would you like that?'

Another nod. Emphatic, this time. It was like handling a child. Promise a lollipop and hope you can deliver. He was so grateful that he even drank the cup of tea she'd poured out for him, while she enjoyed her second one. Ah, there was nothing like a nice cup of tea when you didn't know what to do next.

She saw Freddie off, aware that Rose had come out of the kitchen and was hovering, asking questions without words.

Ellie said, 'Rose, are you all right for the moment? Can you manage something for supper? I want to ring Lesley about Freddie and his pills, and then Evan, who wanted me to go round there but of course I can't, and then the school to explain what's happened and ask one or two questions about Mikey's behaviour there.'

'I'm all right. I've made some soup but I forgot the salt so we'll have to put it in later, and we've got the fish Mikey brought back for supper. I've made some more lemonade, but I don't think my legs will manage the stairs again for a while.'

Ellie didn't think her legs would, either. Not till she'd had a good rest. So she sat down by the phone and tried to reach Lesley Milburn at the station. Lesley was out. Of course. Ellie left a message for her to ring.

Next; Evan. He picked up straight away. 'How are you doing, Evan? I've got Thomas and Vera and her son all down with the flu and whatever, so I don't think I can get over to see you today.'

'I'm having a fine old time. My mobile phone summons ladies of leisure to my side, every hour on the hour. I have some trouble keeping them apart. They're all very sympathetic, which is more than Diana is. She wants me to get out of my wheelchair and doesn't listen when I tell her I'm not ready for that yet.'

'Do the ladies urge you to do your exercises?'

'Of course not. They bring me titbits to eat or a bottle of something good, and they know how to listen. They're all very well brought up. They might fidget, but they don't interrupt.'

Ellie was amused. 'You old fraud. I bet you're milking it for all you're worth.'

'True. I must admit one of them is a bit of a pain, going on about her own aches and pains, but I talk her down. After all, she's not confined to a wheelchair, and I am.'

'One-upmanship?'

'What else can I do?'

'Get back on your feet as soon as you can. Diana won't be able to keep the office going much longer.'

'There, now . . . And I thought she was supposed to be a superwoman.' His tone was sarcastic. Had he fallen out of love with Diana so soon? Or had he married her solely because she was going to give him a son and she was good in bed?

Careful, here. 'She married you because you were Superman.'

'Disappointed, is she?' Jeering.

'No. Distressed. Upset. Trying to be everything you want her to be. You are the strong one now, Evan. It's up to you to take over again, at work and play.'

'You forget, I'm in a wheelchair.'

'With your very own harem to fulfil your every whim. It's a sort of life, I suppose, but will it satisfy you for long?'

Silence.

Ellie wondered if she'd gone too far. Probably. Evan liked his bit of nooky, and he wasn't likely to get it while he was in his wheelchair. Or – nasty thought – was he afraid he'd lost his nerve in that direction, and therefore was in no haste to get out of the wheelchair?

He said, 'I never reckoned on you turning into the mother-in-law of seaside postcards.' But he didn't sound annoyed. He sounded amused.

Ellie grinned. 'We're about the same age, aren't we? And a lot more experienced and wiser than some. You've enjoyed your convalescence and having everyone run around you, but now's the time to reassert yourself as master of all you survey.'

He gave a long, long sigh. 'I suppose you're right.' He clicked off the phone.

As Ellie put the receiver down, the phone rang.

'Lesley Milburn here. You left a message for me?'

'Can you come round?'

'Is it urgent?'

'N-no. Not really. But interesting.'

'How did you get on with the people from Social Services?'

'They came, they saw and they left empty-handed, but only because they thought Mikey was going down with flu.'

'Isn't he?'

'It's hard to say. His temperature goes up and down. Look, I really need to talk to you about Mikey. Something very odd is going on there. He was knocked over by a car that didn't stop today.'

'It's not my case.'

'The disappearing pills are yours, aren't they?'

'You have something for me?'

'I do.'

'I'll be round as soon as I can.'

Now, one more phone call and then she must check on her invalids.

Friday afternoon

Poor Evan.

He was so pathetically grateful for someone to talk to. He'd held her hand as if he'd never let it go.

He'd been so noble, thinking only of what a weakling he was, and how hard it was on Diana and the coming baby. She'd said that of course Diana loved him as he was, but he was so sunk in despair that he couldn't see it. He kept saying they'd be better off without him.

He said Diana had stopped loving him when he had his accident, and that she didn't even share his bed at the moment. Apparently, she had to get up to go to the bathroom a dozen times a night and was so restless that he couldn't get any sleep at all.

She asked what pills he took to go to sleep, and he told her. He said that sometimes he wished he could go to sleep and never wake up.

Well, she'd a few sleeping tablets left.

She supposed she might put some in her handbag for him. He was lonely and depressed. That wife of his ought to be ashamed of herself, neglecting him as she did.

FOURTEEN

Friday afternoon

What to do next?

Ellie felt as if she were going round in circles. She would have screamed if screaming would have done any good, which she knew it wouldn't. Screaming would only upset Rose and, if they heard her, it would upset Thomas, Vera and Mikey, too.

She could go into her study and shut the door and scream. Well, it was a thought.

Instead, she went along to Thomas's quiet room and sat down in his chair. She was worn out. She relaxed. Closed her eyes. Let her hands fall loosely into her lap.

Dear Lord, can you give me a word of advice? Vera is doing well, and if I can stop her fretting over Mikey, I think she'll be all right. I'm worried about Thomas. You know what happens when a cold gets on his chest. And what about Mikey's latest accident? Ought I to call the paramedics again? I wish I knew what to do!

Thomas always said that when he asked God for help he'd get an answer, even though it might not be what he expected. Ellie wasn't at all sure that she could get through to God as if you were talking on a telephone line, but she tried because she was in such a state, not only about Thomas, but also about Mikey, too, and people being helped to commit suicide and Rose getting overtired and . . . oh, everything going round and round in her head till she didn't know what to do for the best.

Dear Lord, tell me what to do next.

Silence.

Nothing was going to happen. Why had she ever thought it would?

At your service, dear Lord. Show me the way forward.

She leaned back in the chair, trying to relax. She would take five minutes off and then traipse upstairs again.

It was very peaceful in this room. No wonder Thomas liked it to much.

Dear Lord, here I am. At your feet.

Every nerve end seemed to quieten down. She smiled, remembering how Thomas had once said she was a fiery angel defending the weak. She had a mental picture of herself as a larger-than-life-size angel, wearing a breastplate and with long wavy hair. Brandishing a sword. Which gave her the giggles.

She smiled and opened her eyes. The rest had done her good. Thomas would be all right, with care. Vera was a strong lass; she'd cope. As for Mikey; well, Ellie could do something about him this very minute.

Back in the hall, she settled herself down by the phone. First off, she rang the school secretary. This call was probably going to take some time, but it had to be done . . .

Lesley Milburn arrived with a gust of wind that blew the front door back on its hinges. Ellie was upstairs seeing to the invalids, so it was Rose who let her in. Ellie hastened down the stairs, talking partly to herself and partly to Lesley. 'I really ought to keep a chart of what painkillers I've given to which person at what time and what their temperature was. Hi, there; Lesley. Only one of my patients' temperatures is anywhere near normal, and he's the one who really ought to be checked out by a doctor. If they'd time to see him, that is. It's an epidemic, isn't it?'

'Flu? Several people at the station have got it.'

Rose said, 'More tea coming up. With chocolate biscuits.'

Lesley shed her coat and went into the sitting room. Ellie followed, collecting dirty cups and saucers and depositing them on the ledge in the hall. She picked the post and the newspapers out of the cage behind the front door and tossed them there, too. It looked like two days' worth of post. Maybe three. Well, her priorities had changed. Invalids first. Mysteries second. Everyday life could be resumed when things calmed down. She turned on the lights and drew the curtains.

'Yes?' said Lesley. 'You have some information for me?'

'The bad news first, or the good? Mikey has—'

A grimace. 'You know I can't discuss Mikey.'

'Let me gossip about him till the tea comes. I've discovered that he played truant because he was being bullied.'

'What? Are you sure?'

'Would I say so, if I wasn't sure? I rang the school. At first they would only say they had a strong policy of dealing with bullies, and they had no knowledge of any of that happening in Mikey's form. So I spoke to his form master. It's Mikey's first term with this man, and it's clear he thought the boy is rubbish. He said that Mikey needed to change his attitude. The words "insolent" and "unteachable" hung in the air.'

Lesley shrugged. 'A lad on the downward path.'

'Unhuh. I needed a second opinion, so I rang an old acquaintance of mine who has a child of Mikey's age at the same school. She keeps her ear to the ground, has three cats, one of whom only has three legs, not that that's of interest to you. She said the boy's teacher this year is fresh out of college and a poor disciplinarian. The kids always know when a teacher hasn't proper control, so they play up. The class bully – and yes, I know his name – has taken advantage of this laxity to target boys who try to stand up to him – which Mikey does, though my informant's son is more circumspect. Apparently, it's well known that this bully and his gang rule the playground and in particular "own" a spot behind the art room where they can smoke or beat people up without being spotted. They also wait round the corner after school and lie in wait for anyone they haven't dealt with during the day.'

'The teachers should have picked up on his problem.'

'So they should. A more experienced teacher would have done so, but this one obviously hasn't. As soon as Vera is better, I'll go along there with her and create the biggest stink in history. Without telling us what was going on, Mikey tried to keep up with his homework but avoided playground times and the after-school exodus. You can see how he became labelled a truant, can't you? Then he was assaulted and hauled off to the police station. He didn't know which day of the week it was when we saw him on Wednesday, did he? He still can't speak.'

Lesley swept this aside. 'I'm sorry, Ellie; I can't get involved in this matter. The social workers now have a file on Mikey, and believe me, they will follow it through. You'd better get the boy to a specialist. The fact that you hadn't even noticed he was mute is going to tell against you. In the meantime, you said you had something for me.'

Ellie stared into space. She understood Lesley's point of view, but the more she thought about what had been happening to Mikey, the more worried she became. Something was very wrong with, well, everything. Especially – and here she frowned – with Hugh's account of the incident in the road.

If Ellie had been asked her opinion of Hugh early that morning, she'd have said she'd trust him with her life. And now, quite simply, she had the gravest of doubts gnawing away at her. Why had he said . . .?

She shook herself back to the present. She would think about that later. Meanwhile, Lesley was waiting for information.

Ellie produced the plastic bag with the pharmacist's box in it. 'Found in the bedside cabinet of a woman who recently committed suicide. Nobody's disputing the fact that she did commit suicide. The return of a cancer motivated her to end her life prematurely. Her husband suspected . . . well, not even suspected, but he was uneasy enough about leaving her to check what medication she had on hand before he went away for the weekend. He had a long-arranged date that she urged him to fulfil.'

'So?'

'The box is not from her usual pharmacy. If it had been, if the lady had obtained the tablets herself, there would have been no need to tear off the label with the name of the patient on it. Conclusion: someone else acquired the tablets for her, which is what you've suspected in the other cases you've mentioned.'

Lesley inspected the bag under the nearest side lamp. 'Names?'

'In a minute. The husband put the box into a plastic bag and brought it to me because he's afraid that his right-hand woman at work, a clinging type called May, might have obtained the tablets and given them to his wife. He wants me to find out if she did. He thinks May has a soft spot for him and therefore might have been keen to help his wife into an early grave. That troubles him a lot. Possibly, it's true.'

'He thinks there may be fingerprints on the box?'

'I suppose there may be several sets: the pharmacist's, the husband because he picked it up out of the drawer, the wife's and—'

'The murderer's?'

'But it's not murder, is it? Helping someone to obtain the means to commit suicide?'

'Helping someone to die is a criminal offence.'

'I agree, but this is not the same thing, is it? No one forced Anita to take the tablets.'

'I need names.'

Ellie gave them. She did not tell Lesley that the funeral service would be on Monday, or that the body would be cremated. Perhaps she ought to have done so, but she didn't. And she didn't feel guilty about that, either.

Friday evening

She thought she was seeing things. Bold as brass, Petra walked out of the Co-op with her shopping and turned up the slip road to the flats. The older woman forgot she'd gone out to fetch some milk and, when the girl started up the stairs, she called out: 'Petra? Is that you? Someone said you were dead.'

'In your dreams! Been in hospital, I have.' Petra let herself into her flat with a key. 'Come in, why don't you? The place is a mess, mind. The boyfriend's done a flit and Phee's with the social people till tomorrow.'

The flat was full of cheap, flashy furniture which had probably looked all right in the showroom but had not been cared for. The upholstery on the three-piece suite was stained, a padded wooden chair lacked an arm. The room stank of fast food, fish and chips, and cigarettes.

The older woman clutched her handbag with gloved hands. She didn't fancy touching anything.

Petra dumped her shopping on the scratched table. 'Peace and quiet tonight, but tomorrow I'm going after my cousin that cheated me of my rights. She thinks she's got away with it, but no one gets one over me, right?'

'She didn't cause your aunt's death.'

'What would you know about it, you old crow?' Petra didn't bother to take off her jacket but collapsed into a chair, chucking off her ill-fitting, down-at-heel shoes. 'My ankle's killing me, and I need a drink.' She scrabbled in her bags to bring out a half bottle of gin. 'Nothing like it for taking the edge off.'

She unscrewed the top and took a long swallow. 'So, what have you come for? I never liked you. As long as I can remember, you've been sneaking around, visiting my aunt, tittle-tattling about me.'

'Your aunt and I were good friends for more years than I can remember.'

Petra took another swallow, and something moved in her eyes. 'Do you mean . . .? It wasn't you that did my aunt in, was it?' Still holding her bottle, she lunged out of her chair and grasped the older lady's forearm. 'Was it you that murdered her? If it was, I'll do you for it.' She gestured with the gin, spraying everything in sight, but as she did so she stumbled over one of her shoes and fell sideways awkwardly, knocking all the breath out of her body. 'Uumph!'

The older lady didn't move. Couldn't. She was trembling.

Petra's eyelids fluttered. She moaned, putting the hand holding the bottle to her head. More gin slopped out. She said, in a thick voice, 'I'll have the police on you for assault.'

Would they believe Petra? No, surely not.

Petra tried to sit up. She dropped the bottle, using both hands to pull herself up by the table. 'You pushed me!' She held on to a nearby chair, wobbling.

The older woman hadn't thought she could kill anyone. It wasn't in her nature. But the next thing she knew, the bottle of gin was in her hand and Petra lay on the floor, gurgling her life away. Her eyes were half open but unseeing. There was blood everywhere, on the carpet, the table. Everywhere.

The visitor dropped the bottle, which splashed gin over her shoes. She brushed her gloved hands down her coat, which felt sticky. Her coat and gloves were black, so the blood didn't

*show, but her legs . . . She must wash them. And her shoes,
her gloves, her handbag.*

*She groped for a chair. She must sit down for a minute. The
room was going round and round and . . . She felt ill, but
mustn't be sick here. She forced herself to find the bathroom
– filthy, but what had she expected? – and cleaned herself up
as best she could. She had a drink of water. She must get
home. Yes, that was what she must do.*

*She left the flat, leaving the front door ajar. Someone would
find the girl, sooner or later. With her reputation the police
would question her boyfriend first, and then they'd conclude
it was some druggy chancing on a woman living alone.*

*She walked home in the dusk. It took her a long time because
she had to stop and rest every now and then. She couldn't risk
getting on the bus, reeking of blood as she did. She would
have to have her coat dry-cleaned. Such a pity, but she'd have
to throw away the gloves, the handbag and the shoes.*

*A nuisance she hadn't any milk. She could have done with
it to make some cocoa, to calm her nerves. Maybe she'd even
have to take one of her last sleeping tablets, the ones she'd
been keeping for Evan.*

*She wished she could find her diary. There's something she
had to do on Monday, she was sure of it.*

Friday night

A difficult evening.

Vera was fretful, wanting Mikey. Thomas demanded to know
what was going on, but drifted off before Ellie had worked
out what to say. Mikey's bright eyes watched Ellie as she
attended to his bruises and the cut on his arm. But would he
talk? No.

Wearily, Ellie tumbled into bed in the guest bedroom,
thinking she'd get more sleep there than in bed with Thomas,
who was so restless that he needed the bed to himself . . .
only to be woken with a cry from Vera, who'd got halfway
down the stairs from the top floor in search of Mikey, before
her legs gave way under her.

Ellie couldn't carry Vera back up the stairs to her own bed, so helped her on down to the first floor where she could see for herself that Mikey was all right, which he was at that moment. Deeply asleep. Ellie put Vera into the bedroom at the end of the corridor beyond Mikey's room, making up the bed in makeshift fashion, fetching more drink and more pain-killers from up top.

She fell back into bed only to be woken by Thomas having a bout of coughing, which had to be soothed with linctus and paracetamol, until he was quieter and she could get back to bed herself.

Then Mikey woke from a nightmare and crawled into bed with Thomas, who woke with a yell, thinking . . . or not thinking, but reacting in alarm. Ellie rescued Mikey and got him into bed with her, where he lay, quivering, until sleep took him again.

Ellie lay awake for a long time after that, worrying away . . . How could she look after everyone . . . keep Mikey safe . . . discover who was helping people to commit suicide . . . encourage Evan to get out of his wheelchair . . . be with Diana when she gave birth . . .?

She must have dozed off because when she woke an hour later, Mikey had gone. So she had to go looking for him again. Upstairs? Had she really left the landing lights on all this time? He wasn't there. She found him in bed with Vera in the room at the end of the corridor. Oh well.

Back to bed.

She was exhausted when the alarm went off at seven, but made herself climb into some clothes and go to check on her patients, who were both sound asleep. Thomas sounded like a train, snoring gently. Vera, with her mouth slightly open, was also snoring.

Mikey nowhere to be seen.

Rose wasn't up, either.

Ellie found Mikey, still in his pyjamas, curled up in Thomas's big chair in the quiet room on the ground floor. 'Budge up,' she said.

He budged. She put her arms around him, and he managed to get on to her lap. He'd been crying, but she wasn't going to notice that, was she?

She thought, Here's a state of things . . .

She'd always relied on Thomas to back her up and give her good advice and on Vera to keep the house running. Now they were out of it. All she had was elderly, frail Rose and a frightened boy who couldn't speak.

The odds weren't good.

Mikey shifted his position, favouring his right side.

A cold anger began to form inside her. How dare they assault this boy? She didn't know who 'they' might happen to be, but *how dare they*!

A nasty thought wormed its way into her head.

You know very well who's behind the sabotage.

No, I don't! How could I?

You've known all along, but you don't want to acknowledge who it is, because you don't know how to deal with it. With her.

Her?

Yes, her. Consult within. What does your gut reaction tell you?

All right, I agree. But—

So. Go get her.

How?

No answer.

There was no connection that she could see between the woman she didn't even want to name inside her head and the workmen on site. Could Mistress No Name possibly be bribing workmen to delay the opening of the hotel? But, why? And what good would that do her?

Well, as Ellie had said at their business meeting, Edwina Pryce knew she couldn't upset the will, but she could stir up so much trouble that they'd be happy to pay her off.

In her dreams!

Yes, but Edwina only ever thought of things from her own point of view. She had a warped mentality, thinking the world owed her a luxurious lifestyle just because she'd been born into the Pryce family.

Ellie had been left the Pryce mansion to do as she wished with it. She could have blown it up, or transported it to Mumbai if she had so wished, only providing that she kept the remaining members of the Pryce family out of debt. And there was the rub. Edwina Pryce could run up what bills she liked and they'd always be paid, in order to keep her out of the debtors' courts. She could engage solicitors and, because she had no money to pay them, the bills would come to Ellie. Edwina shopped at Harrods, she took taxis whenever she wished because she couldn't drive . . .

Which meant that the vague suspicion Ellie had been harbouring about the car which had nearly run Mikey over didn't work. Edwina Pryce had not been responsible for trying to kill Mikey. Even if she'd been behind the sabotage and knew that Mikey had caught Preston and Dave red-handed; even if she'd realized he could bear witness against them; even if she had seen him in the street and decided that here was an opportunity to silence him for good, she couldn't have driven that car at him.

Which meant . . . which meant . . . Ellie didn't know what it meant.

But there was one thing that she was very sure about. Mikey was not a helpless child but had a highly intelligent, computer-literate brain.

'Mikey, before we have breakfast we'll get you washed and dressed and do the hospital rounds. After that, you and I are going to put our heads together to confound the wicked. Right?'

The boy did indeed prove helpful, fetching clean nightwear and toiletries down for Vera from the top floor, bringing up more drinks from the kitchen, and helping Ellie to remake beds which had been ruckled up overnight. Both patients seemed a little better, and Ellie was thankful that Thomas hadn't developed that awful, grinding chest cough which in the past had meant he was going to be seriously unwell.

Only, they found Rose in the kitchen, not attending to breakfast, but sitting in her chair, weeping gently.

Ellie hurried to Rose's side. 'My dear, whatever's the matter?'

'I feel so useless. You've got everything to see to, and Mikey's in trouble, and I'm just a silly old woman who can't climb the stairs any more. I just tried and I couldn't and I can't do anything to help and I'm just in the way . . .'

Ellie gave Rose a hug. 'Listen to me, Rose. Even if you never got another meal ready in your life, even if you never washed a dish, or dusted a room or watered the flowers, you are at the heart of this house. We depend on you to be here for us, to worry about us, to care what happens to us. Please God you don't get the flu because I don't know how we'd cope if you did!'

Ellie tried to make a joke of it, but Rose was beyond joking. 'Yes, but—'

Then Mikey proved his heart was in the right place. Because Midge the cat was his constant companion and best friend, he thought the cat would offer the same love and consolation to Rose. So he picked Midge up and put him in Rose's lap.

Unfortunately, neither Midge nor Rose had expected this, and both overreacted. Rose screamed and flailed her arms around in an effort to fight off her uninvited guest while Midge distended to twice his normal size, leaped off Rose on to the table and overturned a pint of milk.

Mikey looked stricken.

Ellie began to laugh.

The cat fled, and Rose, reluctantly, smiled. 'I'm a silly old billy. Look what that darned animal's done now!'

'Will there be enough milk for breakfast without it?' asked Ellie, seizing some paper towels to mop up the spilt liquid. 'Don't be upset, Mikey. It was a lovely idea of yours to comfort Rose by putting the cat on her lap, even if it did take them both by surprise.'

'There's plenty of milk in the freezer, and look what I found in the washing, when I took it out of the drier.' Rose held up Ellie's watch, which had been missing for days. 'It must have got mixed up with the sheets when you changed the bed, and it's still going.'

'Wonders will never cease. That's a good omen for the day, isn't it? Now, Mikey. What shall we have for breakfast?'

FIFTEEN

Saturday morning

Ellie led the way to her study, followed by Mikey and the cat. 'It may be the weekend and most people won't be working but, even though I may not be the brainiest person in Britain – don't laugh, Mikey – I have advantages which a lot of people lack. I have clever friends, and I have money. And, just occasionally, I know how to make people jump.'

She settled him down with her computer. 'Now, I want you to write down everything you remember about the problems at the site.'

She turned to the phone. First, she must consult her solicitor. He might be playing golf or have gone away or, well, anything. But she had his mobile number and no compunction whatever about interrupting his Saturday.

'Gunnar, it's me, and I'm in trouble again. Yes, I know it's Saturday, but it's urgent. Two things. I may need some backing to fend off Social Services who think they can make out a case to put Mikey into care. Nothing will happen at the weekend but perhaps I can make an appointment to see you about it early next week?'

'I'm in court on Monday. Tuesday afternoon for a short half hour, perhaps?'

'I'll jot that down. Teatime, I assume? If they take action before that, I'll send you an SOS. Even more important than that, could you look out Mrs Pryce's will and let me know how far I need to observe the clause about providing for Edwina Pryce? She's on the warpath again and I've run out of ammunition to use against her. It sounds silly, but she's managed to get the ear of someone high up on the board of directors at the hotel chain, and I'm very much afraid that she's got them thinking her way. I'm going to fax her latest blackmailing letter through to you in a minute, and you'll see what I mean.'

'How long has this been going on?'

'Only this last week. I know I should have contacted you straight away, but there's been complications. Flu. Yes, both Thomas and Vera. Thanks, they're both on the mend now, but it's been an anxious time.'

'What does the pesky woman want?'

Ellie subdued hysteria, because really Edwina's threats were hollow, weren't they? Only, if the director had been persuaded that Ellie was behind the sabotage at the site, then perhaps Edwina might be able to swing things her way. 'She wants me to hand over my shares in the hotel, or alternatively to pay her "compensation". She's been living like a millionaire at our expense, and I'm sure that's not what Mrs Pryce intended. Can you find a hole in the wording of the will to let me off the hook?'

'My dear lady. A pleasure. I'll ring you back.'

She faxed Gunnar a copy of Edwina's letter only to find Mikey was staring at his computer screen, without making any effort to work on it. 'Full statements, Mikey. Times and dates, if you can remember them.'

He shrugged. Perhaps he didn't know where to start?

She said, 'Let me put a question on the computer, and you try to answer it.' She typed in, '*Why have you been missing school?*'

He gave her a look of scorn.

She sighed. 'All right. I know why. Let's try another question.' She typed, '*Do you visit the hotel site often?*' She left a space for him to reply, then tried another question, '*When did you suspect that some of the workmen were not doing their job properly?*'

She turned the screen back to Mikey, who read the questions and nodded. He thought for a bit and then started to type with two fingers, making them dance across the keys.

Ellie pressed more buttons on her telephone. 'Kate? Ellie here. Yes, I know it's a Saturday morning and you're busy but I need financial advice and I need it *now*. Yes, do ring me back. I wouldn't want to interfere with potty training.'

She put the phone down, smiling. Kate was not only an ex-neighbour of hers, but a good friend and also the financial director for the trust. Kate could make figures turn somersaults and jump through hoops. She was also a devoted wife and mother of three children under the age of six, and somehow managed to keep all of them content with their lot.

Ellie tried another number. 'Hugh? Ellie here. Yes, Mikey's all right. Bruised and shaken, but all right. He's at my side at this very moment, preparing his statement for the police.'

A small explosion at the other end of the phone. 'What!'

Ellie said, 'Yes, I thought you might not want him to do it, but look at it from his point of view. He's got to clear his name.'

'How is he giving you his side of the story?'

'He's not talking yet, if that's what you mean, but he can operate a word processor like nobody's business. You didn't know that? Ah, he's quite something on a computer. A useful skill. He's got sharp eyes, too. And ears.'

'I'd rather—'

'I sympathize, Hugh. I do realize that you are in a difficult position, but this has got to stop. For one thing, your man Preston has put Mikey in the clutches of the Social Services, who'd very much like to write the boy off as a proto-delinquent who needs to be taken into care. Yes. I can see it would be convenient for you in some ways if—'

'No, no. You're twisting my—' With some heat.

Ellie raised her eyebrows. 'I'm sorry if I misunderstood you, Hugh. I know you're fond of the boy. Let me finish. I think both of us know who's been at the sharp end of the sabotage at the site and that it's Preston and Dave. I do believe you'd like to shift both of them out of your sight, preferably to the North Pole, but there's someone pulling the strings behind them, isn't there?'

A dull sound to his voice this time. 'No, no.'

'It's hard to discover that you've been betrayed by people you've trusted. You've known all along that they were the saboteurs, haven't you?'

Silence.

Ellie ratcheted up the pressure. 'I'm sure you know, Hugh.

You know all your men, through and through. You know who's at the end of their working life and who's having difficulty paying their bills. You know who might accept a couple of hundred here or there to help pay for Christmas. You know the family relationships that bind their loyalties to one another, rather than to the man who pays their wages. And you recognized the car that tried to kill Mikey. Oh, you gave me a taradiddle about it being this or that make, but I think perhaps the police would get a different answer if they questioned the electrician who watched the incident with you.'

A tired objection. 'You can't—'

'Yes, it's distressing,' said Ellie. 'But it was devastating for Vera and Mikey. Do they deserve what's happened to them? Also, I'm more than slightly concerned that the conspirators see Mikey's existence as a threat. You've been thinking along those lines too, haven't you, because you tried to warn me? Twice he's been attacked. Will he be lucky enough to get away with his life, third time round?'

Silence.

'I understand that you would like to protect your men at all costs, not least so that they don't lose their bonuses for the job. But your loyalty must primarily be to the people who employ you. It is, isn't it?'

A heavy sigh.

'Sorry, sorry,' said Ellie. 'That was uncalled for. I know you'll do the right thing. You wouldn't be you, otherwise. Suppose you drop round here later this morning and we'll go over Mikey's statement and discuss what the next step should be?'

Mikey was frowning at the screen. He turned it to Ellie, so that she could read what he'd written. Wavy red lines were everywhere. Apparently, spelling was not his strong point.

'*I go there neerly every day. I like to see how it's made. I lurned a lot.*'

Ellie corrected his spelling of the words 'nearly' and 'learned'.

The second question was about how soon he'd learned about bodged jobs on the site. He'd written, '*Don't know. Hugh said about water leeking. Preston larfed. I thort, why?*'

Ellie dithered over whether or not to correct the spelling,

then did a double take. Mikey was more than just computer literate. He was a computer whizz kid. So he must know about the spellcheck. Was he trying it on with her? Hm. Probably.

'Mikey, use the spellcheck, please.'

He gave her a slit-eyed stare, sighed, and did as she asked. She typed another question. '*What did you do about it?*'

He responded. '*Watched them. Preston didn't mind at first. Then he got cross. Dave can't hack it. I could do better than him.*' No spelling errors here. So he had been trying it on?

She said, 'I dare say you *could* do a better job than Dave, even at your age. So you shadowed Preston and Dave . . . and then?'

He typed more words. Ellie watched them appear on the screen. She'd guessed correctly. He'd caught Preston and Dave interfering with a plumbing job which had been signed off the day before. It was Preston who had been wielding the wrench, and it was Dave who'd spotted Mikey watching them. She said, 'So they grabbed you and . . .?'

He typed on. Yes, she'd guessed correctly.

'*Was they mad! Dave had a knife. I put my arm up but it stung. Preston shook me. He hit me, here and here.*' He pointed to his jaw and throat. '*He threw me across the landing. I tumbled down the stairs. They shouted. Men came. My voice wouldn't work. Preston carried me downstairs. He shouted, lots, saying I was the bad one. He threw me in the back of his van. I bumped my head. It all went fuzzy. Like, I wasn't there. Then you came and got me.*'

No wavy red lines. Some green ones for grammatical errors. She discounted those.

A damning indictment.

Ellie stared at the screen, trying to imagine how the boy must have felt. It had shaken Mikey up, and it shook her, too.

She said, 'Now we must deal with the matter of the car that tried to run you down.'

Mikey rolled his eyes, but did as he was told.

Ellie read what he'd written and felt depressed. It was no more than she'd guessed, but . . . oh dear. She was about to ask Mikey a further question when she noticed he'd disappeared. Why?

Ah, the doorbell had rung and he'd gone to answer it. His hearing was sharper than hers.

The phone rang, and it was Kate, wanting to know what was up.

Ellie shook her head to clear it. 'Sorry to trouble you at a weekend. As you know, Edwina Pryce is making a nuisance of herself again. More than a nuisance. Now I know that I handed her affairs over to you with the instruction only to pay her bills if she was threatened with court action or the electricity being cut off, or whatever. I didn't want to know the details. But now I've got a horrid feeling that she's put one over us in spite of all our precautions. I need to know if somehow or other she could have managed, perhaps by inflating a bill or two, to scrape a largish sum of money together.'

'You mean, by getting a supplier to charge us more than they charged her? Mm. Well, everything's on my computer, but . . . how could we tell without checking back with all her suppliers, and even then . . .?'

'Yes, I know. It's a long shot. But I'm working myself up to a confrontation with her and I need as much ammunition as you can find. I suspect she's been bribing a workman on the hotel site to do a job badly and thereby delay the opening.'

'You really think she's behind the sabotage at the site? But why?' It didn't take Kate long to work that one out. 'Ah, to jack up the tension and force you to hand over your stake in the hotel? That's, well, extreme.'

'Edwina is extreme. Her bills have all passed through your hands. What do you make of her?'

'Hold on a mo while I boot up the computer.'

As Ellie waited, Mikey came in with a bag of Werther's Original sweets, which he emptied into the bowl Ellie kept on her desk. This meant Tesco's had delivered, so at least they'd have some food for the weekend. And yes, she knew sweets were bad for her teeth, but sucking one when doing a boring job did help to keep her sane.

Mikey vanished.

Kate was talking. 'What do I think of Edwina? She's extravagant, a spendthrift. Wait a mo. I've accessed her account . . .' A pause. 'Yes, every month I get a sheaf of bills from her:

council tax, electricity, gas, phone; her MasterCard account; Waitrose, John Lewis; health treatments; gutting and redecoration of the flat; a new television and computer. I can't see anything amiss, apart from the fact that she's living a life of luxury at our expense. There's only one small query . . . Ellie?' In a sharper tone. 'She used to bill us every month for taxis because she's waiting for a hip replacement – which I suppose she'll have done privately and send us the bill for it – the only thing is, she didn't bill us for the month of June.'

'She went on holiday?'

'Oh. Yes. So she did. Hotel bill, air fare. False alarm. She started using taxis again in August.'

'Well, she can't drive.'

'That's odd. If she can't drive, why has she bought a car?'

'What!'

'A second-hand Volkswagen, taxed for six months, MOT for eleven months, etc., etc. Five thousand five hundred pounds, and probably a bargain at that. Her covering letter says her doctor warned he wouldn't be responsible for the consequences if she walked any distance, so she bought the car from another member of the family thinking she could pay in instalments which she finds she can't manage. He threatened court action unless she paid up, so we cleared the bill.'

Ellie felt faint. 'Yes, a cousin or second cousin of hers did have a car like that, but Kate, to the best of my knowledge, Edwina can't drive.'

Kate was on to this in a flash. 'She may be taking driving lessons, but if so, wouldn't she have billed us for them? Also for the insurance for the car, and a provisional licence?'

'And she hasn't?'

'Definitely not.'

Ellie exhaled. 'You have to admire her nerve! I bet that car never changed hands at all. She got five thousand five hundred pounds out of us, just like that. I suppose she produced a fake invoice for the car. And yes, she does have a car-driving relative with a slightly dodgy background. Perhaps he provided her with the invoice for a consideration. Or perhaps she created it for herself? She never thought we'd check, any more than we've checked any of her other bills.'

'That's fraud.' Kate was scandalized.

'Mm. Good. Well, not "good" exactly, but you know what I mean. If it's true, it gives us a nice lever to get her off our backs.'

'Threatening her with the police might slow her down, but unless you can upset the terms of the will we're still liable for whatever she likes to throw at us.'

'True. Can you dig out that invoice for me, let me have a breakdown of what we've spent on her so far, and we'll take it from there?'

Ellie put the phone down. So Edwina had managed to build up a nice little nest egg of five thousand five hundred pounds. The question was, what had she done with it?

Saturday early afternoon

Ellie, Rose and Mikey were in the kitchen clearing up after a light lunch of soup and sandwiches when the front doorbell rang. They'd done the rounds of the invalids. Both their temperatures were down, thank goodness, and Vera had even managed to swallow some home-made soup though Thomas still couldn't take anything but lemonade.

Ellie was on her way to the front door, when the phone rang in the hall. She opened the door to Hugh, saying, 'Come in. Leave your coat here. Do you mind if I just take this call? Go through to my study. First on the left down the corridor.'

She turned back to the phone, to find the caller had rung off. But the answerphone light was winking. Something urgent? Hugh could wait a moment longer.

A message had been left by someone whose carefully rounded vowels and distinct consonants told Ellie that she'd been brought up to speak 'properly'.

'Mrs Quicke? You have not seen fit to reply to my communications in any way, so I must assume that you have agreed to my terms. I have been in touch with the chair of the board of directors for the hotel chain, and he has been so good as to listen to what I have had to say, and to agree with my conclusions. It is perfectly clear to everyone that you are unable to control your so-called ward, the boy Michael, who has been responsible for so much damage at the hotel site, and who has put the opening date in jeopardy. We must assume you have been aware of his actions and approved of them. The chairman agrees with me that your conduct is indefensible. I have suggested – and he has agreed – that the only way to correct matters is for you to resign from the board and to hand your shares over to me. Naturally, you will no longer have any interest in the project and I, as the most senior surviving relative of the Pryce family, will be cutting the ribbon on Opening Day. I shall be calling on you on Monday morning at ten with my solicitor, to accept your signature on the papers transferring your shares to me. I think that is all quite clear.'

Plock. The phone call finished.

Ellie tried to replace the receiver on its rest at her end and fumbled the job. But, finally, got it there.

She couldn't think straight. One blow after the other.

How to counter them?

And with what? She was completely out of ideas.

Hugh was waiting for her. She went along to her study, trying to sort out what she should do next. Could Hugh help her by clearing Mikey? Maybe, but if he did . . . what then?

Hugh was sitting in a chair by her desk. He didn't look comfortable. She didn't feel comfortable, either. She switched on the lights. It was such a dark day. So depressing. She said, 'Is it still raining? Silly question. Of course it is. Have you had lunch? Yes? Coffee? No. All right, let's get down to it.'

She seated herself at her desk and accessed Mikey's statement on her computer.

'Here's what the boy has written so far. He's prepared to answer questions about it if you need more detail. Then we will run off copies for you, the police and Social Services.'

Hugh said, 'Do we need to be so formal?'

She tried for a light touch. 'Dear Hugh. You're fighting a losing battle on this one. Why not give in gracefully and admit that you have a problem on site?'

Hugh had slumped in his chair. 'I have a problem on site. Yes. Now tell me how to solve it.'

'You know how to solve it. It's your responsibility to hire and fire men.'

'If it were only that simple. The managing director has just been on the phone to me. A Ms Edwina Pryce has been in touch with him, saying that you are behind all the problems we've had, that you've been working through the boy to delay the opening. He tells me that you are resigning from the project and that Ms Edwina Pryce is taking over. Also that she has promised the men a bonus if they finish on time.'

So Edwina had spoken the truth? She had managed to sell her story to the managing director? Ellie felt quite breathless. She tried to smile. 'So first she causes delays to the project and then she urges completion on time?'

'You think she's behind the sabotage? You have proof?'

'I'm getting it. For a start, let's take Mikey's statement about surprising Preston and Dave doing something they shouldn't and what happened afterwards.'

He read it, sucked his teeth, shook his head. 'It's his word against theirs.'

'True. Except that the report on Mikey's injuries docsn't agree with Preston's statement. How do you get round that?'

'I don't propose to.' He fidgeted. He wasn't enjoying this, either.

Ellie knew why. 'Now let's look at what he says about the attempt to run him down in the street.'

Instead of reading it, Hugh got out of his chair and went to look out of the window at the sodden garden. It was getting dark, and he probably couldn't see much. He didn't want to read the statement, did he?

Ellie said, 'Hugh, Mikey says he saw you and his pal the electrician upstairs as he walked along on the other side of the street. He says you signed to him not to go in. He continued on his way to the crossroads. A vehicle was approaching. He waited for it to pass, but it slowed down. He recognized it as a van – not a car – belonging to one of your workforce. There was a string of flowers wound round the driver's mirror. He recognized the driver, who was not wearing a hard hat.

'The driver gestured to Mikey to cross the road in front of him. Mikey hesitated but started to do so. He saw the van's wheels begin to turn and leaped back on to the pavement but not before the mudguard caught him on his side.'

Silence from Hugh.

Ellie said, 'Hugh, you told me that it was hard to see what was happening in the street. You were upstairs looking down on the road, and it was raining. You gave me a description of a car which you said paused to let Mikey cross the road, and then accelerated away. Would you like to revise your statement?'

Hugh pulled a face. 'Mikey may have been mistaken.'

'He gives considerable detail. He's seen the cars and vans your workforce uses often enough to know them. He knows your men. He recognized the van and the driver even in the rain.'

'You think I saw it, too?'

'You know whose van it was, and who was driving it. It was young Dave, wasn't it?'

'I have to look at the bigger picture. I'm responsible for getting the work done to the highest possible standard and completed on time.'

She leaned back in her chair. She'd known, liked and respected this man for a long time. It was hard to believe he would give in so quickly. She couldn't understand why he should. In the rather harsh light in her study she noted fresh and deeper lines on his face, a thinning of his hair, a droop to his shoulders.

'Dear Hugh, you are feeling tired, and no wonder, with all that's been going on with this project.'

'It's my last job for the company.'

'Will you look back on it with satisfaction?'

He repeated, 'I have to look at the bigger picture.'

'At Mikey's expense? At the expense of what is right?'

'You don't know what you're talking about.'

But she did. Oh yes, she did.

He knew it, too. He said, 'Well, I'd best be going. Working double time today, trying to catch up.' He wasn't giving her another chance to talk him round, but made his own way to the front door, picking up his coat on the way. He opened the door and hesitated. Without looking at her, he said, 'I'm really sorry, you know. But this is how it has to be.'

He vanished into the rain, leaving her to shut the door behind him.

She sank into the seat by the phone. For two pins she'd

burst into tears. Even for one pin. Her throat ached, and she wondered if she, too, was going down with flu. It wouldn't be surprising if she did, and it might save her from having to face Edwina on Monday.

She'd never like the word 'defeat', but she couldn't see any way in which she could reverse what was happening. Oh, she could go to the chairman and spin him her tale of woe, try to make him understand what Edwina had been up to, but without proof, why should he or anyone else believe her? And the damage the woman was doing to Mikey and Vera . . . It didn't bear thinking about. Ellie's mind went round and round, thinking about it.

She ran her hands back through her hair. There wasn't a single thing she could do to stop Edwina walking all over them. Well, except for that niggle about buying a car which she couldn't drive. Edwina would probably have a good explanation about that, too. She'd say she'd overlooked an invoice, or was waiting for the driving school to confirm, or something.

If only there were some way Ellie could curb the woman's spending! That would be some solace. But the wording of Mrs Pryce's will had been clear enough. Ellie inherited the estate and Pryce House to do as she wished with, the only proviso being that she had to keep the remaining members of the family out of trouble financially. Or words to that effect.

Ellie couldn't remember the exact wording, although she knew she ought to have it engraved on her heart . . . or whatever organ it should be, as Edwina didn't seem to have much of a heart herself.

Gunnar, her solicitor, hadn't got back to her. It had probably been stupid to ask him to do anything for her on a weekend. Was there anybody else she could ask to help?

Well, just conceivably, there was.

Mrs Pryce's own solicitor had been a round, bouncy, youngish man by the name of Greenbody. It was he who had been responsible for the drawing up of Mrs Pryce's will, so he'd know her exact intentions towards Edwina and the only other surviving member of the family, who was her cousin or second cousin or whatever. Terry Pryce. He'd once owned a yellow Volkswagen, and Ellie would take a bet – and she was not a betting woman – that this was the car which Edwina claimed to have bought recently.

Ellie hadn't had any reason to contact Mr Greenbody recently since her own solicitor had steered Mrs Pryce's will through probate, but she seemed to remember that he'd gone on acting for young Terry in some unrelated problem or other. Something which had involved the police? Nothing desperate. Drunk and disorderly? Driving under the influence?

Ellie had been only too happy to let Mr Greenbody go on looking after Terry while Kate coped with Edwina's demands. For some reason, either inertia or by an oversight, Mr Greenbody had continued to represent Terry in his dealings with the trust. Kate had said this was a good thing as she had more than enough to do, coping with Edwina. She'd also said that Mr Greenbody's requests to help Terry with his finances had been reasonable. There had been the occasional bill for repairs and maintenance for his car, a request for a new washing machine, that sort of thing. By no means unreasonable.

Terry had a job somewhere, didn't he? Ellie wondered how Mr Greenbody had managed to curb young Terry's excesses. It might be interesting to find out.

SIXTEEN

Ellie hunted for and eventually found Mr Greenbody's home number.

'Mrs Quicke? How delightful to hear from you. Keeping well, I trust?' Noises off indicating children at play and a television set on full volume. 'Just a mo, while I shut myself away from the family. They're playing inside in this dreadful weather, but what can one expect at this time of the year? Now, what can I do for you today?'

'Help me murder Edwina Pryce?' She hadn't meant to say that.

Instead of being horrified, Mr Greenbody laughed. 'What's she been up to now?'

'Too long a story to tell you, but I'm wondering how Mrs Pryce coped with her extravagance. Her spending of late has been excessive.'

'She coped more less, and not all the time, by refusing to pay anything except the utility bills. Oh, except when Edwina had a water leak at the flat which did a lot of damage. She had to move out to a hotel while the place was gutted. Everything had to be replaced; wiring, plumbing, carpets, redecoration, everything. Even then—'

'What?' Ellie shot upright in her chair. 'Are you sure? I'm in shock. When was this? We've just paid a bill for doing the same thing.'

'Have you now?' His voice lost all its humour. 'This would be some twelve, maybe thirteen months ago. Mrs Pryce did query the bills. She was going to get them checked, thinking they'd probably been inflated, but she let it go because she was tired of fighting all the time.'

Ellie rubbed her forehead. She was beginning to get a pressure headache. 'You mean Edwina charged Mrs Pryce for all that work over a year ago? I can hardly believe that we've passed bills for the exact same work.'

'Dearie me. What a very enterprising lady she is.'

'I feel quite faint. We never thought to check. We ought to have done, but . . . I'm at fault, I'm afraid. I disliked the woman so much that I handed her affairs over to someone else to deal with. It was only when she presented a bill for buying Terry's car that I—'

'Terry's car? The Volkswagen? When was this? That car's been off the road for months. In fact—'

'What? Are you sure? But . . . No, I'm being stupid. You wouldn't say so if it weren't true. Can you explain?'

'There's no mystery about it. Terry Pryce got drunk once too often. He careered down a hill and clipped a Toyota driving in the other direction. The driver of that car and his passenger got away with shock and minor injuries, for which Terry ought to be grateful to the end of his life, but probably won't. He failed to stop and report the accident. Instead, he ended up at the bottom of the hill, wrapped around a lamp-post. And I mean wrapped around it. The air bag inflated and saved its owner's worthless life. Terry was found wandering across the road, singing a song about survival.'

'And the car?'

'Written off. Carted off on the back of a lorry. He's lost his licence, of course. He hasn't to my knowledge bought another car.'

'The Licensing Agency will have been informed that the car was written off?'

'Certainly.'

Silence.

'I think,' said Ellie, trying out the words for fun, 'that this is good news.'

'Because Edwina's claiming she bought a car which no longer exists?'

'And we paid out for it. And for doing the work on her flat a second time.'

'Fraud.' He sounded plummy with satisfaction.

'I love that word. Fraud. Mr Greenbody, I wonder if I could ask you to spare some time to compare notes on Edwina's spending with my finance director? You may have met Kate at some point during the handover of the estate?'

'The wonderful Kate? Certainly. I'd be delighted. What's your timescale?'

'Appalling. Edwina is setting up a meeting on Monday morning at ten, in which she expects me to hand over . . . Well, that's a long story. Can you spare the time to listen to me rant about her?'

'Delighted.'

So Ellie gave him the gist of what had been going on, including the shenanigans at the hotel site and Mikey's part in it . . . and how Ellie suspected Edwina had first engineered trouble and then complained to the managing director that Ellie had arranged for Mikey to sabotage the work . . . and finally had offered bonuses to the workforce to get the work completed on time.

'Where's she getting the money from, to give bonuses?'

'Indeed. In addition, she's saying I've forfeited the right to hold any shares in the project because I'm responsible for what Mikey is alleged to have done. I'm at a loss how to fight her off. The only way I can think of to get back at her is to query the terms of Mrs Pryce's will, and to look more closely at her accounts. Hence my last-minute plea to you.'

'You want to know the exact wording? Well, I should know, as I argued with Mrs Pryce about it for some time. She wanted to ensure that the remaining members of the family are – and I quote – "never at a loss for the basics".'

Ellie repeated the words in a hollow tone. '"Never at a loss for the basics"? But that could mean I only have to cover the utility bills and her rent, with perhaps a little over?'

'She owns her flat outright. You might pay her council tax, if you felt generous. But yes, that's what Mrs Pryce meant. You'd need to get a second opinion, if you wanted to test it in court.'

Ellie was quiet, trying to reorganize what passed for her mental processes. How come she'd not realized before exactly what the will said? How come she'd let Edwina milk the trust for so much money? And what should she do about it?

'Mr Greenbody, you couldn't spare some time tomorrow to compare accounts with Kate, could you? I know it's a lot to ask, and Kate may not be able to free herself from domesticity, but if I can only get a handle on what Edwina's done I might be able to defeat her. You must bill me for your time, of course.'

'At double my usual rate? No, Mrs Quicke, I'll do it for a minimum fee. I liked old Mrs Pryce and admired her for dealing with that difficult family so well. Edwina and Terry gave her nothing but grief. She thought that perhaps Terry might one day make a decent member of society, though from what I've seen of him it's unlikely. She sorrowed deeply over Edwina. She believed the girl had been so badly warped by her earlier life that it was doubtful she would ever be a rounded personality. The one who died, Edgar, was the best of the bunch, and I gather you are caring for his widow and stepson. That is more than Mrs Pryce could have hoped for, and I'm sure she'd thoroughly approve. Her premature death was a shock. I miss her still and will do whatever I can to help you sort out this mess. I'll go into the office later this afternoon and sort out the relevant papers. Give me a ring when you can arrange for Kate to meet me there tomorrow. Or, wait a minute, I think I might have her home phone number on a card she gave me somewhere. Perhaps I should go to her?'

'Could we meet here at my place? I've got Thomas and Vera down with flu, and I don't want to leave Mikey on his own.'

'Just looking at the diary . . . Yes, I've got nothing on tomorrow that I can't rearrange. There's Anita's funeral on Monday, of course. Did you know her? I suppose you'll be going? Do you want a lift? What time are you supposed to meet Edwina?'

'At ten. Suppose you join us at that meeting as well, and we can go on together to the funeral?'

Ellie put the phone down on what had been a most satisfactory conversation. The house lay quiet about her. A little too quiet? What was Mikey up to now? Before she tracked him down, she'd make one more phone call. It might be difficult for Kate to arrange for the children to be looked after on a Sunday afternoon, but it was worth a try . . .

Ten minutes later, Ellie left the study, switching on lights as she went. Rose would be resting on her bed with the television on, but Ellie had a feeling that she ought to find Mikey and tell him to stop it. Whatever 'it' might happen to be.

He was sitting at the bottom of the stairs with the cat on his lap. Forlorn. Had he been listening to her talk with Hugh and her phone calls? She remembered the old adage about listeners hearing no good of themselves. Mikey certainly couldn't have derived much comfort from listening in.

He was too quiet for her comfort. Boys like Mikey needed lots of physical action to balance their habit of sitting at a computer for hours on end.

Rain was lashing at the conservatory. He couldn't go out to run around in the garden, and until he could use his voice again it wasn't any use suggesting he went to a friend's house to play.

There was a stir in the kitchen as Rose turned on the radio for comfort. So she was up and about after her afternoon nap.

Ellie beckoned Mikey to follow her into the kitchen. 'Rose, what can we find for Mikey to play with? What did you do on a rainy day as a child? I can't remember doing much except playing in our Wendy house with a friend. Sometimes we helped my mother do some cooking. On Sundays we had to visit my auntie, when we played cribbage and had Battenberg cake for tea.'

'We skipped,' said Rose. 'We could teach Mikey how to skip. Not in the kitchen, but in the hall.'

'Brilliant.' Ellie fished out some of the old washing line that they no longer used, cut off a suitable length and tied knots at either end. 'Mind you, I don't think I'd be able to skip much nowadays. Nor you, Rose. We'd best take an end each and have Mikey jump over it as we swing it to and fro, until he gets the hang of it.'

Mikey looked sullen. He didn't want to learn anything, thank you very much.

Rose said, 'Come on, let me have a try first. You two hold the ends, swing it slowly, and I'll see if I can remember how to do it.'

Ellie didn't think Rose ought to be trying such tricks, but the ruse worked, for Mikey soon realized he could do far better than clumsy old Rose, and within five minutes he was begging to be allowed a go himself.

Thump, thump. Mikey made Rose sit down on the chair in the hall, to tell him what to do next. It wasn't long before he was skipping on the spot, and Rose was encouraging him to count how many turns of the rope he could do before he got his feet tangled up in it. So that was him settled for the afternoon.

Ellie ignored the winking light on the answerphone to attend to her other charges. Which meant climbing the stairs again, oh dear.

Thomas had his iPad out and was frowning over it, worrying he'd forgotten something important. Ellie took it off him and said that if he had a nice nap now, he might be fit enough to come downstairs later to watch the telly. She knew she was treating him like a child, but it seemed to work for he snuggled down under the duvet without protesting too much.

Vera was sitting up in bed, brushing out her hair and wondering if Mikey could go upstairs and find her a clean pair of pyjamas. Ellie went, instead. Worrying a bit. Praying a bit. Hoping the rain would stop soon.

Saturday afternoon

She was getting too old for this lark. She hadn't been able to sleep for thinking of Petra. Silly girl, she oughtn't to have threatened to go to the police. Where had she said her son was staying? Well, he'd be properly looked after, no doubt.

Oh, the stink of blood. She wouldn't be able to wear her best black coat again till it had been cleaned. She couldn't take it her local dry cleaners, where questions might be asked because of the blood. Suppose she said she'd had a nosebleed? Yes, that would do. It would save her having to take it to some place where she wasn't known.

One good thing. She'd had to change her handbag over because the black one was saturated with blood and gin and, regretfully, would have to be disposed of in some public refuse bin. What a shame. But she found her diary in the inner pocket

of her brown bag. She was so pleased. She couldn't think what
had happened to it. And she was right, there was something
important she had to do on Monday.

She'd promised to see Evan at the funeral, but she'd have
to wear her navy coat because it was the only other warm
one she'd got. She couldn't find her navy handbag. It must be
somewhere around but she was not going to worry herself
about it. The brown would have to do.

Poor Evan, how are the mighty fallen. Condemned to a
wheelchair with an unfeeling, uncaring wife. She could have
told him what Diana would be like before he married her, but
there, he'd always been a bad picker where women were
concerned.

She wished she didn't feel so tired, but she mustn't be selfish.
So long as she had breath in her body, she must carry out the
tasks she'd been given to do. One last effort. She could manage
that. She'd grind up the pills with her little mortar and pestle
and dissolve them in a miniature bottle of whisky. He liked
whisky. And the bottle would fit nicely into her handbag when
she went to the funeral.

She wondered if they'd sing 'Brother James's Air.' It was
one of her favourites.

Sunday morning

Sunday is a day of rest. Discuss.

It wasn't a day of rest when you had two members of the
household down with flu and a third in trouble with the law.
Not for Ellie, anyway.

The rain had stopped for the moment. Amazing.

Vera seemed to be on the mend. She suggested she return
to her flat upstairs so that she'd be out of Ellie's way. Ellie
wasn't sure the girl was capable of climbing the stairs by
herself, but with a bit of a push from behind she made it,
laughing at how weak she was but glad to be back among her
own things. Also back in his own quarters was Mikey, the
young imp, eating toast in front of the telly, still in his pyjamas.
And Midge, giving himself a once over.

Ellie's spirits lifted. At least the tide had turned for Vera, and soon perhaps she'd be able to join in the fight for Mikey's future.

Now for Thomas. He greeted her with, 'Is it Sunday?' and tried to get out of bed on legs that wobbled. 'Am I supposed to be taking a service somewhere?'

'No, you're not. Get back into bed this minute.' His temperature was almost normal. Praise be, indeed.

'I'm hungry.'

Was he really? Well, perhaps it was time he started to eat again. 'What would you like?'

'Scrambled eggs and smoked salmon. Earl Grey tea.'

Back downstairs, Ellie collected the Sunday papers from the cage behind the door and stacked them with all the other newspapers and post that had been accumulating since the flu bug had struck. She found Rose in the kitchen, looking bright-eyed and bushy-tailed.

She said, 'Both their temperatures are down. Only just above the mark. And Thomas actually wants something to eat.'

'Praise be!' said Rose.

Ellie took a tray of food up to Thomas, who ate the lot and asked for the small portable television they kept for guests and which they hardly ever used themselves. After having some breakfast herself, Ellie decided she really ought at least to listen to the answerphone messages. She thought there'd probably be some on Thomas's separate phone in his study as well, so she started there.

Message number one. A minister wondered if Thomas could take the morning service in a neighbouring church the following Sunday. Ellie rang the number, which went to voicemail, and left a message saying it was unlikely, because he was still in bed with the flu.

Someone – garbled name – rang about an article they'd sent in by email and what did Thomas think about it? They hadn't left a phone number but Ellie punched the reply button and her call went to voicemail. She left a message to say Thomas was in bed and would deal with it when he could.

She booted up his computer, watched the number of incoming emails rise to the thirties and then the forties . . . and go on rising. Well, she couldn't do anything about any of that. She went offline and switched the computer off. She supposed that if she were really clever she might have been able to put a reply message on saying that Thomas was ill, etc., etc. But she wasn't that clever. He could deal with it when he was better.

She moved to her own study and accessed the messages on her own answerphone. What a pleasant surprise! Kate and Mr Greenbody had been liaising like mad, and they planned to bring their Pryce files to Ellie's at noon today, to compare notes. Kate said she'd arranged for her husband to take the children to a Messy Church service, and they were all going to have lunch out afterwards. She proposed to send the bill for lunch to Ellie, if that was all right by her.

Very much so.

Thump, thump. Much faster than before. Mikey must be back in the hall, practising his skipping. At this rate he'd be up to Olympic standards before supper.

The other messages for her were the usual. The cleaners hoped to make it by Tuesday but warned her that it probably wouldn't be the usual team; an old friend put off an arranged meeting in town due to flu having struck in their family; another friend wondered if Ellie could babysit her grandchildren who were staying with her. Well . . . no. Not at the moment.

Thump, thump. Thump, thump, thump. Mikey was getting faster and faster.

Ellie rubbed her eyes. She hadn't slept well and still felt tired. She went and sat in Thomas's quiet room for a while. It was peaceful there. Some quirk of the building meant you couldn't even hear the doorbell or the phone ringing.

She woke with a start. Had she really dropped off for a while? She shook herself back to the present. Was it really Sunday? Yes, it was. How much would the invalids eat? And what was there in the freezer to cook for them?

Sunday at noon

'Yoo-hoo! It's us!'

'Us' was not only Kate, but also Mr Greenbody. They were

burdened with laptops and box files. Ellie came out of the kitchen to see Kate leading Mr Greenbody into the dining room and switching on the lights.

'All right by you if we work in here?' said Kate. As if she'd accept 'no' for an answer.

'Would you like some coffee?'

'No, thanks. We've got just over an hour,' said Kate, dealing out papers on the big table and switching on her laptop with the other hand. 'All right by you, Ken?'

So his name was Ken? Sometimes Kate made Ellie feel her age.

Mikey had disappeared again. Probably up with his mother. Ellie went back to the kitchen to unpack the dishwasher.

Some time later Kate appeared in the doorway to the kitchen. 'Come and see what we've found.' She was grinning, and so was Mr Greenbody. Ken.

Mr Greenbody was tapping away with two fingers at his computer. 'What a clever little woman it's been.'

Kate said, 'We thought at first that we could work out what she's been doing from the figures on our computers but decided in the end that we had to go back to the actual pieces of paper.' She laid her right hand on one pile of paper. 'These are her utility bills. They can't be faked, they haven't been inflated and the ones Mrs Pryce paid in the past compare pretty well with those the trust has paid since.' She moved her hand to a similar pile. 'Here we have the rest of the bills which Mrs Pryce passed and we have allowed. TV licence, Dynorod for a blocked up drain, that sort of thing. These bills were acceptable.'

'But,' said Ellie.

Kate's grinned widened. 'Yes. But. These –' and she indicated a much larger pile – 'are Ken's bills for the water leak which meant she had to move out of her flat while it was gutted. Hotel bill, new plumbing, wiring, new bathroom, kitchen, redecorating, new television and computer, new carpets and furniture. Right? Ken queried these at the time but Mrs Pryce told him, eventually, to pay.'

Ken said, apologetically, 'I asked her if she'd like me to query the amounts charged as I'd had similar work done myself at our house, and thought the bills excessive. But she said to pass them as a one off.'

'I can't blame her,' said Ellie.

'I know, I know.' Kate clearly disapproved of letting anything pass, but reluctantly had to admit that Mrs Pryce had the right to decide. She moved the stacks she'd dealt with further along the table and squared her elbows over yet another, even bigger pile. 'Now we come to the stack of bills which she's been sending us since we took over managing her accounts. The criterion was to pay anything for which she'd received threatening notices. She started small but soon became bolder, and we've paid a lot of stuff which Ken here tells me Mrs Pryce had always refused to accept . . . in particular her food bills, bills for clothing and for taxis. I'm at fault here. I didn't check with Ken to see what Mrs Pryce had or had not allowed. It's only now I'm beginning to see that she's not only billed us for things which Ken had already covered, but inflated the amounts, too.'

Ken nodded. 'The service charge for the flat, for instance. It's payable a year in advance. I paid it six months ago, but she asked Kate to pay it again, two months ago.'

'Oh dear,' said Ellie.

Kate held up her hand. 'That's nothing compared to the duplication of the work on her flat.' She handed Ellie a sheaf of bills. 'These bills covered the same things that Ken had paid out for last year, and for the same reason. She said that a water leak had destroyed her flat and she had to have completely new plumbing, kitchen, electrics, bathroom, carpets, decorating, furniture, plus a new computer and a new television set. Oh, except that she claimed to have gone away on holiday while the work was done this time, instead of moving out to a hotel as she'd done before. That added the cost of her air fares into the equation.'

Ellie clutched her head. 'How have we been so easy to fool?'

'She never thought we'd compare notes. What we think she's done,' said Ken, enjoying himself, 'is to take each one of the original invoices from a supplier and photocopy the heading on to a new sheet of paper. Then she filled in details of the work done or the piece of equipment bought, using different fonts on her own computer. Most times she copied the wording of the original, upped the total, added a new date, and Bob's your uncle.'

'Here,' said Kate, showing Ellie an invoice from a firm of carpet suppliers, 'is the one Mrs Pryce passed. And here –' another bill, which looked identical except for the date – 'is the one she sent to us recently. Note how much more she's charged us than she charged Ken.'

Ellie was bewildered. 'But wouldn't we have paid each supplier individually? She can't have got them all to take a kickback in her efforts to defraud us.'

'No, she didn't. On both occasions she said she'd asked a friend to project manage the whole thing for her while she was away. He submitted a sheaf of unpaid bills, plus one for his time and trouble, amounting to an extra ten per cent. We paid him the total, and he reimbursed everyone. His covering invoice is here—'

'We've just checked, and his name and address don't exist,' said Ken, laughing. 'She made them up, both times. Easy enough to do on a computer. But she made one slip. The telephone number she gave first time is that of a hairdresser in Pimlico, but second time round she can't have photocopied the heading properly and was forced to type in the telephone number herself. I thought it was familiar and checked whose it might be and—'

'It was Terry's?' said Ellie. 'Terry was her "project manager"?'

'And got ten per cent of the total for his trouble first time round. The second time she probably pocketed the lot because it was payment for work already done. We will have to pursue her through the small claims courts to get the money back.'

Oh. That would mean months of hassle and unpleasantness.

Kate wasn't finished yet. 'Now to the even more serious problem. The invoice for the car. Either young Terry supplied her with the bill and they shared the proceeds, or she thought the scam up all by herself. Whichever way, once the Licensing people are informed that she's "bought" a non-existent car, they will be decidedly unpleasant about it.'

'We haven't found everything yet,' said Ken. 'One of the last things Mrs Pryce did was to tell Edwina that we wouldn't accept her food bills any longer, nor pay for her account at Harrods, her subscription to the National Trust, and so on. Yet she's been passing these to Kate for payment recently.'

Ellie cringed. 'So when we took over paying her bills, she tested us out with small amounts at first, to see how much she could get away with? She realized pretty soon that we weren't going to check back to see what Mrs Pryce had allowed before and took us for . . . how much?'

A quick glance between Kate and Ken. 'We're not sure yet. We need to go through things in more detail. But at a conservative guess, over a hundred thousand pounds.'

That took her breath away. Ellie wiped the back of her hand across her forehead.

Silence. The other two looked at her with compassion. Kate stirred, looking at her watch. 'I have to go. I said I'd meet the family at the Carvery.'

'We need to do a lot more work on these papers,' said Ken, 'but it's getting late and I promised to be back for lunch. Mrs Quicke, is there anything else I can do before I go?'

'Give me a brain transplant? This is all my fault,' said Ellie. 'I knew what the woman was like, and I ought to have foreseen that she'd try to take us for a ride. I am so angry with myself I can't think straight, but one thing's for sure: I can't let the trust pay for my mistakes. I'll have to make good our losses.'

'No, no,' said Kate, rapidly packing papers away and shutting down her laptop. 'It's not your fault. It's no one's fault. Or rather, it's Edwina's crime and she will have to pay for it. It'll take a while for us to assess the damage, but then we can turn the car invoice and the rest over to the police, who may or may not decide to prosecute her for fraud. If they don't, we'll have to take out a civil action in the courts to recover what we can.'

Ken frowned. 'I don't think Mrs Pryce would have done that.'

'Mrs Pryce is dead. Long live Ellie Quicke.' Kate gave Ellie a hug and vanished. The front door banged behind her.

Ken slowly gathered his own papers together. 'You look as

if you could do with a stiff drink. It's a shock when people whom you've trusted let you down.'

'I underestimated her capacity to do damage, and I didn't take any sensible precautions to prevent this happening. I suppose it is possible that the trust may wish to write the debt off, but I know that Thomas will agree with me that the money must be repaid.'

'Then get it off her. Another idea. Why not get Terry Pryce to tell on her? You know that I went on acting for him after Mrs Pryce passed away? He'd got himself into trouble, minor stuff. Drunk and disorderly in the town centre, for which he was fined. Speeding; points on his licence and a fine. I saw him through all that so he asked me to represent him when he was interviewed by the police some months ago when he wrote off his car, and later, at the court hearing when he lost his licence. He did manage to keep his job throughout, but it was a near thing. Suppose I threaten to inform his employers that he is alleged to have taken part in this fraud? I suspect he might be anxious to distance himself from Edwina, and to put all the blame on her. Would you like me to try it?'

'If only! But we haven't time. I have to meet her first thing tomorrow. Is it possible – could you spare the time to be here as well, so that we can make it clear to her that we can prove fraud?'

'It would be a pleasure. Then we can go on to the funeral together.'

SEVENTEEN

Ken Greenbody said, 'Preparation is the key word here, isn't it? We must marshal our forces, Mrs Quicke. Prepare our lines of attack.'

Ellie tried to smile. Thomas would say she should put on the armour of God, but she'd always thought armour must have been very uncomfortable to wear, particularly if you were of a well-padded persuasion. Or did the layers of fat insulate you against those bits which would otherwise stick into you in inconvenient places?

She let Ken out of the front door, noticing as she did so that Mikey had left his skipping rope coiled up at the bottom of the stairs. Come to think of it, she hadn't heard his 'thump, thump' lately. She wondered where he might have got to. He was probably up with his mother now. Yes, that would be it. She'd check later on.

For now, she needed a good sit-down and a hard think.

The phone rang. She hesitated. She was in no condition to think sensibly about anything. But she was glad that she did answer it for it was her very own solicitor, Gunnar, booming down the phone at her. 'Sorry, my dear, got held up. Can't get into the office today. Family, you know?'

'Yes. No matter.' She tried to clear her head. 'I think I have the wording I needed. Mrs Pryce's will stated that I must ensure the remaining members of the family would never be at a loss for the basics. How would you interpret that?'

'Utility bills. Rent, possibly.'

'She owns her own flat. Service charges?'

'Mm. She could argue that one. If she is of a certain age and unemployed, she would be receiving a basic pension from the state.'

'She is unemployed and of a certain age, so I assume she would.'

'Has she any savings, shares? Own any property to let? That might affect the issue.'

Ellie thought of the money Edwina had been creaming off them. What would she have done with it? Stashed it abroad in the Canary Islands or whatever? Was she that clued up? Um, possibly not. 'Let us suppose she got into debt and couldn't pay her food bills. Would we have to fork out for them?'

'An interesting point. I'd have to check. Off the top of my head, I'd say we wouldn't pay her debts, but we might be persuaded to pay her an allowance for food. Baked beans, rather than caviar.'

'We don't have time to consult cases that have gone through the courts in the past. Gunnar, I have a meeting with her tomorrow morning. She's run up a ton of bills, some of them fraudulent. I could hand them over to the police, and I may have to . . . but I feel I'm still hamstrung by the terms of the will.'

'You could say that your solicitor has advised you not to pay anything except her utility bills in future. If you're feeling generous and as a gesture of goodwill – remember to put that in, "as a gesture of goodwill" – you could offer to double her state pension. I think a judge would go for that, unless she can represent herself as an orphan being crushed by a wealthy trust.'

'We're all orphans at our age, aren't we?'

He laughed and put the phone down.

Ellie was left looking at the coil of Mikey's skipping rope. She had a horrid feeling that she'd missed something. She listened for the everyday noises which people make when they're living in a house.

She could hear Rose clattering about in the kitchen, with the wireless on. Rose was using the food processor. Making another cake?

Thomas was either talking to himself or on the phone to someone. He had his iPhone with him, didn't he? It was about time she went up with some more drink for him.

At the top of the house a door opened and some light-hearted music drifted down two flights of stairs. Someone – probably

Ellie herself – had left the door to the stairs leading to the top
flat open. Vera had her radio on, tuned to a different station
from Rose.

There was a dearth of Mikey noises. Of course he could be
watching telly up top, with the door closed. Or be closeted
with his computer.

She knew he wasn't. He was nowhere in the house. Which
meant . . . She didn't want to think what it meant.

She went upstairs to check on the invalids. Would they like
something to eat? Perhaps some home-made soup or an egg
on toast? Thomas said, 'I thought you'd forgotten me. Yes,
please.' Playing the neglected spouse. Ellie blew him a kiss
and said she'd bring something up straight away.

Vera said she was sure she could manage to cook for herself,
and Ellie said, 'All right; I'll let you try tomorrow, but I'm
playing chef today.' Vera asked where Mikey was, but didn't
seem too worried when Ellie said vaguely she thought he was
on her computer downstairs.

Ellie checked Vera's sitting room, which was much too tidy
to have been visited by Mikey recently. The window of this
room overlooked Ellie's garden and, as she usually did when
she was up there, she looked over the wall which divided their
property from that of the Pryce mansion. The rain had stopped,
and Ellie could see that although it was Sunday a team of
gardeners was beavering away, planting the last of some low-
maintenance shrubs at the end of the garden. Someone else
was fiddling with the pergola situated at the end of one of the
paths. A man in waders was placing pond plants into the newly
finished water feature. They were working overtime to catch
up. No Mikey.

Hugh had forgotten to sever the rope that Mikey had hung
over the wall. Had the boy made use of it the moment her
back was turned?

Ellie felt a chill race down her back. Didn't he realize how
dangerous this could be?

She went down to fill the food orders for Thomas and Vera.
Rose was putting a chocolate cake into the oven to cook. Ellie
hoped Rose hadn't left out anything important, such as an egg
or the sugar.

'Have you seen Mikey? Did he appear for food at lunchtime?'

Rose shook her head. 'He must have come in when I was having my nap. He left the butter out of the fridge and half a loaf of bread on the table, together with the wrapping from a packet of ham. And my best kitchen scissors are missing.'

'I suppose he's gone over the wall, though what he thinks he can do there . . . and the trouble he can get himself into! Why won't he listen when we tell him not to do something?'

Rose was placid. 'Because he doesn't think we're doing enough to catch the baddies.'

Ellie raised her fists in the air and shook them. 'I could murder him! I suppose I'd better see what I can do to rescue him. But first, I have to feed the invalids.' And hope Mikey makes it home again soon.

Which he didn't.

Ellie cooked light meals for the invalids and only after that did she try phoning Hugh. He must be busy because her call went to voicemail. She left a message for him, saying that Mikey might have gone over the wall again and, if so, could Hugh keep a lookout for him?

Ellie was too worried to eat much herself. Should she go over to the site and look for him herself? No. Not a good idea. Hugh wouldn't like that, and now the men had heard she was dropping out of the project, they wouldn't like it, either.

How to keep the boy safe? Suppose Preston and Dave caught him and . . . No, she wouldn't think about that. Dave had a knife and no compunction about using it. They'd clouted the boy good and hard and thrown him down the stairs before. What would they do to him if they caught him spying on them now?

She shuddered. Tried to pray.

Thomas said she was looking a little tired, and why didn't she have an afternoon nap? She promised she would, but couldn't rest.

Finally, the front doorbell rang. Both Ellie and Rose scurried to answer it.

It was Hugh, with a bedraggled scarecrow of a boy who looked as if he'd been in a mud bath.

The moment before, Ellie had wanted to half kill Mikey but the blank look in his eyes was enough to melt her anger. 'My dear boy! What on earth—'

Rose gave a little scream. 'Whatever have you been doing, you naughty boy?'

Hugh pushed Mikey gently into the middle of the hall. 'I was busy, didn't get your message for a while. Found a couple of the men had cornered him out front, hiding under one of the lorries. You can't blame them for being angry, but I don't think they hurt him much. Just rolled him around in the mud.'

Ellie felt tears start. 'Thank you, Hugh. I'm really grateful. I've told him so many times to keep away but—'

'Let's have your clothes off and dunk you in the shower,' said Rose, laying hands on the boy's muddy jacket. 'I'm not letting you go up to frighten your mother looking like that.'

The boy's left hand was clenched into a fist, and Rose couldn't get his jacket off till Ellie helped her. And even then . . .

'What's he holding?'

The boy let his fingers relax and dropped a string of filthy felt flowers into Ellie's hand. She stared at it. Then at the boy. Then at Hugh.

'I think it's part of the string of flowers which he said was looped around the driving mirror of the van that tried to run him down.'

A voice came from upstairs. 'Mikey, is that you?'

Rose shouted back, 'It's all right, Vera. He's been out in the rain, just come in. I'm going to put him in my shower and clean him up. Can you throw down some warm clothing for him, or he'll catch his death?' She whipped the boy round and shooed him down the corridor into her shower room, scolding all the way. '. . . and I suppose you've lost my best kitchen scissors, right? I should dock your wages, that is, if you'd ever earned any . . .'

Ellie held Mikey's trophy up to the light. 'I'll find a plastic bag to put this in. I suppose he thought that if he cut off part of the string from the van that tried to run him down, it would prove something. But it doesn't, does it?'

Hugh shook his head. 'It proves nothing, except that he was trespassing and did some more damage to the company's property. If I hadn't gone looking for him, I don't know what might have happened.'

Ellie told herself it was no good crying now. It was relief that was making her feel weak. 'Thank you, Hugh. I am so grateful you found him in time.'

He was stiffly formal. 'I can't be responsible for him if he enters the site again.'

'No, I realize that.' She couldn't find a hankie, so sniffed, hard.

He nodded and let himself out.

The phone rang, and this time Ellie ignored it. Mikey was safe for the moment. But for how long?

Heads were hanging over the banister. 'What's up?' said Thomas, bear-like in his dressing gown.

Vera, trailing her own dressing gown, had managed to lower herself down to the first-floor landing, holding a bundle of Mikey's clothes. She looked as washed-out as natural blondes can do on a bad day. And very anxious. 'Is Mikey all right?'

'He's fine,' said Ellie, forcing a smile. 'Drop those clothes over the banister and I'll take them to Rose's shower room. He should have taken his mac if he wanted to go out and play in the rain, but there, you know what he's like. He'll be up to see you as soon as he's been cleaned up.'

'Ellie?' Thomas's voice was as gentle as always, but it held a command. Thomas was getting stronger by the minute, and he wasn't going to be as easy to put off as Vera.

'In a minute,' she said, rescuing Mikey's clothes.

She took them through to Rose, who said, 'Everything that he had on ought to be dumped, including his shoes, but if that rapscallion has left any hairs on my head after all the worry he's given us with his shenanigans, I'll see what I can do to rescue them.'

Ellie trudged up the stairs and into the master bedroom. Thomas sat her down by the windows and seated himself there, too. He took her hand in his. 'Tell me what's going on. Visitors are coming and going without explanation. Phones are ringing, sometimes answered, sometimes not. Mikey has been doing a disappearing act, here one minute and gone the next. Vera's trying to be brave and not making a scene but she knows that something's up, as I do.'

'Leave it till tomorrow, right? You'll feel better then.'

'Ellie, light of my life; if I'm well enough to realize something serious is going on, then I'm well enough to pray about it. Your eyes look tired. I know Vera and I have given you some disturbed nights, but it's more than that, isn't it?'

Was he really up to hearing what was going on? His colour had improved but his hand was a trifle too warm on hers. No, he wasn't fighting fit yet.

She turned her hand in his, holding on to it. 'Prayer would be good. As much as you can manage.'

There was a stir at the door, and Mikey came in, freshly scrubbed, smelling of good soap, warmly clad. With his mother in tow. Vera's eyes looked wild. 'You said not to worry, but Mikey's in trouble, isn't he? Don't shut me out. I have a right to know what's going on.'

Behind her came Rose, panting from the effort of climbing the stairs. 'Council of war, is it? Well, you're not discussing anything behind my back.'

'Take a seat, all of you,' invited Thomas. 'And now, Ellie, tell us what's going on.'

So Ellie did, with Rose interjecting now and then that she didn't understand that bit so Ellie had to go back and fill in. Ellie hadn't intended to go into detail about Mikey's adventures, and she did try to minimize how roughly he'd been treated, but Vera wept and clutched him to her when they got to that part. 'Oh, Mikey! And I knew nothing about it.'

Rose handed Vera the box of tissues. 'It's his own fault. He will *not* be told!'

The boy looked down at his feet.

Thomas stirred in his chair. 'Mikey, we see what you've been trying to do, but a good general doesn't win a war by throwing all his troops into battle against overwhelming odds. That way he's sure to be defeated. A good general thinks long and hard before he acts. He considers the enemy's strengths and weaknesses. He doesn't necessarily attack where he's expected to do so. He makes sure his troops are in good condition, well fed and well armed. He gathers information. He takes advice from his officers. He may not follow that advice because his is the final decision about how to fight the war, but he listens to what they have to say.'

Mikey didn't look up at Thomas, but he did seem to be listening.

Thomas went on, 'When I'm up and about, we'll have a look at stories of some of the great generals of the past and how they won their wars. The Duke of Wellington, for instance, was wily enough to pull his troops back from territory he'd gained in a summer campaign, to overwinter where he was safe from attack. That way he didn't lose men by making them fight under adverse conditions and was well prepared for a spring offensive. You follow me?'

Mikey's mouth twisted, but he managed a tiny nod.

'Good. Your problem is that you only saw one small part of the picture and, without any particular preparation or forethought, you launched into an offensive you couldn't win.'

Mikey flushed.

'Now suppose,' said Thomas, 'you'd taken a camera with you when you first went after Preston and Dave. You might have got some evidence which would have stood up in court, saved yourself considerable aggro and us a lot of worry.'

Mikey ground his teeth. It was clear he hadn't thought of that.

'Remind me to give you a good camera for your birthday. Or suppose,' said Thomas, 'you'd confided your suspicions in me or in Ellie? We could have asked Hugh to investigate and—'

Mikey treated Thomas to a Grade One glare of contempt.

'Sorry to interrupt,' said Ellie, 'but I don't think Hugh could have helped much. He's, well, got a lot of problems at the moment. But Mikey, if you'd told me earlier, I might have been able to help. You were tackling things from the wrong angle. The problem was not what Preston and Dave were doing, nor that someone tried to run you down in the street. The problem was who bribed Dave, or Preston, or both of them to do the damage in the first place.'

Mikey frowned. So did everyone else.

Ellie said, 'I've been thinking a lot about this. The police can't always catch people doing bad things, but sometimes they can deal with the problem another way, by tracing the money the villains have made by their crimes. The Inland Revenue can step in and confiscate the fruits of their wrongdoing. The police couldn't manage to put away the boss of a crime spree in Chicago for the murders he'd committed, but he ended up behind bars because he'd fiddled his income tax. I think I can tackle this problem the same way. With help.'

Thomas nodded approval. 'By taking advice from your friends, by attacking at the weakest point and when least expected. Now Mikey, what you have done so far has brought several crimes to light, and it's time for adults to move in and take action. But we can't concentrate on what we ought to be doing if we're in a state of anxiety as to your whereabouts. I want you to promise your mother that you will keep away from the building site until this matter is cleared up. Agreed?'

Mikey's lower lip came out.

Vera gave him a hug. 'Come on. You know it makes sense. To please me? I shan't have a minute's peace if I think you're going to put yourself in danger again.'

Mikey gave a reluctant nod and then sagged against his mother, who clasped him tightly, murmuring, 'There, there. You've had a rough time but it's over now. Let's go up and have a little nap, shall we? Back in our own little beds.'

Rose bustled to her feet, easing her back. She muttered something about everyone wanting a nice cup of tea, and disappeared.

Ellie said, 'Tell me what to do, Thomas.'

His eyes were closed, his breathing even. He wasn't asleep but praying. She stayed where she was, watching him, being thankful for his presence in her life.

The room stilled around them.

Thomas was a powerful prayer warrior.

She wasn't sure exactly when he fell asleep, for his clasp on her hand remained firm. She heard the phone ring downstairs, and it seemed to disturb him for he stirred, letting her hand drop away. He did not waken. His temperature was the nearest to normal that it had been all week. Rain spat against the window. She sat on in the early dusk, not thinking but resting.

Monday morning

Busy, busy. Lots to do. Thomas to settle. He said he didn't think he was up to much yet, but he'd be praying for her. Rose was in a flurry, dropping things. Mikey and Midge made themselves scarce. Thump, thump. He'd found his skipping rope again.

Ellie, trying not to be distracted, made phone calls. Mr Greenbody – Ken – would be with her on time. He said he had some good news for her. Kate said she'd try to make it but had a whirlwind of a day already booked.

Her own solicitor, Gunnar. 'No, my dear, I haven't forgotten. Do you still need a copy of Mrs Pryce's will? I'll look it out as soon as I get to the office, but I'm afraid I'm in court after that. What? What! Oh. Yes, I suppose I could ask my clerk to fax through a copy for you . . .'

Gunnar wasn't going to be much help, was he?

Vera looked pale but ate a reasonably good breakfast for a change. 'You can't really want me in on this, Ellie? I mean, every time that woman sees me she "forgets" my name and asks when I can go to clean for her.'

'She's afraid of you, that's why.'

'Of me? A cleaner?'

'Be proud of what you did to keep you and Mikey afloat. And you're not a cleaner now. You're a mature student, getting good grades. Yes, I know it will be awkward for you, but I really would like you to join us if you can manage it.'

Set the scene. To offer coffee or not? Possibly not.

Dust and hoover in the dining room, which needed attention in the absence of her cleaners. Turn on the lights. Chase Midge and Mikey out from hiding under the big table. What on earth were they playing at? Hadn't she enough on her plate without . . .? And the phone rang again.

This time it was the fax Gunnar had promised. Well, they'd need that. She scanned it carefully. Yes, and yes. That's what she'd thought. Hoped.

The front doorbell announced the first arrival.

EIGHTEEN

K en Greenbody bustled in carrying a bulging, rather worn leather briefcase and a superb new laptop. 'Rejoice with me, Ellie! I bring good news. I thought it might be a good idea to contact young Terry before Ms Pryce realized we were on to her little schemes and could warn him what was happening, so I called in to see him on my way home yesterday. I explained that some of Edwina's scams had come to light and that she seemed to have involved him, too. I said how worried I was that she might try to drag him down with her in the matter of the fraudulent sale of his car. The very idea caused him to go weak at the knees. He had to sit down and sip a restorative before he could speak coherently.

'Then it all came out. He confessed that he *had* acted as project manager for her when she had a leak at her flat. The leak was genuine and did do a lot of damage although probably not nearly as much as she made out. Terry had been short of the readies at the time and agreed to project manage for ten per cent of whatever it was she managed to get out of Mrs Pryce. And yes, he probably was aware that some of the bills were inflated first time round, but he denies emphatically that he had anything to do with a second leak and a second lot of work on the flat. He was more than happy to give me a statement to that effect. He is not, definitely not, going to prison to save her skin.

'As to the sale of his car . . .' Ken gave a great, chuckling laugh. 'Yes, I suspect he *was* in on the scam but now he knows that she's been rumbled, he's never going to admit it. He looked me in the eye and declared she must have thought up the fraud herself. He has given me a signed statement to the effect that he did not sell his car to Edwina. I suppose we could get the police to look at his bank statements, to see if he was in receipt of any kickbacks from her, but I'm not sure it would be worth it.'

'Bravo, Ken.'

He grinned. 'Oh, by the way, I was late for supper and my wife says I owe her a night out at the opera, strange tastes she has, but there it is. I said you'd be happy to underwrite the cost of the tickets.'

'I shall be delighted. Tell her to pick her programme.' Ellie flicked tears from her eyes. 'I can't tell you how . . . That's just exactly what . . . You know what I mean to say.'

He was pleased with himself. 'There's nothing like sowing dissension in the ranks of the ungodly. Now, where would you like me to set up shop?'

Ellie suggested he sat at the foot of the long dining table, and she offered him coffee.

He declined. 'I wonder, would you like me to be Inquisitor General today?'

'You have all the facts and figures. I'd be grateful.'

The next arrival was Ms Edwina Pryce, who stepped into the hall as if she were the leading lady making an entrance on stage. A Louis Vuitton handbag was hooked over one arm, and she was wearing a cunningly cut ivory cashmere coat over a matching slimline dress. Her four-inch high heeled shoes were exquisite, her hair had been attended to by a master and her make-up was understated but took a good few years off her age. Or maybe she'd been Botoxed?

No, no Botox yet, thought Ellie. Or we'd have had the bills for it.

Edwina looked Ellie up and down. 'You almost disappear into the woodwork on a dark day like this. Going to a funeral?'

'That's right,' said Ellie, who'd been pleased to find only one buttery spot on the midnight blue suit she kept for such occasions, and it had come off nicely with a flannel and some hot water. 'We're meeting in the dining room. May I take your coat?'

'If you can hang it up. I do not want it thrown carelessly over a chair. My solicitor will be with us in a moment. He's just parking his car.' She consulted a tiny watch on her wrist. 'Mustn't take too long. I have an appointment at noon with my manicurist and then I'm going on to meet the carpet people at my new flat.'

Ah-ha, thought Ellie. So Edwina had put her ill-gotten gains into buying another flat, had she? Hadn't Evan said something about her looking for another flat so that she could rent out her old one? Now that *is* something to think about. She said, 'My own solicitor has only just arrived. You know him, of course. Mr Greenbody.'

Edwina's smile tightened. 'What's he here for? Poor little man. He was totally under my stepmother's thumb. But I suppose he'll do as the second of the two witnesses we'll need for your signature.' She stalked into the dining room and seated herself at the head of the table, opposite Mr Greenbody.

Another ring on the doorbell. Ellie let in a youngish, darkish man clutching a spankingly new briefcase. Edwina's solicitor? He beamed at Ellie and held out his hand – chilly and slippery – to shake hers. 'Zach, short for Zachariah.'

Was that his first or surname? He didn't say. He did look pleased with himself, didn't he? The term 'ambulance chaser' came into Ellie's mind. He was keen, all right, but perhaps not very experienced.

Ellie ushered Mr Zachariah into the dining room, where he took a seat on Edwina's right.

Another ring on the doorbell.

This time it was Hugh, looking harassed. 'I'm terribly busy. Are you sure this is necessary?'

'Yes, Hugh. Trust me, it is. Do go through and find yourself a seat . . . perhaps between the two men?'

A stir in the doorway leading to the kitchen and there was Vera, pale of face, dressed in a sweater and jeans, her hair freshly washed and gleaming in the overhead light. She had a reluctant Mikey in tow.

'Come along,' said Ellie. She ushered them into the dining room and seated them opposite Hugh and the new solicitor. She herself took a chair between Vera and Edwina, just in case there was any unpleasantness. She surveyed the scene. Men on one side. Women and children on the other.

Ellie said, 'Does everybody know everybody? Hugh, this is Mr Greenbody, who used to be the deceased Mrs Pryce's solicitor. Ken, Hugh is the project manager for the hotel and is here to represent the board of directors' interests this morning.'

Edwina, predictably, objected to Vera's presence. 'What's your cleaner doing here?'

Mikey's eyes flashed, and he drew closer to his mother. Vera gave a painful half smile and turned her head away from Edwina, which displeased that lady even more.

Ellie kept calm. 'Remiss of me not to introduce everyone. Zach and Hugh, do you know Mrs Edgar Pryce and her son, Michael?' And if she laid the slightest of stresses on the 'Mrs' then who could blame her when Edwina – who had never been married – could only claim the title of 'Ms'?

Ellie continued, 'Mrs Edgar Pryce has had flu but is recovering. As a member of the Pryce family and as Mikey's mother, I thought it only right that she attend this meeting about the future of the Pryce mansion, and also to refute the allegations laid against her son. I did wonder about asking Terry Pryce, too, but decided against it as he's never had anything to do with the hotel.'

'And your cleaner has?' Edwina was not amused.

Ellie smiled as sweetly as she could. 'For some years Mrs Edgar Pryce kept herself off benefits by working as a cleaner, yes. She is now at university, studying for a business degree.'

'Whatever,' said Edwina. She shrugged and waved her hand at Zach. 'Get on with it.'

Zach bared very white teeth in what was meant to be a smile but held no mirth. He produced a pair of dark-rimmed spectacles and flicked open his very new, stiff briefcase to extract a sheaf of important-looking papers. He had a watch with a metal bracelet on his left wrist, but the catch was loose on it and he fiddled with it before proceeding.

He cleared his throat. 'It is understood that—'

Ken Greenbody held up a forefinger. 'Sorry to interrupt, but before you get going I have a quick question for Ms Edwina Pryce.'

'What?' Edwina was not amused.

'An audit is coming up. Solicitors get hammered if they haven't disbursed everything their clients entrusted to them.'

'Well, can't it wait?' She glanced at her watch.

'It can't. Not really.' Apologetic. 'It's only a tiny detail.'

Zach cleared his throat. 'Perhaps . . . after the signing? Since Ms Pryce needs to be elsewhere in an hour's time?'

'Get on with it, Zach,' said Edwina.

Zach revealed his teeth in another grimace. 'I think it has already been accepted that, since Mrs Quicke is no longer the appropriate—'

'It will only take a minute,' said Mr Greenbody. 'A question of dates. Was it March or April? That's all I need to know.'

'What was?'

'The leak at your flat. It isn't clear. March or April?'

Edwina snapped out, 'April. The leak was in the water pipe leading to the washing machine.'

'Oh. Thank you. Do carry on.'

Zach lifted his papers again.

'So sorry to interrupt again,' said Mr Greenbody, who didn't look at all sorry. 'I'm trying to work out how a little leak in the kitchen could have caused so much damage.'

As one humouring a nitwit, Edwina said, 'You know perfectly well why. I was away for the weekend and didn't discover the leak until it had flooded the flat and got into the electrics. The plumber found I'd still got lead piping, so that had to be replaced and so did the electrics. I had to move out while the place was gutted. The carpets and the furniture all had to be thrown out. It was a nightmare!'

'I don't seem to have the surveyor's report from your insurance company.'

Edwina's face flooded with colour. 'You know very well there was no insurance cover. I . . . it had lapsed.'

Zach lifted his papers again, but Mr Greenbody was turning back to his files. 'Yes, yes. I seem to remember, but referring back through my files, yes, here it is . . . Your stepmother sent you a cheque to cover renewing the insurance for a year in . . . Yes, that February. A couple of months before the leak.'

Edwina pinched in her lips. 'I had other calls on my finances at the time, and . . . Let's get on with the real reason why we're here—'

Mr Greenbody said, mildly, 'Ah, did you use the cheque for something else, then?'

Edwina half rose and then sank back into her chair. 'You know perfectly well what happened. I had a stack of other bills which needed paying. My stepmother was impossible. She never understood that I had a position to keep up and that I couldn't go around in rags.'

'So that explains how it happened you had no insurance cover for the leak when it occurred, which is why you asked your stepmother to pay for everything?' He made a note.

'She was most unpleasant about it, but she did agree in the end to cover my bills. I had to get the lowest possible quotes, use local workmen, replace like for like. The disruption was appalling. I don't know what I'd have done if a friend hadn't acted as project manager for me.'

'Ah yes. We'll come to him in a minute. Now, your insurance. I seem to recall that Mrs Pryce renewed it for you? According to my records, she asked me to send a cheque to the insurance people direct?'

'Of course.' Edwina signed to Zach. 'Carry on, or we'll never get through in time.'

Zach raised his papers only to have Mr Greenbody, faint but pursuing, ask one more question.

'These plumbers. I have their invoice here, but I can't find them in the local directory. Preston and somebody?'

Vera looked bemused. Ellie held her breath. Hugh stiffened in his seat. Mikey, whose eyes had glazed over during the preliminaries, sharpened to attention.

Edwina shrugged. 'Someone local. A neighbour recommended them. Can we please get on?'

Ken Greenbody was leafing through his file. 'His invoice doesn't look very professional. Was he moonlighting from a day job?'

'How should I know? He seemed efficient enough to me.'

'His work was satisfactory?'

'Yes, of course. I don't understand why you're asking—'

'Then why did the work have to be completely redone, all over again, not three months ago? And, if his work was so poor that another flood occurred with the same devastating effect on the electrics and furniture within the year, why did you use the same people again?'

'I . . .' Edwina blinked. 'No, I . . . his work was satisfactory, which is why I used them again. These leaks happen.

Most unfortunate.' She blinked rapidly. 'Those people were the cheapest, so—'

'The second leak happened when you were away on holiday this year?'

An attempt at a smile. 'You sound as if you don't think I had a right to take a holiday. Yes, that's right.'

'This time you did have insurance cover because I'd paid that cheque myself, direct to the company. And yes, I have the confirmation from the insurance company here. So why didn't you use your insurance to cover your bills, second time round?'

Edwina went very still.

Silence.

Hugh leaned forward. 'Mr Greenbody, might I see that plumber's invoice?'

'Pleasure.' Ken sent them skimming over the table. 'First time round . . . and the second.'

Hugh looked at them, stone-faced. Then laid them on the table before him, face down. 'Preston has been working for me full time for some years now. Preston is a qualified plumber of many years' experience. He would not – could not – have installed plumbing so badly that it had to be redone within such a short space of time. I would query this second invoice, if I were you.'

Edwina's voice cracked. 'How dare you! Why, that's as good as accusing your own workman of cheating me out of hundreds of pounds.'

Hugh thrust back his chair. He looked at Ken. 'Ms Pryce was paid for this second lot of plumbing?'

'The trust paid, yes. A clerical oversight.'

Hugh pinned Edwina in his sights. 'You passed that money on to Preston?'

'My project manager did. Yes, of course. What else . . .?'

Hugh turned to Ellie. 'You win, Mrs Quicke. I don't like to hear of my men doing jobs on the side when they're supposed to be working full time for me, and I can't believe his work was so shoddy it had to be ripped out and done again within a year. That second invoice must be a fake. And if Preston was paid for doing non-existent work, then I have

to ask why he was given the money, and what he was supposed
to do for it. Much as I hate to think it, I'm beginning to agree
with you that he was given that money as a bribe, and what
could that have been for, except to cause delays to the work
at the hotel?'

'Nonsense!' But red flags flared in Edwina's cheeks. 'I don't
know why . . . I mean, my project manager might have . . .'

'Why should he pay Preston for work which he hadn't
done?'

Edwina bit on her lower lip. Her upper teeth were strong
and large. For a moment Ellie thought the woman looked like
a trapped rat.

Vera was slow to understand what had been happening. 'So,
when Mikey tried to find out what was going wrong and started
watching Preston and Dave, when he came across them
damaging the pipes, they blamed him for a problem they'd
caused themselves?'

Hugh admitted, 'It looks like it.'

Vera was insistent. 'This is the same Preston who threw
Mikey down the stairs, took him to the police station and
accused him of sabotage? It was Preston who set the Social
Services on him?'

'I'm afraid so. If it's any consolation, Mrs Pryce, I will
personally see that he and his nephew are dealt with and Mikey
cleared.'

Edwina's voice climbed. 'What nonsense! Of course the
little bastard was responsible. What else can you expect from
a boy with his background?'

Ellie said, 'You forget that he's your nephew, your brother's
adopted son.'

'He has usurped what should be mine by rights.' She snorted.
'Well, if you prefer to take the word of a child who's been
truanting and trespassing and sabotaging the work at the hotel
instead of mine, then all I can say is that you are making a
grave mistake. I am personally acquainted with the managing
director of the hotel chain, and I can assure you he will not
be impressed by this charade. As if I would dream of bribing
a workman! In any case, I had no contact with the workmen
who renovated my flat. My project manager saw to everything

for me. I don't suppose I would recognize the plumber if I saw him again.'

Mikey made as if to speak and failed. He became agitated. He pulled on his mother's arm, looked imploringly at Ellie.

'Yes, Mikey?'

The boy gestured at Edwina, his throat working. A strange hissing came out of his mouth. He touched his eyes, raised his finger, pointing upwards. And then pointed back at Edwina.

Ellie tried to follow. 'You saw Ms Pryce from up above? From your sitting room at the top of this house, which overlooks the garden of the hotel? When, Mikey?'

Again the boy tried to speak, and again he failed. He ran round the table to push Mr Greenbody aside and type rapidly on his laptop.

Mr Greenbody said, 'He's written, "A long time ago. Before things went wrong. In garden with Preston. She fell. High heels."'

Mike showed how high. Four inches?

'Go on, Mikey,' said Mr Greenbody.

The boy typed again. Ken read out, '"Hurt her foot. Preston and another man carried her in."'

Mr Greenbody said, 'Which men, Mikey?'

Mikey typed again.

Mr Greenbody looked at Hugh. '"Contractors, laying paths." You know which firm it was? Will you ask them if they can confirm?'

Hugh got out his mobile phone, consulted the addresses on it and located a number. Rang it. Spoke to a man at the other end. Listened to the reply. Said, 'Thanks, I'll get back to you,' and shut off the call. 'The boy spoke the truth. His men remembered the incident. They joked about it in the office afterwards. They say some toffee-nosed woman, dressed to the nines, wearing high heels, came on the site after most of the men had gone for the day. She was being shown round by a man whose description matches that of Preston. So she not only knew him but had him show her around the site himself. It was you, Ms Pryce, wasn't it?'

'All lies,' said Edwina, turning the accusation off with a light laugh. 'I'm not staying to listen to this nonsense, and if

I find out you've repeated the slander I shall sue.' She picked up her handbag, ready to leave.

Ellie said, 'The best defence against slander is truth. It isn't just the boy's word against yours, is it? We have asked your "project manager" to give his side of the story, and he has done so. He confirms that he acted for you on the occasion of the first leak and subsequent refurbishment, but not on the second.'

Edwina flushed. 'He's lying through his teeth, and you have no right to bully me like this.'

'Are we bullying you, Edwina? We haven't finished yet. If you leave now, Mr Greenbody will have no choice but to send your false invoices to the police and let them prosecute you for fraud.'

'Fraud? Ridiculous! I don't have to listen to this.' But instead of leaving, she wiped her upper lip with a hankie, took out a compact and redid her lipstick.

Zach was looking from one face to the other, worried, not sure what was going on. 'Please, can we just get on? You know Ms Pryce has other appointments—'

'So she has,' said Ellie. 'There's still a formal agreement to be signed. After, that is, she's explained how she came to bill the trust for a non-existent car.'

Zach looked confused. 'What car? She's bought a car? I understood—'

'You understood that she can't drive. I expect you gave her a lift here this morning, right? No, she can't drive, but she's put in an invoice for a car she's bought recently. What she hasn't done is to apply for a provisional driving licence, or for driving lessons.'

Edwina stared, wide-eyed, at Ellie. Then at Mr Greenbody. 'I need a car. My doctor says so. I shall bill you for lessons when I'm good and ready.'

'Where is this car now? In the breakers' yard, I believe. That's where Terry says it is, anyway. He wrote it off months ago. So how could he have sold it to you?'

She passed her tongue over her lips. 'Well, he did. He needed the money, and I needed the car, so he sold it to me. I bought it in good faith.'

'He denies selling you his car. We have his statement to that effect.'

'I don't have to listen to this.'

'Yes, you do,' said Ellie. 'Think of the alternative.'

Zach was also staring at Edwina. 'Ms Pryce, I would advise you, in your own interests, not to say—'

'She doesn't have to say anything,' said Ellie. 'She just has to listen, and to accept our terms.'

'Terms?' Zach was on his mettle, trying to prove he was worth his fee. 'Well, I wouldn't advise my client to—'

'Perhaps you'd better wait till you understand exactly what's been going on,' said Ellie. 'I dare say Ms Pryce failed to acquaint you with the exact terms of old Mrs Pryce's will? Hm? Perhaps you'd like to read the relevant paragraph. I've had a copy faxed to me today.'

She passed it over to him. 'You will see that Mrs Pryce left everything to me – and I have turned everything over to the trust – with one proviso. I must ensure the surviving members of the family – that is Edgar, Edwina and their cousin Terry Pryce – are never at a loss for the basics. Edgar died shortly after the will was proved but is survived by his wife, Vera, and his adopted son, Michael. The trust will continue to look after them. The trust will also continue to be responsible for Terry and Edwina, within the limits set out in Mrs Pryce's will.'

Zach settled his glasses further up on his nose and glanced at Edwina. Re-read the paragraph. He repeated the words, 'The basics?' and looked hard at his client.

Ellie said, 'I expect you are now wondering who is going to pay your fee? Would you think that came under the heading of "basics"?'

He folded his arms and looked into the middle distance. Then – and she had to admire him – he unfolded his arms. 'Ms Pryce asked me to represent her at this meeting. She is my client, and I will represent her to the best of my ability.'

'Well said. Now you must understand that the trust has two aims to pursue at this meeting. In the first place we must seek to recover the money wrongfully and criminally extracted from us by way of false invoices.'

Edwina said, in a faint voice, 'Don't be ridiculous. Unless

you do as I ask and pass over your shares in the hotel, I will have nothing and will be destitute. So you won't get your money back, whatever happens.'

Ellie smiled. 'What about the second flat you've bought? Where is it and how much did you pay for it?'

Edwina slapped the table. 'No comment.'

Zach opened his mouth, and she turned on him. 'Don't you dare!'

Ellie grinned. 'So you know all about it, do you, Zach? Perhaps you did the conveyancing for it and know exactly how much it's worth? I think you'd better advise your client to sell it and pay us compensation for the money she's taken off us. Less your costs, of course. Or, if it is roughly equal to the amount she's taken off us by fraud, she could simply make it over to us here and now.'

'No! No, I won't! How dare you even suggest—!'

'The other piece of paper we need from her is a confession that she bribed Preston to delay the work at the hotel and confirmation that Michael Pryce had nothing to do with it. She must make it clear that Preston and his assistant assaulted and falsely accused him of criminal damage when he discovered them in the act of sabotaging the plumbing, and that one of them subsequently attempted to run him down in the road.'

'You are out of your tiny mind! I'm not staying to listen to this.' Edwina made it to her feet.

Ellie didn't bother to move. 'By the way, tomorrow morning my secretary will be writing to the newspapers, with copies to all the people to whom you owe money, advising them that in future we will no longer be responsible for your debts.'

Edwina began to shake. 'You can't do that!'

'Oh, except for the utilities, of course. They're basic. We assume you're collecting an old age pension already? You own your flat outright, so if we pay for the utilities that should be quite enough to keep body and soul together.'

Edwina screamed.

NINETEEN

With a vicious swing, Edwina swept her handbag around in an arc.

Zach shoved back his chair to avoid being hit. 'What the—!'

Edwina thrust back her own chair. She staggered, nearly fell. Her eyes were wild.

She swiped at Ellie, using her heavy handbag as a weapon.

Ellie ducked, stumbling to get out of reach, overturning her own chair and ending up on the floor.

Zach shouted, 'Careful!'

Mr Greenbody was on his feet. Hugh, too. Hugh started round the table.

Edwina screamed. She lashed out again, this time at Vera. Missed.

Vera recoiled in her chair, clutching Mikey, trying to protect him.

Edwina struck out at Vera. Caught her on her shoulder.

Edwina raised her handbag above her head, to hit Vera again.

Hugh, lifting both hands to fend Edwina off, managed to step between her and Vera. 'Now, now!' He seemed unwilling to hit her. 'Stop that, right now!'

He took the blow himself.

Ellie disentangled herself from her chair and struggled to her feet out of Edwina's reach. What to do? Send for the police?

Edwina was beyond reason. She danced round Hugh to continue the attack on Vera. 'I'll have you! You and your bastard!'

Zach, arms widespread, closed in on Edwina from behind.

Mikey slipped out of his mother's arms and leaped at Edwina with a strange roar, starting low down and ending in a yell which raised hairs on the back of Ellie's neck.

Vera screamed, 'Mikey!'

Bullet-headed, the boy went for Edwina. She rained a blow at him. Missed.

He caught her around the waist and drove her back into Zach's arms.

She struggled, beating against Mikey's head and Zach's restraining hands.

Ellie and Vera between them caught hold of Mikey and hauled him away.

Hugh caught hold of one of Edwina's thrashing arms and held fast. She was frenzied. Too strong for the men to hold her, shaking them to and fro. Zach held on, somehow. As did Hugh.

Screaming, Edwina kicked the men. Her eyes and teeth snapped together. She caught one of the men on his shin, then got Ellie, too.

Mikey disappeared from view. So did Vera.

Ellie felt a tug on her leg. Mikey pulled her down to join him and Vera under the table. Ellie joined them on the floor, watching the drama played out via the fighters' legs.

The three men were all around Edwina. Shouting at her to keep calm. She went on screaming. Kicking. Tearing at the hands which held her with clawing nails.

Ellie saw the door open and Rose's thin legs appear. Rose was holding something in either hand. A pair of saucepan lids? She crashed them together. 'Isn't anyone going to answer the phone?'

Her concentration broken, Edwina gulped and was quiet.

In the silence they heard the phone ringing in the hall.

Panting, Edwina allowed herself to be supported back to the chair, which Mr Greenbody righted for her. He removed Edwina's handbag from her loosened grasp and laid it on the table. Edwina began to weep.

They were all breathing hard.

Hugh said, 'If you try that again, Ms Pryce, we'll have to tie you up and send for the police. Understood?' He bent down to look under the table. 'Are you all right, down there?'

Ellie crawled out and hauled herself upright, wincing. She really was too old for this sort of thing. Her leg hurt; grazed, but not bleeding. Her tights were ruined.

Vera was drawn out by Hugh. Mikey followed. Mikey was grinning. Vera wasn't. She looked pale enough to pass out.

Thankfully, the phone stopped ringing.

Rose said, 'Thomas said I had to interfere. He seemed to think I'd know how to help, but I couldn't think what to do.'

Ellie said, 'You did exactly the right thing, Rose.' Pulling herself together, she said, 'Have we any cake or biscuits left in the tin? I think we could all do with a cuppa.'

'Of course.' Rose disappeared.

Mr Greenbody nursed grazed knuckles. Had he actually hit the woman? 'What an exhibition!'

Ellie eased herself on to the nearest chair. She hadn't felt fear when the woman had gone berserk but now she did feel a little tired. A cuppa might help. And perhaps some chocolate.

Hugh was favouring one leg. 'She's got a kick on her like a mule.'

Zach stood over Edwina. Very close. Making sure she didn't get up, nursing the backs of his hands where she'd clawed him.

Edwina wept, 'You're all being horrible to me. I only want what's my due.' Her hands fluttered around. 'My handbag. A hankie. I'm all shaken up. I need a doctor.'

'You need a psychiatrist,' said Ellie, feeling grim. She didn't like the way Vera was biting her lip and shivering. 'Vera, my dear. Go and lie down. Mikey, see that she does so, and stay with her.'

Hugh helped Vera and Mikey to the door and returned to his chair, righting two others which had been overturned in the fight. 'What happens now?'

Edwina wailed, 'I need a lift. I'm going to be late for my next appointment.'

'Forget it,' said Ellie. 'There are more important things in life than seeing your manicurist.'

'Don't be ridiculous!' cried Edwina, holding up a jagged fingernail. 'Look what's happened!'

'Yes, just look at what's happened,' snarled Hugh, rubbing his shin. 'When I think of the trouble you've caused . . .!'

Silence, except for some heavy breathing. The phone started to ring again. No one moved to answer it.

Finally, Zach picked up the papers he'd brought to the

meeting, signing over Ellie's shares in the hotel chain to Edwina. He tore them across once, twice. 'My client is prepared to cooperate, without prejudice—'

'It was Terry who put me up to it,' said Edwina, taking a compact and comb out of her handbag and attending to her hair. 'It was he who suggested various ways of, well, getting what was only my due out of the trust.'

'You paid him well for doing so?' asked Ellie.

Edwina gave a flick of her fingers. 'I was completely under his influence.'

'Are you prepared to sign a confession to that effect?'

'I'm not confessing anything, but I'm perfectly willing to lay the blame where blame is due. Provided, of course, that no further action is contemplated against me.'

Rose butted the door open and came in with a trolley holding a slightly-lopsided cake and tea for all, plus biscuits in a tin. 'Thomas says, are you all right?'

Ellie did her best to smile. 'Tell him everything's perfect.' She was shaking, but managed to pour out tea and hand round the cake and biscuits. Everyone except Edwina accepted refreshments.

Hugh spoke round a mouthful of cake. 'Let's start at the beginning, shall we? We need a statement from you about bribing Preston—'

'I need the loo!'

Ellie had to admire the woman.

Ken Greenbody wiped crumbs from his mouth. 'Mr Zach, would you care to advise your client that if she doesn't clear Mikey's name, admit what she's done and offer restitution, we shall have to turn the faked invoices over to the police.'

'Perhaps I could confer with my client in another room?'

'I think not,' said Ellie. 'Your client seems to have only a vague understanding of the truth, and you are not personally familiar with everything that she's been doing. It's best if you consult with her in this room, in front of us. Then if she comes up with any more lies, we can show you the evidence confirming or refuting what she says. That should save some time. All agreed?'

Hugh had his mobile out again. 'I'm going to have to report

to Head Office.' He took his phone over to the windows and spoke into it, softly, behind his hand.

'I'm not staying here to be libelled,' said Edwina, picking up her handbag and making as if to rise.

'If you leave here without making restitution,' said Ellie, 'we go straight to the police.'

Ken Greenbody squared his papers. 'Ms Pryce, suppose we start with how much money you've made false claims for. Zach –' he turned to Edwina's solicitor – 'we've worked it out that she photocopied the headings from various suppliers and used them to create fictitious invoices. Shall I show you how . . .?'

The front doorbell rang, and Ellie went to answer it.

Kate swept in on a gust of wind and rain, holding a bulging file of papers and her laptop. 'Sorry I'm late. Are we in here?' She flew into the dining room, dropped her bundles on the table and opened her laptop in one swift movement. 'Morning, Ken. Morning, Edwina. This your solicitor? Haven't come across you before, have I?'

Ellie wanted to introduce Hugh, who was still on his phone, but Kate was already seating herself and booting up her computer. 'Ken, I've done some more work on Her Ladyship's frauds, and I think, if we can quickly put the totals together, we ought to be able to agree a grand total, subject to—'

Ellie left the room, quietly closing the door behind her.

Heads were bobbing over the banister from the first floor. She could hear Mikey's rather hoarse voice, recounting his exploits: '. . . so I headbutted her, should have been on her nose, but I got her in the middle, and she folded up, just like you see on the telly . . .'

Thomas was looking worried. 'You all right, Ellie?'

Vera had managed to climb the stairs to the first floor landing and was sitting on the top step, laughing and crying. 'Oh, Ellie! He's got his voice back!'

'About time, too,' said Rose, pulling herself up the stairs to join them. 'Now, Ellie; you tell Thomas he ought to be back in bed. He's not fit—'

'And you, Rose,' said Thomas, also hoarse of voice, 'ought not to be climbing stairs—'

'There's thanks for stopping the fight for you! Such goings on!'

'And I tried to kick her—'

Ellie followed Rose up the stairs. Slowly. Thomas was sitting on a bedroom chair but looked as if he were about to fall off it any minute. Rose was looking pale, but still on her feet. Vera probably couldn't get up, even if she wanted to. And Mikey was dancing around, waving his arms and crowing like a cock.

Ellie got to the top and seated herself beside Vera. Suddenly, she wanted to cry.

Rose said, 'Well, now! A good morning's work, but Thomas ought to go back to bed, and Vera needs to rest, too. Mikey, if you don't shut up, I'll . . .' She aimed a blow at him.

He ducked, laughing. The cat Midge wandered up the stairs, not wanting to be left out. Mikey picked him up and gave him a cuddle.

Ellie said, 'Back to school tomorrow, my lad.' And then, 'I don't know whether to laugh or cry.'

Thomas's colour was poor. 'I was praying, all the time. But yes, perhaps it might be as well to have a little nap now.'

Ellie helped him back to bed. By the time she'd got Vera settled as well, there were sounds of movement down below. And the phone was ringing.

She went down to answer it.

Diana, almost hysterical. 'Mother, I've been trying to get you all morning. Where have you been? Why don't you answer the phone?'

'Business, dear. Are you all right? The baby not come yet?'

'I'm on my mobile. We're on our way to the funeral at church. I wanted to wait for you to come with us, but Evan insisted we have to be there in good time. Look for us when you arrive.' Diana disconnected, and Ellie returned to the dining room to find out what had been resolved.

Kate was, predictably, on her way out. 'All settled, Ellie. Grand total of her bills is roughly equivalent to the price she paid for the flat she's just bought. She's signed it over to the trust, which wipes out her debt and covers her solicitor's fees.' Kate checked the time on her watch, compared it with the grandmother clock in the hall and opened the front door. 'Must go, or I'll be late.' She vanished.

Ellie murmured to herself, 'I'm late, I'm late, for a very important date.'

Zach appeared next, brushing back his hair, stowing away his glasses. 'All settled, Mrs Quicke. My client insists that Terry Pryce put her up to the whole thing, and that it was he who paid Preston to delay the work at the hotel. She has signed a statement to that effect. This should clear your ward, Michael Pryce. Hugh has a copy for the board of directors. I have persuaded her to drop her suit against you.'

'Well done, Mr Zach. Are you giving Ms Pryce a lift somewhere?'

'Out of your way, you mean?' Zach was not without a sense of humour. 'Yes. I'll drop her at her manicurist's with the proviso that she can't charge that bill, or any more such bills to the trust.'

He held the front door open. Edwina stalked through the hall, ignoring Ellie completely. The door closed behind them.

Hugh was next. 'Preston and Dave are dismissed as from now, and I'll see if I can clear up exactly what happened when Mikey was nearly run over.'

'But you know exactly what happened, Hugh. You've known—'

'Suspected, yes. Been able to prove, no. It *was* one of our workmen's vans which we saw, and it *did* have a string of flowers wound around the driver's mirror. It was either Preston or Dave who drove it at Mikey but I'm not sure which. One of them went to collect the load of tiles which we needed to finish that bathroom, but by the time I'd brought Mikey round here and returned, they were both back at work. Nobody else noticed which of them had taken the van out. It was raining, everyone was busy. I'm sorry. That's the nearest I can get without involving the police.'

Ellie was silent. She could see why he was avoiding that.

He said, 'I'll get the workmen together and tell them what's been going on. I'll tell them that Preston and Dave are out and that Mikey was the hero who saved the day. I'll make sure the police dismiss all charges against him. One more thing; I've suggested to Head Office, and they've agreed, that it should be not only you, but you with Vera and Mikey, all three of you together, who cut the ribbon and hand the building over on Opening Day.'

'Splendid. It was Edgar Pryce who suggested the house be turned into a hotel, so it's only fitting that his wife and son should do the honours. Well done, Hugh.'

He twitched a smile. 'I'm sorry it all took so long to sort out.' He went off to face his workforce.

Ken Greenbody was now the only one left, putting away his papers, closing his laptop. He looked as weary as Ellie felt.

She said, 'You did well. Thank you.'

'Part of me thinks that Edwina ought to be hauled off to the police station with Terry and charged with everything under the sun, not excepting parking on double yellow lines and spitting in the street. I told her we'd do that if she caused any more trouble, but I'm not sure she can take it in.'

'Her punishment is that she's going to have to live on a much reduced income. She won't like that. Every day she'll be reminded of what she's lost.'

'Of what she never ought to have had.'

'Poor woman,' said Ellie. 'It must be awful to be her. I've never heard her say a kind word to anyone. Think how horrible it must be to live like that.'

'You, Mrs Quicke, are almost too good for this world.'

'Er, not quite,' said Ellie. 'Part of me is jumping up and down and screaming with joy that she's been cut down to size. It's only a tiny, weeny bit of me that feels sorry for her.'

Ken laughed. He looked at his watch. 'Shall we go? We might even get to the church in time, but if not, we'll turn up at the house, shall we?'

'Give me a minute to change my tights, and I'll be right with you.'

Monday at noon

Ellie and Ken reached the church just as the second hymn was announced. The place was packed, and they had to search for seats. A good turnout for Anita.

Family flowers only. Donations to Cancer Research.

Jolly hymns. Good-oh. No dirges, by request.

Ellie looked round and saw some familiar faces. Evan and Diana were at the front, where there was space for his wheelchair.

Ellie hoped that Anita was at peace now and that Freddie would not exactly 'get over it' quickly, but 'come to terms' with what his wife had done very soon.

Ellie hoped the police wouldn't bother him any more but, remembering Lesley Milburn's interest, she suspected the affair would drag on until some new and greater crime pushed it off the police radar.

The last hymn thundered out, and the coffin was taken out and put into the hearse. Out of sight, out of mind? Well, not exactly. Anita had been much liked and would, hopefully, be remembered for her bright personality rather than for the manner of her death.

Freddie and a large woman – presumably the bossy sister? – stood at the door to receive condolences as the mourners left. Freddie seemed content to stand in his sister's shadow. He looked as if he hadn't slept much recently. Small talk. Everyone looking subdued. Everyone looking at their watches. A general move back to the cars. Relief. Only immediate family were going on to the crematorium. Everyone else was expected back at the house.

Diana spotted Ellie and waved. 'Got a lift? See you at the house, then.' Diana climbed into a black taxi, which had Evan's wheelchair already inside.

Ken Greenbody made sure Ellie had done up her seat belt. He looked at his watch. 'I'm peckish, aren't you? I believe there's food laid on back at the house. Time enough for a sandwich and a glass of something, and then I must get back to the office. Will you stay on after I leave, or shall I drop you off at home when I go?'

Ellie stifled a yawn. 'I won't stay long, but I'll probably get a lift back with my daughter.' She wondered if Freddie had switched on his Christmas lights yet. Or not. Probably not.

No, he hadn't. His house was warm and full of flowers. It was a dark and dismal day, but someone had had the common sense to switch on all the lights and bump up the heating. A couple of small children ran around. The offspring of relatives? In Freddie's absence at the crematorium, an elderly relative received the guests.

A glass of not very good wine. Platters of canapés. Ellie hoped there'd be something more substantial as they passed through into the dining room.

Diana arrived, with some difficulty managing to push Evan in his wheelchair. 'Mother, I hope you're not going to set a bad example to Evan and drink too much.'

'Fiddle faddle,' said Evan in a sharp voice. He grinned at Ellie and gave her an enormous wink. 'Watch this space. I've just remembered a rather risqué joke which Anita told me a while ago. I shan't leave till I've passed it on to Freddie.'

'*Not* appropriate,' said Diana, who seemed to be perspiring. She looked sallow, and when she'd parked the wheelchair, she held on to her lumbar region with both hands.

Ellie was separated from them by an influx of guests. 'Hello there!'

Who was this? Ah. Marcia double-barrelled, looking by turns solemn and full of mischief. 'Nice to meet you again,' said Ellie, truthfully.

Marcia treated Ellie to another wink. 'We shall see . . . eh?'

More people came in, moving Ellie on to where a large female in a purple outfit stood blocking the way to a conservatory at the back of the house. The conversation level was rising, and it was becoming hard to hear what people said unless you leaned close.

'I'm Pauline,' said the purple outfit. 'I remember you from the golf club. Eleanor, isn't it? I never forget a face. Your poor dear husband couldn't get you on to the golf course, could he? What a shame. I think a wife should take an interest in her husband's activities, don't you?'

'Did yours?' asked Ellie, thinking she didn't have to suffer insults in silence.

'Until he passed away.' The woman lifted her glass to make the rings on her fourth finger dance. 'Then my sciatica took over. After that, I had shingles, and you've no idea how I've suffered from that. Three times it's returned, and though they say each time it should be less painful, I really can't agree. There are days when . . .'

Ellie thought she could identify Pauline as the visitor Evan liked the least, because she went on about her own afflictions, and not his.

Platters of sandwiches and yet more canapés were brought in. Very welcome. Ellie managed to lose Pauline in the crush. She looked around for Diana. There was something about her daughter which disturbed. Not much, but enough to want to keep an eye on her.

The events of the morning were catching up on Ellie. She needed to sit down. There were chairs lined around the walls but they were all occupied. What about the conservatory? Yes, there was a two-seater settee, rather worn but with large cushions. An elderly woman was sitting on it, but there was room for Ellie. 'Are you keeping this seat for someone?'

The woman shook her head. 'I need to speak to a friend before I go, but I haven't seen him yet.'

Ellie produced a social smile and seated herself with a sigh. She wanted to lie back and close her eyes but if she did she'd fall asleep and that would never do. Perhaps she was going down with flu?

There was something odd about the woman. Ah yes. Tobacco brown boots, brown handbag, and a *navy* coat and hat. Navy did not go with brown. If you had a navy coat, you usually wore navy or black accessories, not brown.

Odd, really. The woman was otherwise well-turned out. Her hair had been expertly cut; the blouse showing at the neck of her coat was a Liberty print. She'd been a beauty in her day and hadn't resorted to Botox or a face lift to delay natural ageing. Ellie didn't think she'd met her before.

She made small talk. 'You've known the family long?'

'My dear husband was their doctor until he died, and Anita was one of my best friends. I miss her terribly.'

Ellie nodded. 'Cancer. So sad.'

'You knew her?'

'My husband was a member of the golf club. We met on social occasions, as one does. I admired her spirit.'

'She always knew her own mind.'

'Such a pity,' said Ellie, not really thinking what she was saying. She didn't like her wine much. Should she tip it into a plant pot nearby?

'No, no. Don't say that. She knew what she was doing.'

Ellie felt something cold at the back of her neck. She didn't turn her head, but let her subconscious work out what the woman had implied. Or maybe not even implied. What she'd hinted? Ellie told herself that she couldn't possibly *know* that this was the woman who had helped Anita to die. It was ridiculous even to suspect her.

Ellie turned to look at the woman, who looked back at her without embarrassment. Knowledge passed from eye to eye. Yes, this was the person who had helped Anita to die, and who was not ashamed of it.

Ellie's mouth felt woolly. She grimaced. 'Not very nice wine. Though I suppose I ought not to complain.'

'We don't do enough complaining nowadays. That's what I think. Why put up with things when they go wrong?'

'You may be right.' Ellie couldn't think what she ought to do with what she'd discovered. Or thought she'd discovered.

What *could* she do, anyway? Stand up and scream that this woman was a murderess? Well, not a murderess, exactly. But someone who . . . hang on! Had a crime of any sort been committed?

'I'm Ellie Quicke,' she said.

'I know who you are. Evan told me about you. You were in his wedding photos.'

'You know Evan well?'

'Well enough.' The woman began to rock to and fro, her face contorting. 'It's hard, very hard. I tell myself I can do it, but it is hard.'

'Do what?'

The woman was still, her eyes wide. A little wild. She smiled, and her skin broke into a hundred lines. She was older than Ellie had thought at first. 'I brought some whisky for him. He likes that.'

Ellie looked at the expensive brown handbag which the woman was clutching to herself. 'In your bag? Your brown bag?'

'I couldn't find the navy one, and the black one is . . . hush!' She put her finger to her lips.

'You brought a special drink for Evan?'

'My name's Rosemary. What's yours?'

Rosemary? That was the name of another member of Evan's harem, wasn't it? Someone Ellie had been asked to visit, only she'd never got round to it, what with the flu and all. 'Ellie. Ellie Quicke. Evan is my son-in-law.'

'I don't think much of his new wife, do you? She's a burden round his neck. It's terrible to live in pain, and for such an active man to be confined to a wheelchair, it must be hell on earth.'

'Yes,' said Ellie, watching the woman, 'he's been through a bad patch, but there are signs of improvement. His life is not yet over.'

'He said it was, and I believe him.' The woman nodded, emphatically. 'Yes, yes. It's the best way. The only thing to do. I have to help him. Only, I didn't think there'd be so many people here. I may have to wait and visit him at home, but . . . I'm getting to the end of the day.'

'Getting tired of it all?'

Another emphatic nod. 'One more and that's it. I shall be glad to have finished with it, I can tell you. It's a burden I've carried for too long. What did you say your name was?'

'Ellie Quicke. Evan is my son-in-law.' Was the woman suffering from short term memory loss?

'He told me about you, I think.'

There was a stir, and Evan forced his wheelchair through guests into the conservatory. 'Ah, there you are. Enjoying yourself, Rosemary? Ellie, Diana says to tell you she wants to go home, but I told her to hang on a bit and we'll all go together.' He was in high spirits. He flourished a cut-glass tumbler which had definitely not contained the inferior wine offered to most of the guests. 'Good stuff, this. I'll just get a top up. Want one, Ellie? Rosemary?'

'I brought one for you,' said Rosemary, diving into her bag and producing a miniature whisky bottle. 'Never say I forget you.'

'There's a friend for you! Forget-me-not,' said Evan, pouring the contents of the miniature into his glass. 'That's what we used to call you. I can't remember why.'

Ellie couldn't think what to do. Had Rosemary given Evan unadulterated whisky, or . . . what? Should she snatch the glass out of his hand and pour it on the floor? No, no. Too melodramatic, and difficult to get the stain out of the carpet.

She tried to get out of the settee but the cushions were soft and yielding and she didn't make it. 'Please, Evan. Don't drink any more.'

He took that the wrong way, lifting the glass to his mouth. 'What! You, too? I'll drink as much as I like.' He took a sip.

'Evan, stop! Rosemary put something in it.'

'Did she?' He looked at his drink. 'Looks all right to me. Rosemary knows what I like.'

'Rosemary is in love with death.'

Evan froze.

Rosemary shook her head, 'No, no. You've got it all wrong. Drink up, Evan.'

'She helps people to die,' said Ellie, trying once more to rise.

Rosemary caught Ellie's arm, pulling her back down again. 'Don't you interfere. We know what we're doing, don't we, Evan?'

Evan stared, narrow-eyed, at his glass. Then at Rosemary. 'Why would you . . .?'

Ellie tried to pull away from Rosemary, whose grasp on her arm was surprisingly strong. 'Evan, suppose you exchange your glass for Rosemary's? If the whisky she's brought is harmless, it won't hurt her.'

Patches of red stood out on Rosemary's cheeks. 'Don't be absurd. I don't like whisky.'

Evan held his glass up to the light. 'It looks all right to me.'

Rosemary insisted, 'It's good whisky; the best. I bought it for you specially.'

Ellie said, 'Pour it away, Evan. To be on the safe side.'

TWENTY

'**R**idiculous!' Rosemary was now as pale as she had been flushed before. 'Evan, let me have your drink. I'll pour it back into the bottle and use it another time.'

It was impossible to pour the contents of a tumbler back into a miniature bottle and they all knew it. Evan, puzzled, held on to his glass.

Ellie couldn't think what to do. If she got Evan to ditch the drink, what was to stop the woman from trying again later?

Rosemary began to weep. 'Oh, this is so awful! I can't bear it.'

'Oh, for heavens' . . .!' said Evan, and made as if to drink up.

Ellie said, 'Anita!'

Evan paused with the glass at his lips.

Ellie said, 'Rosemary, it was you who helped Anita to die, wasn't it?'

Rosemary sought in her pockets for a hankie and used it. Her words were indistinct. 'What if I did? It's no crime to run an errand for an old friend.'

Evan's jaw dropped. 'It was you who gave her the extra tablets?'

Rosemary tossed her head. 'She asked me to help her, and I did. She took the pills as and when she wanted to.'

Evan looked at the glass in his hand, his eyes wide.

'Petra,' said Ellie, disinterring the name from her memory banks. 'She blamed a cousin for supplying her aunt with the pills that killed her. Was that you, as well?'

'Petra?' Rosemary began to rock to and fro, clutching her handbag. 'Nasty little girl. Never liked her. Her aunt used to work for me; we've always kept in touch.'

'Was it you who gave Petra's aunt a Prada handbag?'

'Why not? She kept it for best, only used it at Christmas

time. Petra is a nasty, snivelling brat. Always looking for handouts. Deserved what she got.'

Evan met Ellie's eyes. Did she look as appalled as he did? Ellie said, in a soft voice, 'Did you hurt Petra? How?'

A toss of the head. 'She tripped and fell over.'

'How many people have you helped to die, Rosemary?'

'I don't know, do I? I'm never there when they do whatever it is that they want to do.'

Evan was fascinated. 'Rosemary, what's in the drink you've given me?'

'The usual. It's the very last of the sleeping pills. I've been so careful, eking them out, and yours are the last, the very last. You said you wanted to die, and I trusted you. What are old friends for but helping you out? And now, you've made a fool of me and I wish I were dead!'

'Here, then,' said Evan, passing his drink over to her.

'No!' cried Ellie.

Rosemary, gasping, laughing, still with tears on her cheeks, took the glass and tipped it into her mouth. She gagged once but continued to drink, even licking out the last drop.

'You see,' said Evan, half daring and half regretting his impulse. 'There was nothing wrong with the drink.'

Ellie withdrew her mobile from her handbag. 'She needs pumping out. I'll dial for an ambulance.'

'No, no!' said Rosemary, mopping herself up, blowing her nose. Laughing gently. 'How I've fooled you! Did you really think there was something nasty in the whisky? Of course there wasn't. There was nothing in it but a calming powder I got from the alternative medicine shop. It would have done Evan good, and it certainly won't harm me. Dear me, Evan! Don't look so distressed. I'm perfectly all right and, goodness me, will you look at the time? I'd best be on my way.'

Ellie wasn't sure what to think, but tried one last word. 'Why did you wear a brown handbag with your navy coat?'

'Why ever not?' Rosemary stood up, with some difficulty heaving herself out of the soft cushions of the settee. 'My best black coat's at the cleaners and my black handbag's still wet from the gin and . . .' Her voice trailed away.

'Gin?'

'Petra got gin all over it and maybe some blood.' She stopped short. Blinked. 'I suppose you'll need to tell someone that she's dead. It's not going to make any difference to me now, is it? I really must be going.' She made her way out through the few remaining guests in the main room.

'Do you think she really . . .?' said Evan.

Ellie dialled Lesley Milburn's number and for once was connected straight away. 'Lesley, I've just learned who's been providing people who want to die with extra pills. She also says she killed that girl who's been making such a nuisance of herself over her aunt's death. Petra. Is Petra really dead, or is this woman imagining it? She's called Rosemary something. A doctor's widow. She's on her way home now from the wake at Freddie's house, and I think she's taken enough sleeping pills to kill her. I'll hand you on to someone who can give you her full name and where she lives.'

She passed her phone to Evan, just as Marcia double-barrelled hove into sight, with one arm around Diana, who looked ghastly.

Ellie didn't exactly shoot to her feet, but did manage to pull herself out of the cushions.

'Her contractions are coming every five minutes,' said Marcia. 'I think it's time to go to the hospital. I'll drive you, if you like.'

Evan stood up.

Evan . . .

stood . . .

. . . up.

He handed the mobile phone back to Ellie and did his imitation of the crocodile's smile. 'Well, on with the game.'

'You've been practising!' said Ellie.

Marcia laughed. 'Every minute he could.'

'What a lovely surprise,' muttered Diana, not smiling at all. 'But if you don't mind . . .'

Rosemary was forgotten.

Marcia and Ellie sat side by side in the waiting room of the maternity unit, making small talk.

Marcia said, 'I challenged him to a game of chair-bound

golf, and of course he couldn't stand being beaten by a woman so he soon forgot he couldn't stand. At first he was wobbly on his feet. He didn't want to let anyone know he was getting better until he could walk properly. So we practised in secret. Diana probably suspected but went along with his little game.'

Ellie didn't think Diana had known. Diana wasn't very observant. 'Marcia, you're a gem. They should put up a statue to you somewhere.'

Marcia waved the compliment away but looked pleased. 'Men never think things through. He's left his wheelchair in Freddie's house, and I suppose I'll have to retrieve it for him tomorrow. And what about Diana's maternity case? Where is that, do you suppose?'

Ellie switched her eyes away from the door. The waiting seemed to go on for ever. 'Are you going to work your magic on Freddie next?'

'Too soft a target. I was at school with his sister, older than me but a legend for bullying even in those days. Going on past behaviour, she'll boss him about till one day he cracks and throws her out. After that, he'll start living again.'

Evan staggered in on uncertain legs. Grinning. 'Congratulations are in order. A fine boy. Perfect, they say. Diana's being cleaned up and will have a rest. They'll be home tomorrow, if all is well.'

Monday evening

The house seemed peaceful, after the uproar of the party at Freddie's. Ellie relaxed. What a day it had been! First the confrontation with Edwina, then the wake at Freddie's, and to cap all, Diana going into labour.

She shed her coat and the phone rang.

Lesley Milburn. 'Ellie, you there for a change? This friend of yours, Rosemary something. I arrived to find she'd collapsed in the street outside her house. A neighbour had just called an ambulance. I followed them to the hospital, who want to know what she's taken before they pump her out.'

'Sleeping pills, probably. In whisky. Will she make it?'

'Possibly. She understood I was with the police, and she

pressed a diary and a dry-cleaner's ticket on me. Have you any idea what that's about?'

'Well, if she did kill Petra – can you check? – there may be some blood on a black coat, the one she was wearing at the time, and which she's taken to be dry-cleaned.'

'I'll have someone collect it. The doctors are going to work on her now. If she makes it . . . but at her age . . .'

'Would you want her to make it?'

'That's not the point. If she's been helping other people to die, and if she really has killed Petra, she's got to answer for it. I'll see if I can get her to talk later. Must go, the nurse is calling me.'

Ellie returned the phone to its rest. The matter was out of her hands now, and if Rosemary died, then God and not man would be Rosemary's judge.

Rose must be having her afternoon nap, as she hadn't appeared in the hall. She could wait.

Ellie went upstairs to tell Thomas what had been happening. He laid aside his iPad to listen, and when she'd finished, he said, 'Well done all round. I think I'll get up for a bit, later.'

Up in the top flat, Ellie found Vera making sure Mikey did his homework. Vera said she'd rung the school and told them he'd be back tomorrow and that she'd go in to explain what had been happening as soon as she could.

Ellie rushed downstairs on hearing Rose scream. Midge had brought a field mouse into the kitchen. Alive. Rose caught it in a tumbler and threw it back into the garden. Midge was furious. Hadn't he just given her the best possible present? He stalked off to find Mikey.

Ellie sat down for a nice cup of tea to tell Rose all about everything, but in the middle of telling her about Evan, she remembered that ages ago – was it only last week? – she'd been potting up some bulbs for the winter. Where had they gone? Had Rose seen them?

'I put them in the big cupboard in the hall, out of the way. I meant to tell you but I forgot. I think one of them has started to grow already. So what's your new grandson like? Does he have a full head of hair, or is he as bald as a billiard ball?'

Monday evening

As Ellie arrived at the maternity unit with Diana's suitcase – retrieved from Freddie's house – she could hear a baby wailing.

Not a weakly cry. A full-blooded you'll-be-sorry-if-you-don't-feed-me-NOW! sort of cry. This was a baby determined to get his own way and prepared to give the world hell if it didn't oblige immediately. Ellie supposed that wasn't surprising, given the genes he'd inherited.

Diana was glaring into space. 'Can't you make him stop? He's driving me crazy.'

'That's what babies do when they're hungry. Where's Evan?'

'Gone to the golf club to celebrate.'

'That's what men do. Your job is to feed the baby.'

'That's what the nurses say. But I didn't feed my first, and I'm not ruining my figure by feeding this one, either. I asked the nurse to bring him a bottle but so far there's no sign of it.'

Ellie picked the baby up, tugged Diana's gown out of the way, and guided him on to his mother's breast. He didn't need showing what to do. The howling ceased.

Suck, suck. The top of his little head pulsed with the rhythm of his feeding.

Diana looked horrified. 'What!' And then, 'What the . . .' Her arms closed round her son. 'What a strange sensation.' She smiled, actually smiled.

'Enjoy,' said Ellie, and sat down to watch Diana bond with her son.